PRAISE FOR

THE MAIDENS

"Irresistible." — *THE NEW YORK TIMES*

"Dazzling." — *ESQUIRE*

"A masterful, slow-burn blend of Greek mythology and a knife-edged plot."

— *NEWSWEEK*

"*The Maidens* is a page-turner of the first order."

— DAVID BALDACCI

"A deliciously dark, elegant, utterly compulsive read—with a twist that blew my mind. I loved this even more than I loved *The Silent Patient*, and that's saying something!"

— LUCY FOLEY, *New York Times* bestselling author of *The Guest List*

"How do you go about following one of the biggest thrillers of the past decade? You write something even better."

— CHRIS WHITAKER, *New York Times* bestselling author of *We Begin at the End*

"Stunning."

— *PUBLISHERS WEEKLY* (starred review)

"Tautly plotted and impeccably paced."

— *THE OBSERVER* (UK)

Praise for *The Maidens*

A Barnes & Noble Best Book of 2021
A *Parade* Best Book of 2021

"Alex Michaelides's long-awaited next novel, *The Maidens*, is finally here. . . . The premise is enticing and the elements irresistible."
—*The New York Times*

"Fans of *The Secret History* will fall hard for *The Maidens*, Michaelides's dazzling chaser to 2019's bestselling *The Silent Patient*, a challenging act to follow. . . . Layered in dreamlike references to Greek mythology and ancient ritualized murders, this clever literary page-turner firmly establishes Michaelides as an unstoppable force in the thriller space."
—*Esquire*

"The author of the critically acclaimed *The Silent Patient* permanently cements himself as a top modern author with this new work, a masterful, slow-burn blend of Greek mythology and a knife-edged plot."
—*Newsweek*

"A deliciously dark, elegant, utterly compulsive read—with a twist that blew my mind. I loved this even more than I loved *The Silent Patient* and that's saying something!"
—Lucy Foley, *New York Times* bestselling author of *The Guest List*

"Alex Michaelides hits a home run in his sophomore effort. *The Maidens* is a page-turner of the first order."
—David Baldacci

"Stunning . . . The intelligent, cerebral plot finds contemporary parallels in Euripides's tragedies, Jacobean dramas such as *The Duchess of Malfi*, and Tennyson's poetry. The devastating ending shows just how little the troubled Mariana knows about the human psyche or herself. Michaelides is on a roll."
—*Publishers Weekly* (starred review)

"Michaelides's stage-setting skills are as masterful here as they were in *The Silent Patient* (2019); another tense, cleverly twisted winner." —*Booklist* (starred review)

"Michaelides has proven that he is no one-hit wonder and is well on his way to becoming one of the world's most influential and well-read thriller writers." —*Bookreporter*

"Tautly plotted and impeccably paced, it's an intelligent and propulsive second novel." —*The Observer* (UK)

"Elegant, sinister, stylish, and thrilling, *The Maidens* answers the weighty question: How do you go about following one of the biggest thrillers of the past decade? You write something even better." —Chris Whitaker, *New York Times* bestselling author of *We Begin at the End*

"Enticingly dark and compulsively page-turning . . . If you liked *The Silent Patient*, then you already know Michaelides's new book will be up your alley. With similar page-turning cliff-hangers, this utterly compulsive read will make you question which book you like better." —*PopSugar*

"Fans of *The Silent Patient* will love *The Maidens*. . . . Set in the world of academia, it features Greek mythology, multiple murders, and a twist that made my jaw hit the floor." —Riley Sager, *Parade*

"*The Maidens* is an intricately plotted mystery-thriller for the discerning reader. It's an atmospheric story set on Cambridge University's campus, merging cliff-hanging twists with artful suspense." —*New York Journal of Books*

Praise for *The Silent Patient*

"An unforgettable—and Hollywood-bound—new thriller . . . A mix of Hitchcockian suspense, Agatha Christie plotting, and Greek tragedy."   —*Entertainment Weekly*

"Disturbing."   —*The New York Times*

"Impressive first novel . . . with an ending worthy of a classic Agatha Christie mystery."   —*The Wall Street Journal*

"The perfect thriller."   —A. J. Finn

"Superb . . . This edgy, intricately plotted psychological thriller establishes Michaelides as a major player in the field."   —*Publishers Weekly* (starred review)

"Smart, sophisticated storytelling freighted with real suspense—a very fine novel by any standard."   —Lee Child

"A totally original, spellbinding psychological mystery so quirky, so unique that it should have its own genre."   —David Baldacci

"Destined to go down as one of the most shocking, mind-blowing twists in recent memory."   —Blake Crouch

"Unputdownable, emotionally chilling, and intense, with a twist that will make even the most seasoned suspense readers break out in a cold sweat."   —*Booklist*

ALSO BY ALEX MICHAELIDES

The Silent Patient

ALEX MICHAELIDES

THE MAIDENS

CELADON
BOOKS

NEW YORK

THE MAIDENS. Copyright © 2021 by Astramare Limited. All rights reserved. Printed in the United States of America. For information, address Celadon Books, a Division of Macmillan Publishers, 120 Broadway, New York, NY 10271.

www.celadonbooks.com

Designed by Michelle McMillian

The Library of Congress has cataloged the hardcover edition as follows:

Names: Michaelides, Alex, 1977– author.
Title: The maidens / Alex Michaelides.
Description: First Edition. | New York, NY : Celadon Books, 2021.
Identifiers: LCCN 2020057506 | ISBN 9781250304452 (hardcover) |
    ISBN 9781250792969 (international, sold outside the U.S., subject to
    rights availability) | ISBN 9781250304476 (ebook)
Classification: LCC PR6113.I2645 M35 2021 | DDC 823/.92—dc23
LC record available at https://lccn.loc.gov/2020057506

ISBN 978-1-250-30446-9 (trade paperback)

Our books may be purchased in bulk for promotional, educational, or business use. Please contact your local bookseller or the Macmillan Corporate and Premium Sales Department at 1-800-221-7945, extension 5442, or by email at MacmillanSpecialMarkets@macmillan.com.

First U.S. Edition: 2021

First Celadon Books Paperback Edition: 2022

10   9   8   7

*To Sophie Hannah, for giving me
the courage of my convictions*

Tell me tales of thy first love—
April hopes, the fools of chance;
Till the graves begin to move,
And the dead begin to dance.

—ALFRED, LORD TENNYSON, *The Vision of Sin*

Prologue

Edward Fosca was a murderer.

This was a fact. This wasn't something Mariana knew just on an intellectual level, as an idea. Her body knew it. She felt it in her bones, along her blood, and deep within every cell.

Edward Fosca was guilty.

And yet—she couldn't prove it, and might never prove it. This man, this monster, who had killed at least two people, might, in all likelihood, walk free.

He was so smug, so sure of himself. *He thinks he's got away with it,* she thought. He thought he had won.

But he hadn't. Not yet.

Mariana was determined to outsmart him. She had to.

She would sit up all night and remember everything that had happened. She would sit here, in this small, dark room in Cambridge, and think, and work it out. She stared at the red bar of the electric heater on the wall, burning, glowing in the dark, willing herself into a kind of trance.

In her mind, she would go back to the very beginning and remember it all. Every single detail.

And she would catch him.

Part One

No one ever told me that grief felt so like fear.

—C. S. Lewis, *A Grief Observed*

I

A few days earlier, Mariana was at home, in London.

She was on her knees, on the floor, surrounded by boxes. She was making yet another halfhearted attempt to sort through Sebastian's belongings.

It wasn't going well. A year on from his death, the majority of his things remained spread around the house in various piles and half-empty boxes. She seemed unable to complete the task.

Mariana was still in love with him—that was the problem. Even though she knew she'd never see Sebastian again—even though he was gone for good—she was still in love and didn't know what to do with all this love of hers. There was so much of it, and it was so messy: leaking, spilling, tumbling out of her, like stuffing falling out of an old rag doll that was coming apart at the seams.

If only she could box up her love, as she was attempting to do with his possessions. What a pitiful sight it was—a man's life reduced to a collection of unwanted items for a jumble sale.

Mariana reached into the nearest box. She pulled out a pair of shoes.

She considered them—the old green trainers he had for running on the beach. They still had a slightly sodden feel about them, with grains of sand embedded in the soles.

Get rid of them, she said to herself. *Throw them in the bin. Do it.*

Even as she thought this, she knew it was an impossibility. They weren't him; they weren't Sebastian—they weren't the man she loved and would love forever—they were just a pair of old shoes. Even so, parting with them would be an act of self-harm, like pressing a knife to her arm and slicing off a sliver of skin.

Instead, Mariana brought the shoes close to her chest. She cradled them tight, as she might a child. And she wept.

How had she ended up like this?

In the space of just a year, which once would have slipped by almost imperceptibly—and now stretched out behind her like a desolate landscape flattened by a hurricane—the life she had known had been obliterated, leaving Mariana here: thirty-six years old, alone and drunk on a Sunday night; clutching a dead man's shoes as if they were holy relics—which, in a way, they were.

Something beautiful, something holy, had died. All that remained were the books he read, the clothes he wore, the things he touched. She could still smell him on them, still taste him on the tip of her tongue.

That's why she couldn't throw away his possessions—by holding on to them, she could keep Sebastian alive, somehow, just a little bit—if she let go, she'd lose him entirely.

Recently, out of morbid curiosity, and in an attempt to understand what she was wrestling with, Mariana had reread all of Freud's writings about grief and loss. And he argued that, following the death of a loved one, the loss had to be psychologically accepted and that person relinquished, or else you ran the risk of succumbing to pathological mourning, which he called melancholia—and we call depression.

Mariana understood this. She knew she should relinquish Sebastian, but she couldn't—because she was still in love with him.

She was in love even though he was gone forever, gone behind the veil—"behind the veil, behind the veil"—where was that from? Tennyson, probably.

Behind the veil.

That's how it felt. Since Sebastian died, Mariana no longer saw the world in color. Life was muted and gray and far away, behind a veil—behind a mist of sadness.

She wanted to hide from the world, all its noise and pain, and cocoon herself here, in her work, and in her little yellow house.

And that's where she would have stayed, if Zoe hadn't phoned her from Cambridge, that night in October.

Zoe's phone call, after the Monday-evening group—that was how it started.

That was how the nightmare began.

2

The Monday-evening group met in Mariana's front room.

It was a good-sized room. It had been given over to the use of therapy soon after Mariana and Sebastian moved into the yellow house.

They were very fond of that house. It was at the foot of Primrose Hill in Northwest London, and painted the same bright yellow as the primroses that grew on the hill in the summer. Honeysuckle climbed up one of the outside walls, covering it with white, sweet-smelling flowers, and in the summer months their scent crept into the house through the open windows, climbing up the stairs and lingering in the passages and rooms, filling them with sweetness.

It was unseasonably warm that Monday evening. Even though it was early October, the Indian summer prevailed, like an obstinate party guest, refusing to heed the hints from the dying leaves on the trees that it might be time to go. The late-afternoon sun flooded into the front room, drenching it with a golden light, tinged with red. Before the session, Mariana drew the blinds, but left the sash windows open a few inches to let in some air.

Next, she readjusted the chairs into a circle.

Nine chairs. A chair for each member of the group, and one for Mariana. In theory, the chairs were meant to be identical—but life didn't work like that. Despite her best intentions, she had accumulated an assortment of upright chairs over the years, in different materials and in various shapes and sizes. Her relaxed attitude to the chairs was perhaps typical of how she conducted her groups. Mariana was informal, even unconventional, in her approach.

Therapy, particularly group therapy, was an ironic choice of profession for Mariana. She had always been ambivalent about groups—even suspicious of them—ever since she was a child.

She'd grown up in Greece, on the outskirts of Athens. They'd lived in a large ramshackle old house, on top of a hill that was covered with a black-and-green shroud of olive trees. As a young girl, Mariana would sit on the rusty swing in the garden and ponder the ancient city beneath her, sprawling all the way to the columns of the Parthenon on top of another hill in the distance. It seemed so vast, endless; she felt so small and insignificant, and she viewed it with a superstitious foreboding.

Accompanying the housekeeper on shopping trips to the crowded and frenetic market in the center of Athens always made Mariana nervous. And she was relieved, and a little surprised, to return home unscathed. Large groups continued to intimidate her as she grew older. At school, she found herself on the sidelines, feeling as if she didn't fit in with her classmates. And this feeling of not fitting in was hard to shake. Years later, in therapy, she came to understand that the schoolyard was simply a macrocosm of the family unit: meaning her uneasiness was less about the here and now—less about the schoolyard itself, or the market in Athens, or any other group in which she might find herself—and more to do with the family in which she grew up, and the lonely house she grew up in.

Their house was always cold, even in sunny Greece. And there was an emptiness to it—a lack of warmth, physical and emotional. This was due in large part to Mariana's father, who, although a remarkable man in many ways—good-looking, powerful, razor sharp—was also highly complicated. Mariana suspected he had been damaged beyond repair by his childhood. She never met her

father's parents, and he rarely mentioned them. His father was a
sailor, and the less said about his mother, the better. She worked
at the docks, he said, with such a look of shame, Mariana thought
she must have been a prostitute.

Her father grew up in the slums of Athens and around the port
of Piraeus—he started working on the ships as a boy, quickly
becoming involved with trade and the import of coffee and wheat
and—Mariana imagined—less savory items. By the time he was
twenty-five, he had bought his own boat, and built his shipping
business from there. Through a combination of ruthlessness, blood,
and sweat, he created a small empire for himself.

He was a bit like a king, Mariana thought—or a dictator. She
was later to discover he was an extremely wealthy man—not that
you would have guessed it from the austere, Spartan way they
lived. Perhaps her mother—her gentle, delicate English mother—
might have softened him, had she lived. But she died tragically
young, soon after Mariana was born.

Mariana grew up with a keen awareness of this loss. As a therapist, she knew a baby's first sense of self comes through its parents'
gaze. We are born being watched—our parents' expressions, what
we see reflected in the mirror of their eyes, determines how we
see ourselves. Mariana had lost her mother's gaze—and her father,
well, he found it hard to look at her directly. He'd usually glance
just over her shoulder when addressing her. Mariana would con-
tinually adjust and readjust her position, shuffling, edging her way
into his sight line, hoping to be seen—but somehow always remaining peripheral.

On the rare occasions she did catch a glimpse into his eyes,
there was such disdain there, such burning disappointment. His
eyes told her the truth: she wasn't good enough. No matter how
hard she tried, Mariana always sensed she fell short, managing to
do or say the wrong thing—just by existing, she seemed to irritate
him. He disagreed with her endlessly, no matter what, performing
Petruchio to her Kate—if she said it was cold, he said it was hot;
if she said it was sunny, he insisted it was raining. But despite his

criticism and contrariness, Mariana loved him. He was all she had, and she longed to be worthy of his love.

There was precious little love in her childhood. She had an elder sister, but they weren't close. Elisa was seven years her senior, with no interest in her shy younger sibling. And so Mariana would spend the long summer months alone, playing by herself in the garden under the stern eye of the housekeeper. No wonder, then, she grew up a little isolated, and uneasy around other people.

The irony that Mariana ended up becoming a group therapist was not lost on her. But paradoxically, this ambivalence about others served her well. In group therapy, the group, not the individual, is the focus of treatment: to be a successful group therapist is—to some extent—to be invisible.

Mariana was good at this.

In her sessions, she always kept out of the group's way as much as possible. She only intervened when communication broke down, or when it might be helpful to make an interpretation, or when something went wrong.

On this particular Monday, a bone of contention arose almost immediately, requiring a rare intervention. The problem—as usual—was Henry.

3

Henry arrived later than the others. He was flushed and out of breath, and he seemed a little unsteady on his feet. Mariana wondered if he was high. She wouldn't have been surprised. She suspected Henry was abusing his medication—but being his therapist, not his medical doctor, there was little she could do about that.

Henry Booth was only thirty-five years old, but he looked older. His reddish hair was speckled with gray, and his face was covered with creases, like the crumpled shirt he wore. He also wore a perpetual frown, and gave the impression of being permanently tense, like a coiled spring. He reminded Mariana of a boxer or a fighter, preparing to give—or receive—the next blow.

Henry grunted an apology for being late; then he sat down—clutching a paper coffee cup.

And the coffee cup was the problem.

Liz spoke up immediately. Liz was in her mid-seventies, a retired schoolteacher; a prim stickler for things being done "properly," as she put it. Mariana experienced her as rather trying, even irritating. And she had guessed what Liz was about to say.

"That's not allowed," Liz said, pointing a finger, quivering with indignation, at Henry's coffee cup. "We're not allowed to bring in *anything* from outside. We all know that."

Henry grunted. "Why not?"

"Because it's the rules, Henry."

"Fuck off, Liz."

"What? Mariana, did you hear what he just said to me?"

Liz promptly burst into tears, and things degenerated from there—ending in yet another heated confrontation between Henry and the other members of the group, all united in fury against him.

Mariana was watching closely, keeping a protective eye on Henry, to see how he was taking this. For all of his bravado, he was a highly vulnerable individual. As a child, Henry had suffered horrific physical and sexual abuse at the hands of his father before he was taken into care and shunted around a series of foster homes. And yet, despite all this trauma, Henry was a remarkably intelligent person—and it had seemed, for a while, as if his intelligence might be enough to save him: at eighteen he got a place at university, to study physics. But he only lasted a few weeks before his past caught up with him; he had a massive breakdown—and never fully recovered. There followed a sad history of self-harm, drug addiction, and recurring breakdowns landing him in and out of hospital—until his psychiatrist referred him to Mariana.

Mariana had a soft spot for Henry, probably because he'd had such rotten luck. But even so, she was unsure about admitting him into the group. It wasn't just that he was significantly more unwell than the other members: seriously ill patients could be held and healed very effectively by groups—but they could also disrupt them to the point of disintegration. As soon as any group establishes itself, it always arouses envy and attack—and not just from forces on the outside, those excluded from the group, but also from dark and dangerous forces *within* the group itself. And ever since he'd joined them a few months ago, Henry had been a constant source of conflict. He brought it with him. There was a latent aggression in him, a bubbling anger, that was often difficult to contain.

But Mariana didn't give up easily; as long as she was able to maintain control of the group, she felt determined to work with him. She believed in the group, in these eight individuals sitting in a circle—she believed in the circle, and its power to heal. In her more fanciful moments, Mariana could be quite mystical about the power of circles: the circle in the sun, the moon, or the earth; the planets spinning through the heavens; the circle in a wheel; the dome of a church—or a wedding ring. Plato said the soul was a circle—which made sense to Mariana. Life was a circle too, wasn't it?—from birth to death.

And when group therapy was working well, a kind of miracle would occur within this circle—the birth of a separate entity: a group spirit, a group mind; a "big mind," it was often called, more than the sum of its parts; more intelligent than the therapist or the individual members. It was wise, healing, and powerfully containing. Mariana had seen its power firsthand many times. In her front room, over the years, many ghosts had been conjured up in this circle, and laid to rest.

Today, it was Liz's turn to be spooked. She just couldn't let go of the coffee cup. It brought up so much anger and resentment in her—the fact Henry thought the rules didn't apply to him, that he could break them with such disdain; then Liz suddenly realized how much Henry reminded her of her older brother, who had been so entitled, and such a bully. All Liz's repressed anger toward her brother started surfacing, which was good, Mariana thought—it needed to surface. Provided Henry could stand being used as a psychological punching bag.

Which, of course, he couldn't.

Henry leaped up suddenly, letting out an anguished cry. He flung his coffee cup onto the floor. It split open in the center of the circle—and a growing pool of black coffee spread out onto the floorboards.

The other members of the group were immediately vocal and somewhat hysterical in their outrage. Liz burst into tears again, and Henry tried to leave. But Mariana persuaded him to stay and talk through what had happened.

"It's just a fucking coffee cup, what's the big deal?" Henry said, sounding like an indignant child.

"It's not about the coffee cup," said Mariana. "It's about boundaries—the boundaries of this group, the rules we abide by here. We've spoken about this before. We can't take part in therapy if we feel unsafe. Boundaries make us feel safe. Boundaries are what therapy is about."

Henry looked at her blankly. Mariana knew he didn't understand. Boundaries, by definition, are the first thing to go when a child is abused. All Henry's boundaries had been torn to shreds when he was just a little boy. Consequently, he didn't understand the concept. Nor did he know when he was making someone uncomfortable, as he usually was, by invading their personal or psychological space—he would stand too near when he spoke to you, and exhibited a level of neediness Mariana had never experienced in a patient before. Nothing was enough. He would have moved in with her if she'd let him. It was up to her to maintain the boundary between them: to define the parameters of their relationship in a healthy way. That was her job as his therapist.

But Henry was always pushing at her, needling at her, trying to get under her skin . . . and in ways she was finding increasingly hard to handle.

4

Henry hung around afterward, after the others had left—ostensibly to help clean up the mess. But Mariana knew there was more to it; there always was with him. He hovered silently, watching her. She gave him some encouragement:

"Come on, Henry. Time to go . . . Is there something you want?"

Henry nodded but didn't answer. Then he reached into his pocket.

"Here," he said. "I got you something."

He pulled out a ring. A red gaudy plastic thing. It looked like it had come out of a cereal box.

"It's for you. A present."

Mariana shook her head. "You know I can't accept that."

"Why not?"

"You need to stop bringing me things, Henry. Okay? You should really go home now."

But he didn't move. Mariana thought for a moment. She hadn't been planning on confronting him like this, not now—but somehow it felt right.

"Listen, Henry," she said. "There's something we need to talk about."

"What?"

"On Thursday night—after my evening group finished, I looked out of the window. And I saw you, outside. Across the street, by the lamppost. Watching the house."

"It wasn't me, mate."

"Yes, it was. I saw your face. And it's not the first time I've seen you there."

Henry went bright red and evaded eye contact. He shook his head. "Not me, not—"

"Listen. It's okay for you to be curious about the other groups I conduct. But that's something we talk about *here*, in the group. It's not okay to act on it. It's not okay to spy on me. That kind of behavior makes me feel invaded and threatened, and—"

"I'm not spying! I was just standing there. So fucking what?"

"So you admit you were there?"

Henry took a step toward her. "Why can't it just be us? Why can't you see me without *them*?"

"You know why. Because I see you as part of a group—I can't see you individually as well. If you need individual therapy, I can recommend a colleague—"

"No, I want *you*—"

Henry made another, sudden move toward her. Mariana stood her ground. She held up her hand.

"No. Stop. Okay? That's way too close. Henry—"

"Wait. Look—"

Before she could prevent him, Henry lifted up his heavy black sweater—and there, on his pale, hairless torso, was a grisly sight.

A razor blade had been used, and deep crosses carved into his skin. Bloodred crosses, different sizes, cut into his chest and abdomen. Some of the crosses were wet, still bleeding, dripping blood; others were scabby, and weeping hard red beads—like congealed, bloody tears.

Mariana felt her stomach turn. She felt sick with repulsion, and wanted to look away, but wouldn't let herself. This was a cry for help, of course it was, an attempt to elicit a caregiving response—but it was more than that: it was also an emotional attack, a psychological assault upon her senses. Henry at last had managed to get under Mariana's guard, under her skin, and she hated him for it.

"What have you done, Henry?"

"I—I couldn't help it. I had to do it. And you—had to see it."

"And now I've seen it, how do you think it makes me feel? Can you conceive of how upset I am? I want to help you but—"

"But what?" He laughed. "What's stopping you?"

"The appropriate time for me to give you support is during the group. You had that opportunity this evening, but you didn't take it. We all could have helped. We are all here to help you—"

"I don't want *their* help—I want *you*. Mariana, I need you—"

Mariana knew she should make him leave. It wasn't her job to clean his wounds. He needed medical attention. She should be firm, for his sake as well as her own. But she couldn't quite bring herself to throw him out, and not for the first time, Mariana's empathy prevailed over her common sense.

"Wait—wait a second."

She went to the dresser, opened a drawer, rummaged around. She pulled out a first aid kit. She was about to open it when her phone rang.

She checked the number. It was Zoe. She answered.

"Zoe?"

"Can you talk? It's important."

"Give me a sec. I'll call you back." Mariana ended the call and turned to Henry. She thrust the first aid kit at him.

"Henry—take this. Clean yourself up. See your GP if you need to. Okay? I'll call you tomorrow."

"That's it? And you call yourself a fucking therapist?"

"Enough. Stop. You have to go."

Ignoring his protestations, Mariana firmly guided Henry into the hallway, and out of the front door. She shut the door behind him. She felt an impulse to lock it, which she resisted.

Then she went to the kitchen. She opened the fridge and took out a bottle of sauvignon blanc.

She felt quite shaken. She had to pull herself together before she called Zoe back. She didn't want to burden that girl more than she already had. Their relationship had been imbalanced ever since Sebastian's death—and from now on, Mariana was determined to correct that balance. She took a deep breath to calm down. Then she poured herself a large glass of wine, and made the call.

Zoe answered on the first ring.

"Mariana?"

Mariana knew at once something was wrong. There was a tension in Zoe's voice, an urgency that Mariana associated with moments of crisis. *She sounds afraid,* she thought. She felt her heart beat a little faster.

"Darling, is—is everything all right? What's happened?"

There was a second's pause before Zoe answered. She spoke in a small voice. "Turn on the TV," she said. "Turn on the news."

5

Mariana reached for the remote control.

She switched on the old, battered portable TV sitting upon the microwave—one of Sebastian's sacred possessions, bought when he was still a student, used for watching cricket and rugby while he pretended to help Mariana prepare weekend meals. It was rather temperamental, and it flickered for a moment before coming to life.

Mariana turned on the BBC news channel. A middle-aged male journalist was delivering a report. He was standing outside; it was getting dark and hard to see exactly where—a field, perhaps, or a meadow. He was speaking directly to the camera.

"—and it was found in Cambridge, in the nature reserve known as Paradise. I'm here with the man who made the discovery . . . Can you tell me what happened?"

The question was addressed to someone off camera—and the camera swung around to a short, nervous, red-faced man in his mid-sixties. He blinked in the light, looking dazzled. He spoke hesitantly.

"It was a few hours ago . . . I always take the dog out at four, so it must have been about then—maybe quarter past, twenty past. I take him down by the river, along the path . . . We were walking through Paradise—and . . ."

He stumbled for a moment, and didn't complete the sentence. He tried again: "It was the dog—he disappeared in the tall grass, by the marsh. He wouldn't come when I called. I thought he'd found a bird or a fox or something—so I went to have a look. I walked through the trees . . . to the edge of the marsh, by the water . . . and there, there it was . . ."

A strange look came into the man's eyes. A look Mariana recognized all too well. *He's seen something horrible,* she thought. *I don't want to hear. I don't want to know what it is.*

The man went on, relentlessly, faster now, as if he needed to expel it.

"It was a girl—she couldn't have been more than twenty. She had long red hair. At least, I think it was red. There was blood everywhere, so much of it . . ." He trailed off, and the journalist prompted him.

"She was dead?"

"That's right." The man nodded. "She'd been stabbed. Many times. And . . . her face . . . God, it was horrible—her eyes—her eyes were open . . . staring . . . staring—"

He broke off, and tears filled his eyes. *He's in shock,* thought Mariana. *They shouldn't be interviewing him—someone should stop this.*

Sure enough, at that moment—perhaps recognizing it had gone too far—the journalist cut short the interview, and the camera panned back to him.

"Breaking news here in Cambridge—police are investigating the discovery of a body. The victim of a frenzied knife attack is believed to be a young woman in her early twenties—"

Mariana turned off the television. She stared at it for a second, stunned, unable to move. Then she remembered the phone in her hand. She held it up to her ear.

"Zoe? Are you still there?"

"I—I think it's Tara."

"What?"

Tara was a close friend of Zoe's. They were in the same year at

St. Christopher's College at Cambridge University. Mariana hesitated, trying not to sound anxious.

"Why do you say that?"

"It sounds like Tara—and no one's seen her—not since yesterday—I keep asking everyone, and I—I'm so scared, I don't know
what to—"

"Slow down. When was the last time you saw Tara?"

"Last night." Zoe paused. "And Mariana, she—she was being
so weird, I—"

"What do you mean, weird?"

"She said things—crazy things."

"What do you mean, crazy?"

There was a pause, and Zoe replied in a whisper, "I can't get
into it now. But will you come?"

"Of course I will. But Zoe, listen. Have you spoken to the college? You must tell them—tell the dean."

"I don't know what to say."

"Tell them what you just said to me. That you're worried about
her. They'll contact the police, and Tara's parents—"

"Her parents? But—what if I'm wrong?"

"I'm sure you *are* wrong," Mariana said, sounding a lot more
confident than she felt. "I'm sure Tara's fine, but we need to make
sure. You understand that, don't you? Do you want me to call
them for you?"

"No, no, it's okay . . . I'll do it."

"Good. Then go to bed, okay? I'll be there first thing in the
morning."

"Thanks, Mariana. I love you."

"I love you too."

Mariana ended the call. The white wine she had poured was
sitting on the counter untouched. She picked it up, and drained it
in one go.

Her hand was trembling as she reached for the bottle and
poured herself another glass.

6

Mariana went upstairs and began packing a small bag, in case she had to stay a night or two in Cambridge.

She tried not to let her thoughts run away with her—but it was difficult—she was feeling incredibly anxious. Somewhere out there was a man—presumably it was a man, given the extreme violence of the attack—who was dangerously ill, and had horrifically murdered a young woman . . . a young woman who possibly lived a few feet away from where her beloved Zoe slept.

The possibility the victim might have been Zoe instead was a thought Mariana tried to ignore, but couldn't entirely repress. She was feeling sick with a kind of fear she had only felt once before in her life—the day Sebastian died. A feeling of impotence; a powerlessness, a horrible inability to protect those you love.

She glanced at her right hand. She couldn't stop it trembling. She clenched it into a fist and squeezed it tight. She would not do this—she would not fall apart. Not now. She would stay calm. She would focus.

Zoe needed her—that was all that mattered.

If only Sebastian were here; he'd know what to do. He wouldn't deliberate, procrastinate, pack an overnight bag. He would have grabbed his keys and run out the door the second he got off the phone with Zoe. That's what Sebastian would have done. Why hadn't she?

Because you're a coward, she thought.

That was the truth. If only she had some of Sebastian's strength. Some of his courage. *Come on, love,* she could hear him saying, *give me your hand and we'll face the bastards together.*

Mariana climbed into bed and lay there, thinking, drifting to sleep. For the first time in over a year, her last thoughts as she lost consciousness were not about her late husband.

Instead, she found herself thinking about another man: a shadowy figure with a knife who had wreaked such horror upon that poor girl. Mariana's mind meditated on him as her eyelids fluttered and closed. She wondered about this man. She wondered what he was doing right now, where he was . . .

And what he was thinking.

7

Once you kill another human being, there's no going back.

I see that now. I see I have become altogether a different person.

It's a bit like being reborn, I suppose. But no ordinary birth—it's a meta-morphosis. What emerges from the ashes is not a phoenix, but an uglier creature: deformed, incapable of flight, a predator using its claws to cut and rip.

I feel in control now, writing this. At this moment in time, I am calm, and sane.

But there is more than one of me.

It's only a matter of time before the other me rises, bloodthirsty, mad, and seeking revenge. And he won't rest until he finds it.

I am two people in one mind. Part of me keeps my secrets—he alone knows the truth—but he's kept prisoner, locked up, sedated, denied a voice. He finds an outlet only when his jailer is momentarily distracted. When I am drunk, or falling asleep, he tries to speak. But it's not easy. Communication comes in fits and starts—a coded escape plan from a POW camp. The moment he gets too close, a guard scrambles the message. A wall comes up. A blankness fills my mind. The memory I was striving for evaporates.

But I'll persevere. I must. Somehow, I will find my way through the smoke and darkness and contact him—the sane part of me. The part that doesn't want to hurt people. There is much he can tell me. Much I need to know. How, and why, I ended up like this—so removed from who I wanted to be—so full of hate and anger—so twisted inside . . .

Or am I lying to myself? Was I always this way, and didn't want to admit it?

No—I won't believe that.

After all, everyone's entitled to be the hero of their own story. So I must be permitted to be the hero of mine. Even though I'm not.

I'm the villain.

8

The next morning, as Mariana left the house, she thought she saw Henry.

He was standing across the street, hovering behind a tree.

But when she looked back, there was no one to be seen. She must have been imagining it, she decided—and even if she weren't, she had more important things to worry about right now. She banished Henry from her mind, and took the tube to King's Cross.

At the station, she got on the fast train to Cambridge. It was a sunny day, and the sky was a perfect blue, streaked with only a few wisps of white cloud. She sat by the window, looking out as the train sped past green hedgerows and expanses of golden wheat swaying in the breeze like a shifting yellow sea.

Mariana was grateful to have the sun on her face—she was shivering, but from anxiety, not lack of warmth. She couldn't stop worrying about what had happened. She'd not heard from Zoe since last night. Mariana had texted her this morning but had yet to receive a reply.

Perhaps it was all a false alarm; perhaps Zoe had been wrong?

Mariana sincerely hoped so—and not just because she knew Tara personally: they'd had her to stay for a weekend in London a few months before Sebastian died. But Mariana was mainly, self-ishly, concerned with Tara for Zoe's sake.

Zoe had had a difficult adolescence for a variety of reasons, which she had managed to overcome, more than overcome—"triumphantly transcend" was how Sebastian put it—culminating with her being offered a place to read English at Cambridge University. Tara was the first friend Zoe made there, and losing Tara, Mariana thought, and in such unimaginably awful circumstances, might well derail Zoe entirely.

For some reason, Mariana couldn't stop thinking about their phone call. Something was bothering her.

She couldn't quite put her finger on what, exactly.

Was it Zoe's tone? Mariana had a feeling Zoe was holding something back. Was it the slight hesitation, even evasion, when she asked Zoe what were the "crazy" things that Tara had said?

I can't get into it now.

Why not?

What exactly had Tara said to her?

Perhaps it's nothing, Mariana thought. *Stop it—stop doing this.* She had nearly an hour to go on the train; she couldn't sit here driving herself crazy. She'd be a wreck when she arrived. She needed to distract herself.

She reached into her bag and pulled out a magazine—the *British Journal of Psychiatry*. She flicked through it but couldn't concentrate on any of the articles.

Inevitably, her mind kept returning to Sebastian. The thought of going back to Cambridge without him filled Mariana with dread. She hadn't been back since his death.

They would often go and see Zoe together, and Mariana had fond memories of those visits: she remembered the day they moved Zoe into St. Christopher's College, and helped her unpack and settle in. It was one of the happiest times they spent together, feeling like the proud parents of their little surrogate daughter, whom they loved so much.

Zoe had seemed so small and vulnerable as they prepared to

leave her that day, and as they said their goodbyes, Mariana saw Sebastian looking at Zoe with such fondness, such love, mingled with trepidation; as if he were gazing at his own child, which, in a way, he was. Once they left Zoe's room, they couldn't quite bring themselves to leave Cambridge, so they walked along the river together, arm in arm, like they used to when they were young. For they had both been students here—and Cambridge University, like the city itself, was intricately bound up in their romance.

It was where they met, when Mariana was just nineteen.

That meeting happened quite by chance. There was no reason for it—they were at different colleges at the university and doing different subjects: Sebastian was studying economics; Mariana was an English student. It frightened her how easily they might never have encountered each other. What then? What would her life have been like? Better—or worse?

Mariana was forever searching her memory these days—looking for the past, trying to see it clearly; trying to understand and contextualize the journey they had been on together. She would try to remember little things they did, re-create forgotten conversations in her mind, imagine what Sebastian might have said or done at each moment. But she was unsure how much that she recalled was real; the more remembering she did, the more it seemed Sebastian was turning into myth. He was all spirit now—all story.

Mariana was eighteen years old when she moved to England. It was a country she had romanticized since childhood. Perhaps this was inevitable, given that her English mother had left so much of it behind in that house in Athens: bookcases and shelves in every room, a small library, crammed with English books—novels, plays, poetry—all mysteriously transported there before Mariana was born.

She fondly imagined her mother's arrival in Athens—armed with trunks and suitcases full of books instead of clothes. And in her absence, the lonely girl would turn to her mother's books for solace and companionship. During the long summer afternoons, Mariana grew to love the feel of a book in her hands, the smell of paper, the sensation of turning a page. She would sit on the rusty swing in the shade, bite into a crisp green apple, or an overripe peach, and lose herself in a story.

Through these stories, Mariana fell in love with a vision of England and Englishness—an England that had quite possibly never existed beyond the pages of these books: an England of warm summer rain, and wet greenery, and apple blossom; winding rivers and willow trees, and country pubs with roaring fires. The England of the Famous Five, and Peter Pan and Wendy; King Arthur and Camelot; *Wuthering Heights* and Jane Austen, Shakespeare—and Tennyson.

And it was here that Sebastian first entered Mariana's story, when she was just a little girl. Like all good heroes, he made his presence felt long before his appearance. Mariana didn't know what he looked like yet, this romantic hero in her head, but she was sure he was real.

He was out there—and one day, she'd find him.

And then, years later, when she first arrived in Cambridge as a student, it was so beautiful, so dreamlike, she felt as if she had stepped into a fairy tale—into an enchanted city from a poem by Tennyson. And Mariana felt sure she would find him here, in this magical place. She would find love.

But the sad reality, of course, was that Cambridge wasn't a fairy tale; it was just a place, like any other. And the problem with Mariana's flight of fancy—as she discovered years later in therapy—was that she had brought herself with her. As a child at school, struggling to fit in, she had wandered the corridors during the break times, lonely and restless as a ghost—gravitating toward the library, where she felt comfortable, finding refuge. And now, as a student at St. Christopher's College, the same pattern repeated itself: Mariana spent most of her time in the library, making only a few friends with other similarly shy, bookish students. She received no interest from any of the boys in her year, and no one asked her out.

Perhaps she wasn't attractive enough? She looked less like her mother than like her father, with his dark hair and striking dark eyes. Years later, Sebastian would often tell Mariana how beautiful she was, but the problem was she never really felt it, inside. And she suspected, if she *was* beautiful, it was solely because of Sebastian: basking in the warmth of his sunlight, she blossomed like a flower. But that came later—initially, as a teenager, Mariana had little confidence in her appearance, which wasn't helped by the fact she had such bad eyesight, forcing her to wear ugly, thick glasses from the age of ten. At fifteen, she started wearing contact lenses, and wondered if that might make her look and feel different about herself. She'd stand in front of the mirror, peering at her reflection—trying but failing to see herself clearly, and never quite happy with what she saw. Even at that age, Mariana was dimly aware that attractiveness had something to do with the internal world: an inner confidence that she lacked.

Nonetheless, like the fictional characters she adored, Mariana believed in love. Despite an inauspicious first two terms at university, she refused to give up hope.

Like Cinderella, she held out for the ball.

St. Christopher's College ball was held on the Backs—large stretches of grass leading down to the water's edge. Marquees were erected, filled with food and drink, music and dancing. Mariana had arranged to meet some friends but couldn't find them in the crowd. It had taken all her courage to come alone to the ball, and she was regretting it. She stood by the river, feeling horribly out of place among these beautiful girls in ball gowns and young men in evening dress—all of whom brimmed with boundless sophistication and confidence. Her own feelings, Mariana realized, her sadness and shyness, were totally incongruous with the merriment of her surroundings. Standing here on the sidelines—looking at life from the fringes—was clearly Mariana's proper place; it had been a mistake for her ever to have imagined otherwise. She decided to give up, and return to her room.

And at that moment, she heard a loud splash.

She looked around. There were further splashes, and sounds

of laughter and shouting. Nearby, on the river, some boys were messing about on rowing boats and punts—and one of the boys had lost his balance and toppled in.

Mariana watched the young man splashing around, and then surfacing in the river. He swam to the bank and pulled himself out, emerging like some strange mythical creature, a demigod born in water. He was only nineteen then, but he looked like a man, not a boy. He was tall, muscular, and soaking wet; his shirt and trousers were sticking to him, his blond hair plastered across his face, blinding him. He reached up, parted his hair, peered out—and saw Mariana.

It was a strange, timeless moment—that first moment they saw each other. Time seemed to slow down, flatten, and stretch. Mariana was transfixed, held in his gaze, unable to look away. It was an odd feeling, a bit like recognizing someone—someone she had once known intimately, and couldn't quite place where or when they had lost touch.

The young man ignored the jeering calls of his friends. And with a curious, widening smile, he made his way over to her.

"Hello," he said. "I'm Sebastian."

And that was it.

"It was written" is the Greek expression. Meaning, quite simply, from that moment on, their destinies were sealed. Looking back, Mariana would often try to recall the details of that fateful first night—what they spoke about, how long they danced, when they had their first kiss. But try as she might, the specifics slipped through her fingers like grains of sand. She could only remember they were kissing as the sun came up—and from that moment on, they were inseparable.

They spent their first summer together in Cambridge—three months cocooned in each other's arms, untroubled by the outside world. Time stood still in this timeless place; it was always sunny, and they spent their days making love, or having long drunken picnics on the Backs, or on the river, sailing under stone bridges and past willow trees and cows grazing in open fields. Sebastian would punt, standing on the back of the boat and plunging the pole down into the riverbed to propel them along, while Mariana, tingling with alcohol, trailed her fingers in the water, gazing at the swans gliding past. Although she didn't know it at the time, she was already so deeply in love, there was no way out again.

On some level, they became each other—they joined, like mercury.

That's not to say they didn't have their differences. In contrast to Mariana's privileged upbringing, Sebastian was brought up with no money. His parents were divorced and he wasn't close to either of them. He felt they hadn't given him a good start in life; and that he had to make his own way, right from the beginning. In many ways, Sebastian said he related to Mariana's father, and the old man's drive to succeed. Money mattered to Sebastian too, because, unlike Mariana, he grew up without it, so he respected it, and was determined to make a good living in the city, "so we can build something secure for us and the future—and for our kids."

That's how he spoke at just twenty: so ridiculously grown-up. And so naive to assume they would spend the rest of their lives together. They lived in the future in those days, endlessly planning it—and never speaking of the past, and of the unhappy years leading up to their meeting. In many ways, Mariana's and Sebastian's lives began when they found each other—in that instant they first saw each other by the river. Mariana believed their love would go on forever. That it would never end—

Looking back, was there something sacrilegious in that assumption? A kind of hubris?

Perhaps.

For here she was, alone on this train, on this journey they had made together countless times, at various stages in their lives and in different moods—mostly happy, sometimes not—talking, reading, or sleeping, Mariana's head resting on his shoulder. These were the uneventful mundane moments she would give anything to have back again.

She could almost imagine him here—in the carriage, sitting next to her—and if she glanced at the window, she half expected to see Sebastian's face reflected there, next to hers, superimposed on the passing landscape.

But instead, Mariana saw a different face.

A man's face, staring at her.

She blinked, unnerved. She turned from the window to glance at him. The man was sitting opposite her, eating an apple. He smiled.

9

The man continued staring at Mariana—although to call him a man was, she decided, rather generous.

He looked as if he were barely in his twenties: he had a boyish face and curly brown hair, and a sprinkling of freckles on his hairless cheeks that made him seem even younger.

He was tall and thin as a rake, dressed in a dark corduroy jacket, creased white shirt, and a college scarf in blue and red and yellow. His brown eyes, partly disguised by his old-fashioned steel-rimmed glasses, brimmed with intelligence and curiosity, and contemplated Mariana with obvious interest.

"How's it going?" he said.

Mariana peered at him, a little confused. "Do we—know each other?"

He grinned. "Not yet. But hopefully."

Mariana didn't reply. She turned away. There was a pause. Then he tried again.

"Would you like one?"

He held out a large brown paper bag, bulging with fruit—grapes, bananas, and apples. "Take one," he said, offering it to Mariana. "Have a banana."

Mariana smiled politely. He had a nice voice, she thought. She shook her head.

"No, thanks."

"You're absolutely sure?"

"Positive."

Mariana turned and looked outside, hoping that would end the interaction. She could see his reflection in the window, and watched him shrug, disappointed. He was, apparently, not quite in control of his long limbs—and ended up knocking over his cup and spilling it. Some of his tea went on the table, but most landed in his lap.

"Bloody hell."

He jumped up, pulling a tissue from his pocket. He mopped up the pool of tea on the table, and dabbed at the stain on his trousers. He gave her an apologetic look. "Sorry about that. Didn't splash you, did I?"

"No."

"Good."

He sat down again. She could feel his eyes on her. After a moment, he said, "You're . . . a student?"

Mariana shook her head. "No."

"Ah. You work in Cambridge?"

Mariana shook her head. "No."

"Then you're . . . a tourist?"

"No."

"Hmm." He frowned, evidently perplexed.

There was a pause. Mariana gave in, and said, "I'm visiting someone . . . My niece."

"Oh, you're an *aunt*."

He looked relieved to have placed Mariana in a category. He smiled.

"I'm doing a Ph.D.," he said, volunteering the information, as Mariana didn't seem about to ask. "I'm a mathematician—well, theoretical physics, really."

He paused, taking off his glasses to wipe them with a tissue. He looked quite naked without them. And Mariana saw, for the first time, that he was handsome; or would be, when his face grew up a bit.

He put his glasses back on, and peered at her.

"I'm Frederick, by the way. Or Fred. What's your name?"

Mariana didn't want to tell Fred her name. Probably because she had the feeling—flattering but also unnerving—that he was trying to flirt with her. Apart from the obvious fact he was too young for her, she wasn't ready, never would be ready—even thinking about it felt like a sickening betrayal. She answered with strained politeness.

"My name . . . is Mariana."

"Ah, that's a beautiful name."

Fred went on talking, attempting to engage her in conversation. But Mariana's responses became increasingly monosyllabic. She silently counted the minutes until she could make her escape.

When they arrived in Cambridge, Mariana tried to slip away and disappear in the crowd. But Fred caught up with her outside the railway station.

"Can I accompany you to town? On the bus, perhaps?"

"I'd rather walk."

"Great—I have my bike here—I can walk with you. Or you can ride it if you prefer?"

He looked at her hopefully. Mariana felt sorry for him, despite herself. But she spoke more firmly this time.

"I—prefer to be alone. If that's okay."

"Of course . . . I see. I understand. Perhaps—a coffee, later? Or a drink? Tonight?"

Mariana shook her head and pretended to check her watch. "I won't be here that long."

"Well, perhaps I can have your number?" He blushed a little, and the freckles on his cheeks burned red. "Would that be—?"

Mariana shook her head. "I don't think—"

"No?"

"No." Mariana looked away, embarrassed. "I'm sorry, I—"

"Don't be sorry. I'm not discouraged. We'll meet again soon."

Something about his tone made her feel a little irritated. "I don't think so."

"Oh, we will. I *foresee* it. I have a gift for that sort of thing, you know—runs in my family—foresight, premonitions. I see things others do not."

Fred smiled and stepped onto the road. A cyclist swerved to avoid him.

"Watch out," said Mariana, touching his arm. The cyclist swore at Fred as he rode past.

"Sorry," he said. "I'm a little clumsy, I'm afraid."

"Only a little." Mariana smiled. "Goodbye, Fred."

"Until we meet again, Mariana."

He went over to the row of bicycles. Mariana watched as he got on his bike and cycled past, waving at her. Then Fred turned the corner and vanished.

Mariana breathed a sigh of relief. And she began walking into town.

10

As she made her way to St. Christopher's, Mariana's anxiety grew about what she might find there.

She had no idea what to expect—there might be police or press, which seemed hard to believe, looking around the Cambridge streets: there was no sign that anything untoward had happened, no indication a murder had even taken place.

It seemed remarkably peaceful after London. Barely any traffic, the only sound was birdsong, punctuated by a chorus of chirruping bicycle bells as students cycled past in black academic gowns, like flocks of birds.

Mariana had the feeling, a couple of times, as she walked, that she was being watched—or followed—and she wondered if perhaps it was Fred, having doubled back on his bicycle to tail her, but she dismissed the thought as paranoid.

All the same, she glanced over her shoulder a few times, to make sure—and of course no one was there.

As she neared the college, her surroundings grew more and more beautiful with each step: there were spires and turrets above her head, and beech trees lining the streets, shedding golden leaves that collected in piles along the pavement. Long rows of black bicycles were chained against the wrought iron railings. And above the railings, boxes of geraniums enlivened the redbrick college walls with splashes of pink and white.

Mariana glanced at a group of students, presumably first-years, intently studying the posters attached to railings that were advertising events for Freshers' Week.

They looked so young, these students, these freshers—like babies. Did she and Sebastian ever look that young? It seemed impossible, somehow. It was harder still to imagine anything bad ever happening to those innocent, unblemished faces. And yet she wondered how many of them had tragedy waiting in their future.

Mariana's mind went back to that poor girl, murdered by the marsh—whoever she was. Even if she wasn't Zoe's friend Tara, she was someone's friend, someone's daughter. That was the horror of it. We all secretly hope that tragedy will only ever happen to other people. But Mariana knew, sooner or later, it happens to you.

Death was no stranger to Mariana; it had been her traveling companion since she was a child—keeping close behind her, hovering just over her shoulder. She sometimes felt she had been cursed, as if by some malevolent goddess in a Greek myth, to lose everyone she ever loved. It was cancer that killed her mother when Mariana was just a baby. And then, years later, a horrific car crash claimed Mariana's sister and her husband, making Zoe an orphan. And a heart attack crept upon Mariana's father in the olive grove, leaving him dead on a bed of sticky, squashed olives.

Finally—and most catastrophically—there was Sebastian.

They had so few years together, really. After graduating, they moved to London, and Mariana began the circuitous journey that ended in her becoming a group therapist, while Sebastian worked in the City. But he had a stubborn entrepreneurial spirit and wanted to go into business for himself. So Mariana suggested he speak to her father about it.

She should have known better, really—but she cherished a secret, sentimental hope that her father might take Sebastian under his wing, bring him into the family business; let him inherit, before passing it on, one day, to their children. This was how far

Mariana's imagination carried her—but she knew better than to mention any of this to her father, or Sebastian. In any case, their first meeting was a disaster—Sebastian flew to Athens on a romantic mission, to ask permission to marry Mariana—and her father took an instant dislike to him. Far from offering him employment, he accused Sebastian of being a gold digger. He told Mariana he would disinherit her the day she married Sebastian.

The irony was that, in the end, Sebastian did go into shipping—but in the opposite end of the market to her father. Sebastian turned his back on the commercial sector, instead setting up businesses to help transport much-needed goods—food and other essentials—to vulnerable and underprivileged communities around the world. He was in many ways, Mariana thought, the mirror image of her father. And this was a constant source of pride for her.

When the troubled old man eventually died, he surprised them all once again. In the end, he left Mariana everything. A fortune. Sebastian was astounded that, being as wealthy as he was, her father lived the way he did—"I mean, like a pauper. He got no enjoyment out of it at all. What was the point of it?"

Mariana had to think for a moment. "Security," she said. "He believed all the money would protect him, somehow. I think—he was afraid."

"Afraid . . . of what?"

For this, Mariana had no answer. She shook her head, at a loss. "I'm not sure he knew himself."

Despite this inheritance, she and Sebastian indulged themselves with only one extravagant purchase: they bought the little yellow house at the foot of Primrose Hill, which they had fallen in love with at first sight. The rest of the money was put aside—at Sebastian's insistence—for the future, and for their children.

This issue of children was the only sore point between them, a bruise Sebastian couldn't help pressing on every now and then, bringing it up after one drink too many, or during a rare broody moment. He desperately wanted children—a boy and a girl—to complete the picture of the family he had in his head. And while Mariana also wanted kids, she wanted to wait. She wanted to finish her training and establish her psychotherapy practice—which might take a few years, but so what? They had all the time in the world, didn't they?

Except they didn't—and this was Mariana's only regret: that she had been so arrogant, so foolish, as to take the future for granted.

When, in her early thirties, she consented to start trying, she found it difficult to conceive. This sudden and unexpected stumbling block made her anxious—which her doctor said wouldn't help.

Dr. Beck was an older man with a fatherly air, which Mariana found reassuring. He suggested that, before embarking on fertility testing and possible treatment, Mariana and Sebastian go away for a holiday, away from any kind of stress.

"Enjoy yourselves, relax on a beach for a couple of weeks," Dr. Beck said with a wink. "See what happens. A little relaxation can often work wonders."

Sebastian wasn't keen—he had a lot of work lined up and didn't want to leave London. Mariana later discovered he was under a great deal of pressure financially, that summer, as several of his businesses were struggling. He was too proud to come to her for money—he'd never once taken a penny from her. And it broke her heart to find out, after his death, that he had been carrying around all this unnecessary worry about money for the last few months of his life. How could she not have noticed? The truth was, she was selfishly consumed with her own worries, that summer, about having a child.

And so she bullied Sebastian into taking two weeks off, in August, for a trip to Greece; to visit Mariana's family's summer home—a cliff-top house on the island of Naxos.

They took a plane to Athens, and then, from the port, they got the ferry to the island. It was an auspicious crossing, Mariana thought—not a cloud in the sky, and the water was calm and glassy flat.

At the Naxos harbor, they hired a car, and drove along the coast to the house. It had belonged to Mariana's father and now, technically, to Mariana and Sebastian—although they had never used it.

The house itself was dusty and dilapidated—but stunningly situated, perched on a cliff overlooking the deep blue Aegean Sea. Steps had been carved into the rock, going down the cliff face, leading to the beach below. And there, on the shore, over millions of years, infinite pieces of pink coral had broken up and mingled with grains of sand—making the beach glow pink against the blue sea and sky.

It was idyllic, Mariana thought—and magical. She could feel herself relaxing already, and felt secretly hopeful that Naxos might perform the little miracle that was being asked of it.

They spent the first couple of days unwinding and lazing on the beach. Sebastian said that in the end, he was glad they had come—he was relaxing for the first time in months. He had a schoolboy habit of reading old thrillers on the beach, and he lay in the surf, happily engrossed in *The ABC Murders* by Agatha Christie, while Mariana slept under an umbrella on the sand.

Then, on the third day, Mariana suggested driving up into the hills—to see the temple.

Mariana remembered visiting the ancient temple as a child, wandering the ruin and investing it with all kinds of magic in her imagination. She wanted Sebastian to experience it. So they packed a picnic, and set off.

They took the old, winding mountain road, which got narrower and narrower as they climbed higher into the hills, eventually deteriorating into a dirt track littered with goat droppings.

And there, at the very top, on a plateau—was the ruined temple itself.

The Ancient Greek temple was built from Naxian marble, once

gleaming but now dirty white and weather-beaten. All that stood, after three thousand years, was a handful of broken columns silhouetted against a blue sky.

The temple was dedicated to Demeter, goddess of the harvest—goddess of life—and to her daughter, Persephone—goddess of death. The two goddesses were often worshipped together, two sides of the same coin—mother and daughter, life and death. In Greek, Persephone was known simply as *Kore,* meaning "maiden."

It was a beautiful spot for a picnic. They laid out the blue blanket under the dappled shade of an olive tree, and unpacked the contents of their cold-box—a bottle of sauvignon blanc, a watermelon, and chunks of salty Greek cheese. They had forgotten to bring a knife—so Sebastian smashed the watermelon against a rock like a skull, breaking it into bits. They ate the sweet flesh, spitting out the bony seeds.

Sebastian gave her a messy, sticky kiss. "I love you," he whispered. "Forever and ever—"

"—and ever and ever," she said, kissing him back.

After the picnic, they wandered the ruins. Mariana watched Sebastian clambering up ahead, like an excited kid. And as she watched him, Mariana said a silent prayer to Demeter, and to the Maiden. She prayed for Sebastian and for herself—for their happiness—and for their love.

And as she whispered this prayer, a cloud suddenly snaked in front of the sun—and for an instant, Sebastian's body was thrown into darkness, silhouetted against the blue sky. Mariana shivered, and she felt afraid without knowing why.

The moment passed as quickly as it arose. In a second, the sun came out, and Mariana forgot all about it.

But she remembered it later, of course.

The next morning, Sebastian got up at dawn. He put on his old green trainers, and whispered to Mariana he was going for a run on the beach. He kissed her, and left.

Mariana lay in bed, half asleep, half awake, conscious of time passing—listening to the wind outside. What began as a breeze was picking up strength and speed, tearing through the olive branches with a kind of wail, rattling the trees against the windows, like long fingers impatiently rapping against the glass.

Mariana wondered for a moment how big the waves were—and if Sebastian had gone swimming, as he often did after a run. But she wasn't worried. He was such a strong swimmer, such a strong man. He was indestructible, she thought.

The wind grew and grew, whirling in from the sea. But still, he didn't come home.

Starting to worry, but trying not to, Mariana left the house.

She made her way down the steps in the cliff face, holding tightly on to the rock as she descended, for fear of being hurled off by the gale.

On the beach, there was no sign of Sebastian. The wind was whirling up the pink sand and hurling it at her face; she had to shield her eyes as she searched. She couldn't see him in the water either—all she saw were massive black waves, churning up the sea all the way to the horizon.

She called his name: "Sebastian! Sebastian! Seb—"

But the wind flung the words back in her face. She felt herself starting to panic. She couldn't think, not with that wind whistling in her ears—and, behind it, a never-ending chorus of cicadas, like hyenas screeching.

And fainter still, in the far distance, was that the sound of laughter?

The cold, mocking laugh of a goddess?

No, stop, stop—she had to focus, she had to concentrate, she had to find him. Where was he? He couldn't possibly have gone swimming—not in this weather. He never would have been so stupid—

And then she saw them.

His shoes.

His old green trainers, neatly placed together on the sand . . . just by the water's edge.

After that, everything was a blur. Mariana waded into the water, hysterical, howling like a harpy—screaming, screaming . . .

And then . . . nothing.

Three days later, Sebastian's body washed up along the coast.

II

Nearly fourteen months had passed since then, since Sebastian's death. But in many ways, Mariana was still there, still trapped on the beach in Naxos, and she would be forever.

She was stuck, paralyzed—as Demeter had once been, when Hades kidnapped her beloved daughter, Persephone, and took her to the Underworld to be his bride. Demeter broke down—overwhelmed by grief. She refused to move or be moved. She simply sat and wept. And all around her, the natural world grieved with Demeter: summer turned to winter; day turned to night. The earth fell into mourning; or, more accurately, melancholia.

Mariana related to this. And now, as she drew closer and closer to St. Christopher's, she found herself walking with increasing trepidation, as the familiar streets made it hard to hold back the memories flooding into her mind—ghosts of Sebastian were waiting on every corner. She kept her head low, not looking up, like a soldier trying to pass unnoticed in enemy territory. She had to pull herself together if she were to be any use to Zoe.

That's why she was here—for Zoe. God knew Mariana would rather never see Cambridge again. And it was proving harder than she thought—but she'd do it for Zoe. Zoe was all she had left.

Mariana turned off King's Parade, onto the uneven cobbled

street she knew so well. She made her way along the cobbles, up to an old wooden gate at the end of the street. She looked up at it.

St. Christopher's College gate was at least twice her height, and set in an ancient, ivy-clad redbrick wall. She remembered the first time she ever approached this gate—when she came from Greece for an admissions interview, barely seventeen years old, feeling so small and fraudulent, so scared and alone.

How funny, to be feeling exactly the same way now, nearly twenty years later.

She pushed open the gate and went inside.

12

St. Christopher's College was there, just as she remembered it.

Mariana had been afraid to see it again—the backdrop to her love story—but thankfully, the college's beauty came to her rescue. And her heart didn't break—it sang.

St. Christopher's was among the oldest and the prettiest of the Cambridge colleges. It was made up of several courtyards and gardens leading down to the river, and built in a combination of architectural styles—Gothic, neoclassical, Renaissance—as the college had been rebuilt and expanded over the centuries. It was a haphazard, organic growth—and, Mariana thought, all the lovelier for it.

She was standing by the porter's lodge in Main Court—the first and largest courtyard. An immaculate green lawn spread out in front of her, up to the dark-green wisteria-covered wall at the opposite end of the courtyard. The greenery, peppered by splashes of white climbing roses, hung over the bricks like an elaborate tapestry, all the way to the walls of the chapel. There, the stained-glass windows gleamed green and blue and red in the sunlight, and from inside, the college choir could be heard practicing, their voices soaring in harmony.

A whispering voice—Sebastian's voice, perhaps?—told Mariana she was safe here. She could rest, and find the peace she craved.

Her body relaxed, almost with a sigh. She felt a sudden and unfamiliar sense of contentment: the age of these walls, these columns and arches, untouched by time or change, made her momentarily able to put her grief into some kind of perspective. She saw that this magical place did not belong to her or Sebastian; it was not theirs—it belonged to itself. And their story was only one in a myriad that had taken place here, no more important than any other.

She looked around, smiling, taking in the hive of activity around her. Although term had recently begun, last-minute preparations were ongoing, and there was a palpable sense of anticipation, like in a theater just before a performance. A gardener was mowing the grass on the other side of the lawn. A college porter, in a black suit and bowler hat, and a large green apron, was reaching up into the archways and nooks and crannies high above, using a long pole with a feather duster at the end of it, whisking away cobwebs. Several other porters were lining up long wooden benches on the lawn, presumably for matriculation photographs.

Mariana watched a nervous-looking teenager, obviously a first-year student, making his way through the courtyard, accompanied by a pair of bickering parents clutching suitcases. She smiled fondly.

And then, across the courtyard, she saw something else—a dark cluster of uniformed police officers.

And Mariana's smile slowly faded.

The police officers were emerging from the dean's office, accompanied by the dean. Even from this distance Mariana could see the dean was red-faced and flustered.

This could only mean one thing. The worst had happened. The police were here—and so Zoe was right: Tara was dead, and it was her body that had been found by the marsh.

Mariana needed to find Zoe. Now. She turned and hurried toward the next courtyard.

Distracted by her thoughts, she didn't hear the man calling her name until he said it twice.

"Mariana? Mariana!"

She turned around. A man was waving at her. She squinted at him, unclear who he was. But he seemed to know her.

"Mariana," he said again, this time with more confidence. "Wait there."

Mariana stopped. She waited as the man crossed the cobbles toward her, smiling broadly.

Of course, she thought. *It's Julian.*

It was his smile Mariana recognized, rather a famous smile these days.

Julian Ashcroft and Mariana had studied psychotherapy together in London. She hadn't seen him in years, except on television—he was a frequent talking head on news shows or true-crime documentaries. He specialized in forensic psychology—having written a bestselling book about British serial killers and their mothers. He seemed to take a prurient delight in madness and death, which Mariana found slightly distasteful.

She studied him as he approached. Julian was in his late thirties now, and about medium height, wearing a smart blue blazer, crisp white shirt, and navy-blue jeans. His hair was artfully messy, and he had striking light-blue eyes—and a perfect white smile, which he frequently employed. There was something slightly artificial about him, Mariana thought, which probably made him just right for television.

"Hello, Julian."

"Mariana," he said as he reached her. "What a surprise. I thought it was you. What are you doing here? Not with the police, are you?"

"No, no. My niece is a student here."

"Oh—I see. Damn. I thought we might be working together."

Julian flashed a smile at her. He lowered his voice, confidentially. "They called me in, to give them a hand."

Mariana guessed what he was talking about, but she felt a sense of dread all the same. She didn't want it confirmed, but had no choice.

"It's Tara Hampton. Isn't it?"

Julian gave her a slight look of surprise, and nodded. "That's right. She was identified just now. How did you know?"

Mariana shrugged. "She's been missing for a day or so. My niece told me."

She realized her eyes had filled with tears, and she quickly wiped them away. She fixed her gaze on Julian. "Any leads yet?"

"No." Julian shook his head. "Not yet. Soon, hopefully. The sooner, the better, quite frankly. It was horribly violent."

"Do you think she knew him?"

Julian nodded. "It seems likely. We usually reserve that level of anger for our nearest and dearest, don't you think?"

"Possibly." Mariana mulled it over.

"Ten to one it's her boyfriend."

"I don't think she had a boyfriend."

Julian checked his watch. "I've got to meet the chief inspector now, but you know, I'd be happy to discuss this further . . . perhaps over a drink?" He smiled. "Good to see you, Mariana. It's been years. We should catch up—"

But Mariana was already walking away. "Sorry, Julian—I have to find my niece."

13

Zoe's room was in Eros Court—one of the smaller courtyards, consisting of student accommodations built around a rectangular lawn.

In the center of the lawn stood a discolored statue of Eros clutching a bow and arrow. Centuries of rain and rust had aged him considerably, turning him from a cherub into a small, old green man.

All the way around the courtyard, various staircases led off to the student rooms. A tall gray stone turret stood in each corner. As Mariana approached one of the turrets, she glanced up at the third-floor window and saw Zoe sitting there.

Zoe hadn't seen her, and Mariana stood there, watching her for a moment. The arched windows were latticed, with diamond-shaped panes of glass set in lead; the small panes broke up Zoe's image, fracturing it into a jigsaw of diamond shapes—and, for a second, Mariana assembled another image from the jigsaw: not a twenty-year-old woman but a girl of six, silly and sweet, red-faced, with pigtails.

Mariana felt such concern and affection for that little girl. Poor little Zoe—she had been through so much; Mariana dreaded having to hurt her further and break this terrible news. She shook her head, stopped procrastinating, and hurried into the turret.

She climbed the old, circular, warped wooden staircase up to Zoe's room. The door was ajar, so she went inside.

It was a cozy little room—a little messy at present, with clothes strewn on the armchairs and dirty cups in the sink. There was a writing desk, a small fireplace, and a cushioned seat in the bay window, where Zoe was sitting, surrounded by books.

When she saw Mariana, she let out a little cry. She leaped up and threw herself into Mariana's arms.

"You came. I didn't think you'd come."

"Of course I came."

Mariana tried to take a step backward, but Zoe wouldn't let go, and Mariana had no choice but to submit to the hug. She felt its warmth, its affection. It was so unfamiliar to be touched like this. She realized how happy she was to see Zoe. She felt quite emotional, suddenly.

After Sebastian, Zoe had always been Mariana's favorite human being. She went to boarding school in England, and so Mariana and Sebastian had unofficially adopted her—Zoe had a bedroom in the little yellow house, and would stay over with them over half-term and during holidays. She was educated in England because her father had been English; Zoe, in fact, was only a quarter Greek. She had her father's fair coloring and his blue eyes—so it didn't particularly show, this quarter Greekness; Mariana used to wonder how and if it would one day manifest itself—that's if it hadn't been smothered by the great wet blanket of an English private school education.

Zoe eventually released Mariana from the hug. And, gently as she could, Mariana broke the news about Tara's body being identified.

Zoe stared at her. Tears streamed down her cheeks as she took in the news. Mariana pulled her back into her arms. Zoe clung to her as she wept.

"It's okay," Mariana whispered. "Everything's going to be okay."

She slowly guided Zoe to the bed and sat her down. When Zoe managed to stop sobbing, Mariana made them some tea. She washed out a couple of mugs in the small sink, and boiled the kettle.

All the time, Zoe sat upright in bed, her knees up against her chest, staring into space, not bothering to wipe away the tears that rolled down her cheeks. She was clutching her ancient soft toy—a battered black-and-white-striped zebra. Zebra had one eye missing and was falling apart at the seams—having been Zoe's companion since she was a baby, and suffering much abuse and receiving much love. Zoe held on to him now, squeezing him tight, rocking back and forth.

Mariana placed the steaming mug of sweet tea on the cluttered coffee table. She watched Zoe with concern. The truth was Zoe had suffered badly from depression as a teenager. She had frequent fits of crying, punctuated by low, flat, emotionless moods, too depressed even to cry—which Mariana found harder to deal with than the tears. It was difficult to reach Zoe during those years, although her problems were hardly surprising, given the traumatic loss of her parents at such a young age.

Zoe had been staying with them during that half-term, one April, when they received the phone call that would change her life forever. Sebastian answered the phone, and had to tell Zoe that her parents, Mariana's sister and her husband, had been killed in a car crash. Zoe broke down, and Sebastian reached out and held her close. From then on, he and Mariana had doted on Zoe, probably a little too much—but having lost her own mother, Mariana felt determined to provide Zoe with everything she herself had longed for at a young age: maternal love, warmth, affection. It went both ways, of course—she felt Zoe gave back as much love as she received.

Eventually, to their relief, bit by bit, Zoe managed to turn the corner on her grief—as she grew older, she suffered from depression less; she was able to apply herself at school, finishing her adolescence in much better shape than she had started it. But Mariana

and Sebastian both had been worried how Zoe would cope with
the social pressures of university—so when she made a close friend
in Tara, they were relieved. And later on, after Sebastian died,
Mariana was grateful Zoe had a best friend to lean on. Mariana
didn't have one; she had just lost him.

But now, this new loss of Tara—the horrific loss of a good
friend—how would it affect Zoe? That remained to be seen.

"Zoe, here, drink some tea. It's for the shock."

No response.

"Zoe?"

Zoe suddenly seemed to hear her. She looked up at Mariana
with glassy eyes, filled with tears.

"It's my fault," she whispered. "*It's all my fault she's dead.*"

"Don't say that. It's not true—"

"It is true. Listen to me. You don't understand."

"Understand what?"

Mariana sat on the edge of the bed, and waited for Zoe to go on.

"It's my fault, Mariana. I should have done something—that
night—after I saw Tara—I should have told someone—I should
have phoned the police. Then she might still be alive . . ."

"The police? Why?"

Zoe didn't reply. Mariana frowned.

"What did Tara say to you? You said—she sounded crazy?"

Zoe's eyes welled up with tears. She rocked back and forth in
morose silence. Mariana knew the best approach was simply to
be present, and patient, and let Zoe unburden herself in her own
time. But there was no time. She spoke in a low voice, reassuring
but firm.

"What did she say to you, Zoe?"

"I shouldn't have told you. Tara made me swear not to tell
anyone."

"I understand—you don't want to betray her confidence. But
I'm afraid it's too late for that."

Zoe stared at her. As Mariana looked into her face, her cheeks
flushed and eyes wide, she saw the eyes of a child: a little girl,

scared, bursting with a secret she didn't want to keep but was too afraid to tell.

Then, eventually, Zoe gave in:

"The night before last, Tara came and found me in my room. She was a real mess. She was high on something, I don't know what. She was really upset . . . And she said—she was afraid . . ."

"Afraid? Of what?"

"She said—someone was going to kill her."

Mariana stared at Zoe for a second. "Go on."

"She made me promise not to tell anyone—she said if I said anything, and he found out, he'd kill her."

"'He'? Who was she talking about? Did she say who threatened to kill her?"

Zoe nodded, but didn't answer.

Mariana repeated the question. "Who was it, Zoe?"

Zoe shook her head, unsure. "She sounded so crazy—"

"It doesn't matter, just tell me."

"She said—it was one of the tutors here. A professor."

Mariana blinked, taken aback. "Here, at St. Christopher's?"

Zoe nodded. "Yes."

"I see. What's his name?"

Zoe paused. She spoke in a low voice.

"Edward Fosca."

14

Just under an hour later, Zoe was repeating her story to Chief Inspector Sadhu Sangha.

The inspector had commandeered the dean's office. It was a spacious room overlooking Main Court. On one wall, there was a beautifully carved mahogany bookcase and a leather-bound collection of books. The other walls were covered with portraits of past deans—watching the police officers with undisguised suspicion.

Chief Inspector Sangha sat behind the large desk. He opened the flask he carried with him, and poured himself a cup of tea. He was in his early fifties, with dark eyes and a short-cropped salt-and-pepper beard, smartly dressed in a gray blazer and tie. As he was a Sikh, he was wearing a turban, in eye-catching royal blue. He was a commanding, powerful presence, but had a nervous energy about him—a lean and hungry look—forever tapping his foot or drumming his fingers.

To Mariana he seemed faintly irritable. He gave her the impression that he wasn't paying full attention to what Zoe was saying. He didn't seem particularly interested. *He's not taking her seriously,* thought Mariana.

But she was wrong. He *was* taking her seriously. He put down his tea, and fixed his large dark eyes on Zoe.

"And what did you think—when she told you this?" he said. "Did you believe her?"

"I don't know . . ." Zoe said. "She was a mess, you know, she was high. But she was always high, so . . ." Zoe shrugged, and thought about it for a second. "I mean, it sounded so weird . . ."

"Did she say *why* Professor Fosca had threatened to kill her?"

Zoe looked a little uncomfortable. "She said they were sleeping together. And they had a fight or something . . . and she threatened to tell the college and get him fired. And he said, if she did . . ."

"He'd kill her?"

Zoe nodded. She looked relieved to have got it off her chest. "That's right."

The inspector seemed to mull this over for a moment. Then he abruptly stood up.

"I'm going to talk to Professor Fosca. Wait here, will you? And, Zoe—we'll need you to make a statement."

He left the room, and in his absence, Zoe repeated her story to a junior officer, who wrote it down. Mariana waited uneasily, wondering what was going on.

A long hour passed. And then Inspector Sangha returned. He sat down again.

"Professor Fosca was most cooperative," he said. "I've taken a statement from him—and he says that, at the time of Tara's death—at ten P.M.—he was finishing a class in his rooms. It went from eight until ten P.M., and was attended by six students. He gave me their names. We've spoken to two of them so far, and they both corroborate his story." The inspector gave Zoe a thoughtful look. "As a result, I am not charging the professor with any crime, and I feel perfectly satisfied that—despite what Tara may have said—he is not responsible for her death."

"I see," said Zoe in a whisper.

Zoe kept her gaze down, staring at her lap. Mariana thought she looked worried.

"I'm wondering what you can tell me about Conrad Ellis?" said the inspector. "He's not a student here—he lives in town, I believe. He was Tara's boyfriend?"

Zoe shook her head. "He wasn't her boyfriend. They hung out, that's all."

"I see." The inspector consulted his notes. "It seems he has two prior convictions—for drug dealing, and for aggravated assault . . ." He glanced at Zoe. "And his neighbors heard them having violent arguments on several occasions."

Zoe shrugged. "He's a mess, like she was . . . but—he'd never hurt her, if that's what you mean. He's not like that. He's a nice guy."

"Hmm. He sounds lovely." The inspector didn't look convinced. He drained his tea, then screwed the lid back onto the flask.

Case closed, Mariana thought.

"You know, Inspector," she said, indignant on Zoe's behalf, "I do think you ought to listen to her."

"Excuse me?" Inspector Sangha blinked. He looked surprised to hear Mariana speak. "Remind me," he said, "who are you again?"

"I'm Zoe's aunt, and guardian. And—if necessary—her advocate."

Inspector Sangha seemed faintly amused by this. "Your niece seems perfectly capable of being her own advocate, as far as I can tell."

"Well, Zoe is a good judge of character. She always has been. If she knows Conrad—and thinks he is innocent—you should take her seriously."

The inspector's smile faded. "When I interview him, I'll form my own opinion—if you don't mind. Just so we're clear, I'm in charge here, and I don't respond well to being told what to do—"

"I'm not telling you what to—"

"Or to being interrupted. So I would strongly suggest that you keep out of my way—and out of my investigation. Understood?"

Mariana was about to argue back—but restrained herself. She forced a smile.

"Perfectly," she said.

15

After leaving the dean's office, Zoe and Mariana walked through the colonnade at the end of the courtyard—a series of twelve marble columns, which supported the library above. The columns were very old and discolored, with cracks running through them like veins. They cast long shadows on the floor, plunging the women into occasional darkness as they wandered between them.

Mariana put her arm around Zoe. "Darling, are you all right?" she said.

Zoe shrugged. "I—I don't know."

"Do you think, perhaps, Tara was lying to you?"

Zoe looked pained. "I don't know. I—"

Zoe suddenly froze and stopped walking. From nowhere, stepping out from behind a column—a man had appeared in front of them.

He stood there, blocking their path. He stared at her.

"Hello, Zoe."

"Professor Fosca," Zoe said, with a slight intake of breath.

"How are you? Are you okay? I can't believe this has happened. I'm in shock."

He had an American accent, Mariana noticed, with a soft, lilt-ing cadence to his speech—ever-so-slightly Anglicized around the edges.

"You poor thing," he said. "I'm so sorry, Zoe. You must be absolutely devastated—"

He spoke in an impassioned tone, and seemed genuinely dis-tressed. He reached out to her—and Zoe made a slight, invol-untary movement backward. Mariana noticed it, and so did the professor. He gave Zoe an awkward look.

"Listen," he said. "I'll tell you exactly what I told the inspector. It's important you hear this from me—right now."

Fosca ignored Mariana, addressing himself solely to Zoe. And Mariana studied him as he spoke. He was younger than she'd expected, and considerably more handsome. He was in his early forties, tall, with an athletic build. He had strong cheek-bones and striking dark eyes. Everything about him was dark—his black eyes, his beard, his clothes. His long black hair was tied up in a messy knot at the back of his head. And he was wearing a black academic gown, an untucked shirt, and a loose tie. There was something charismatic, even Byronic, about the whole effect.

"The truth is," he said, "I probably handled it badly. I'm sure you can vouch for this, Zoe—but Tara was barely coping, aca-demically. In fact she was failing abysmally, despite my repeated efforts to get her to improve her attendance record and complete the coursework. And she left me with no choice. I had a very frank chat with her. I said that I didn't know if drugs were involved, or if it was relationship problems, but she hadn't done enough to pro-gress this year. I told her she had to resit the entirety of last year. It was either that, or send her down."

He gave a weary shake of the head. "And when I told Tara this, she became quite hysterical. She said her father would kill her. She begged me to change my mind. I said it was out of the ques-tion. And then her attitude changed. She became quite aggressive.

She threatened me. She said she would ruin my career and get me fired." He sighed. "It seems this is what she attempted. Everything she said to you—these sexual allegations—it's an obvious attempt to damage my reputation."

He lowered his voice. "I would never have sex with any of my students—it would be the most gross betrayal of trust, and an abuse of power. As you know, I was extremely fond of Tara. That's why hearing she made this accusation is so hurtful."

Despite herself, Mariana found Fosca entirely convincing. There was nothing remotely in his manner to suggest he was lying. Everything he said had the ring of truth. Tara had often spoken about her father in fearful terms, and Zoe had reported, from her visit to their estate in Scotland, that Tara's father had been a strict host—even draconian. Mariana could well imagine his reaction to Tara failing the year. She could also imagine that the prospect of telling him might make Tara hysterical—and desperate.

Mariana glanced at Zoe to see how she was taking it. It was hard to tell. Zoe was clearly tense, and staring at the stone floor with a look of embarrassment.

"I hope that clears it up," Fosca said. "What's important now is we help the police catch whoever did this. I have suggested they investigate Conrad Ellis, that man Tara was involved with. By all accounts, he's a nasty piece of work."

Zoe didn't reply. Fosca stared at her.

"Zoe? Are we okay? God knows we have enough to deal with right now—without you suspecting me of something like this."

Zoe looked up and stared at him. She slowly nodded.

"We're fine," she said.

"Good." But he didn't look entirely satisfied. "I have to go. I'll see you later. Look after yourself, okay?"

Fosca glanced at Mariana for the first time, acknowledging her with a brief nod. Then he turned and walked away, vanishing behind a column.

There was a pause. Zoe turned to Mariana. She looked apprehensive.

"Well?" she said, with a slight sigh. "What now?"

Mariana thought for a second. "I'm going to talk to Conrad."

"But how? You heard the Inspector."

Mariana didn't reply. She caught sight of Julian Ashcroft leaving the dean's office. She watched him walk across the courtyard.

She nodded to herself. "I have an idea," she said.

16

Later that afternoon, Mariana managed to see Conrad Ellis at the police station.

"Hello, Conrad," she said. "I'm Mariana."

Conrad had been arrested immediately following his interview with Chief Inspector Sangha—the police were confident he was their man, despite a lack of evidence, circumstantial or otherwise.

Tara was last seen alive at eight o'clock by the head porter, Mr. Morris, who saw her leave college by the main gate. And Conrad said he was waiting for Tara at his flat, but she never turned up— although there was only Conrad's word for this; he had no alibi for the entire evening.

No murder weapon was discovered at his flat, despite a thorough search. And his clothes and other belongings were taken away for forensic testing, in the hope they would provide something to link Conrad to the murder.

To Mariana's surprise, Julian readily agreed to help her see him.

"I can get you in on my pass," Julian said. "I need to do the psych evaluation anyway, and you can observe, if you want." Then he winked at her. "As long as Sangha doesn't catch us."

"Thanks. I owe you one."

Julian seemed to enjoy the subterfuge. They entered the police station, and he winked at her as he requested Conrad Ellis be brought up from the cells.

A few minutes later, they were sitting with Conrad in the interview room. It was a cold room, windowless, airless. It was unpleasant to be in—but presumably that was the point.

"Conrad, I'm a psychotherapist," said Mariana. "I'm also Zoe's aunt. You know Zoe, don't you? At St. Christopher's?"

Conrad looked confused for a second; then there was a dim light in his eyes and he nodded absently. "Zoe—Tara's mate?"

"That's right. She wants you to know how sorry she is—about Tara."

"She's all right, Zoe . . . I like her. She's not like the others."

"The others?"

"Tara's mates." Conrad pulled a face. "I call them the witches."

"Really? You don't like her friends?"

"It's me they don't like."

"Why is that?"

Conrad shrugged. Blank, expressionless. Mariana had been hoping to get some kind of emotional response from him, something that would help her read him better—but none came. She was reminded of her patient Henry. He had that same clouded look, from years of relentless alcohol and drug abuse.

Conrad's appearance went against him—that was part of the problem. He was lumbering, huge, heavily tattooed. And yet Zoe was right; there was a niceness to him, a gentleness. When he spoke, his speech was slow and confused; he didn't seem quite clear about what was happening to him.

"I don't understand—why do they think I hurt her? I didn't hurt her. I love—loved her."

Mariana glanced at Julian to see his reaction. He didn't look remotely moved. He proceeded to ask Conrad all kinds of intrusive questions about his life and his upbringing—the longer it went on, the more torturous the interview became, the blacker things looked for Conrad.

And all the more Mariana felt he was innocent. He wasn't

lying; this man was heartbroken. At one point, exhausted by Julian's questioning, he broke down, held his head in his hands—and quietly wept.

At the end of the interview, Mariana spoke again.

"Do you know Professor Fosca?" she asked. "Tara's tutor?"

"Yeah."

"And how did you know him? Through Tara?"

He nodded. "I scored for him a few times."

Mariana blinked. She glanced at Julian. "You mean drugs?"

"What kind?" asked Julian.

He shrugged. "Depends what he wanted."

"So you saw him regularly? Professor Fosca?"

Another shrug. "Often enough."

"What did you make of his relationship with Tara? Did it seem in any way strange to you?"

"Well," Conrad said with a shrug, "I mean, he fancied her, didn't he?"

Mariana exchanged a glance with Julian.

"Did he?"

Mariana was going to press him further, but Julian abruptly ended the interview. He said he had enough to make his report.

"I hope you found that informative," said Julian as they left the station. "Quite a performance, don't you think?"

Mariana looked at him with astonishment. "He didn't fake that. He's not capable of faking it."

"Trust me, Mariana, the tears are all an act. Or else it's self-pity. I've seen it all before. When you've been doing this as long as I have, you realize every case is depressingly similar."

She looked at him. "You don't think it's concerning—that he sold Professor Fosca drugs?"

Julian dismissed it with a shrug. "Buying a little weed every now and then doesn't make him a murderer."

"And what about Conrad saying Fosca fancied her?"

"What if he did? By all accounts, she was gorgeous. You knew her, didn't you? What was she doing with that moron?"

Mariana shook her head sadly. "I imagine Conrad was simply a means to an end."

"Drugs?"

Mariana sighed and nodded.

Julian glanced at her.

"Come on. I'll drive you back—unless you fancy a drink?"

"I can't, I have to get back to college. They're holding a special service for Tara at six."

"Well, one evening, I hope?" He winked. "You owe me, remember? Tomorrow?"

"I won't be here, I'm afraid—I'm leaving tomorrow."

"Okay, we'll work something out. I can hunt you down in London if necessary."

Julian laughed—but not, Mariana noticed, with his eyes. They remained cold, hard, unkind. There was something about the way he looked at her that made Mariana feel distinctly uncomfortable.

She was rather relieved when they got back to St. Christopher's, and she could make her escape.

17

At six o'clock, a special service for Tara was held in the chapel.

The college chapel had been constructed in 1612 from stone and timber. There was an ebony marble floor; stained-glass windows in vibrant blues and reds and greens, illustrating incidents from the life of St. Christopher; and a high molded ceiling decorated with heraldic shields and Latin mottos painted in gold.

The pews were packed with fellows and students. Mariana and Zoe sat near the front. Tara's parents were sitting with the dean and the master.

Tara's parents, Lord and Lady Hampton, had flown down from Scotland to identify the body. Mariana imagined how their minds must have tortured them all the way from their remote country estate; the long drive to Edinburgh Airport, then the flight to Stansted, giving them time to think—hope and fear and worry—before a final trip to the mortuary in Cambridge cruelly resolved their suspense: reuniting them with their daughter—and showing them what had happened to her.

Lord and Lady Hampton sat rigidly; their faces were white, contorted—frozen. Mariana watched them with fascination—she remembered that feeling: like being plunged into a freezer, icy cold, numb with shock. It didn't last long—and it was a blessed state compared with what came next, when the frost melted and the shock wore off, and they began to experience the enormity of their loss.

Mariana saw Professor Fosca appear in the chapel. He walked down the aisle, followed by a group of six distinctive young women—distinctive because they were all extremely beautiful and because they were all dressed in long white dresses. They walked with an air of self-assurance, and also self-consciousness, aware they were being watched. The other students stared as they passed.

Were these Tara's friends, Mariana wondered, who Conrad disliked so much? The "witches"?

A somber silence fell upon the mourners as the service began. Accompanied by the pipe organ, a procession of choirboys, wearing red cassocks with white lace ruffs around their necks, sang a Latin hymn by candlelight, their angelic voices spiraling into the dark.

This was not a funeral; the actual burial would take place in Scotland. There was no body here to mourn. Mariana thought of that poor broken girl lying alone in the morgue.

And she couldn't help but remember how her lover had been returned to her, on a concrete slab in the hospital in Naxos. Sebastian's body was still wet when she saw him, dripping water onto the floor, with sand in his hair and eyes. There were holes in his skin, small chunks of flesh bitten off by fish. And one of his fingertips was missing, claimed by the sea.

As soon as Mariana saw this lifeless, waxy corpse, she knew at once it wasn't Sebastian. It was just a shell. Sebastian was gone—but where?

In the days after his death, Mariana was numb. She remained in a prolonged state of shock, unable to accept what had happened—or believe it. It seemed impossible that she would never see him again, never hear his voice, never feel his touch.

Where is he? she kept thinking. *Where's he gone?*

And then, as reality began to sink in, she had a kind of delayed breakdown—and, like a dam breaking, all her tears came rushing forth, a waterfall of grief, washing away her life and who she thought she was.

And then—came the anger.

A burning rage, a blind fury—which threatened to consume her and anyone near her. For the first time in her life, Mariana wanted to cause actual physical pain—she wanted to lash out and hurt someone, herself mostly.

She blamed herself—of course she did. She'd insisted they go to Naxos; if they'd stayed in London, as Sebastian had wanted, he would still be alive.

And she blamed Sebastian too. How dare he be so reckless; how dare he go out swimming in that weather, be so careless with his life—and with hers?

Mariana's days were bad; her nights were worse. At first, combining enough alcohol and sleeping pills bought her a kind of temporary, medicated refuge; albeit with recurring nightmares filled with disasters like sinking ships, train crashes, and floods. She'd dream of endless journeys—expeditions through desolate arctic landscapes, trudging through icy winds and snow, searching endlessly for Sebastian but never finding him.

Then, the pills stopped working and she would lie awake until three or four in the morning—lie there longing for him, with nothing to quench her thirst but her memories projected against the darkness: flickering images of their days together, their nights, their winters and summers. Finally, driven half mad with grief and lack of sleep, she went back to her doctor. As it was obvious she had been abusing the sleeping pills, Dr. Beck refused to write her another prescription. Instead, he suggested a change of scene.

"You're a wealthy woman," he said—adding callously, "with no children to support. Why not go abroad? Travel? See the world?"

Considering the last trip Dr. Beck had sent Mariana on had ended in the death of her husband, she elected not to follow his advice. Instead, she retreated to her imagination.

She would shut her eyes and think of the ruined temple on Naxos—the dirty white columns against the blue sky—and remember her whispered prayer to the Maiden—for their happiness, for their love.

Was that her mistake? Had the goddess somehow been offended? Was Persephone jealous? Or perhaps she fell for that handsome man at first sight, and claimed him, as she herself had once been claimed, taking him to the Underworld?

This seemed easier to bear, somehow—blaming Sebastian's death on the supernatural, on the capricious whim of a goddess. The alternative—that it was meaningless, random, signifying nothing . . . was more than she could bear.

Stop it, she thought. *Stop, stop it.* She could feel pathetic, self-pitying tears welling up in her eyes. She wiped them away. She didn't want to break down, not here. She had to get out of here, out of the chapel.

"I need some air," she whispered to Zoe.

Zoe nodded, and gave her hand a quick, supportive squeeze. Mariana got up, and hurried outside.

As she left the dimly lit and crowded chapel, emerging into the empty courtyard, she felt an immediate sense of relief.

There was no one in sight. Main Court was silent and still. It was dark, apart from the tall lampposts spaced out through the courtyard—their lanterns were glowing in the darkness, with halos around them. A heavy mist was seeping in from the river, creeping through the college.

Mariana wiped away her tears. She looked up at the sky. All the stars, invisible in London, shone here so brightly—billions of shimmering diamonds, in an infinite blackness.

He must be there, somewhere.

"Sebastian?" she whispered. "Where are you?"

She listened and watched, and waited for some kind of sign—for a shooting star, or a cloud passing in front of the moon—something; anything.

But there was nothing.

Only darkness.

18

After the service, people mingled outside in the courtyard, talking in small groups. Mariana and Zoe stood apart from the others, and Mariana quickly told Zoe about her visit to Conrad, and that she agreed with her assessment.

"You see?" Zoe said. "Conrad is innocent. He didn't do it. We have to help him somehow."

"I don't know what else we can do," said Mariana.

"We have to do something. I'm pretty sure Tara was sleeping with someone else. Apart from Conrad. She hinted at it a couple of times . . . Maybe there's a clue on her phone? Or her laptop? Let's try and get into her room—"

Mariana shook her head. "We can't do that, Zoe."

"Why not?"

"I think we need to leave all that to the police."

"But you heard the inspector. They're not looking—they made up their minds. We need to do something." She sighed heavily. "I wish Sebastian was here. He'd know what to do."

Mariana accepted the implied rebuke. "I wish he were here too." She paused. "I was thinking. How about you come back to London with me for a few days?"

She knew, as soon as she said this, that it was the wrong thing to say. Zoe stared at her with a look of astonishment.

"What?"

"It might help, to get away."

"I can't just *run away*. That won't make any difference. Do you think that's what Sebastian would say?"

"No," said Mariana, suddenly feeling irritated. "But I'm not Sebastian."

"No," said Zoe, mirroring her irritation. "You're not. Sebastian would want you to stay. That's what he'd say."

Mariana didn't say anything for a moment. Then she decided to voice something—a worry that had been bothering her since their phone call last night.

"Zoe. Are you sure . . . you're telling me everything?"

"About what?"

"I don't know. About this—about Tara. I keep thinking—I can't escape the feeling you're holding something back."

Zoe shook her head. "No, nothing."

She looked away. Mariana had a continuing feeling of doubt. It concerned her.

"Zoe. Do you trust me?"

"Don't even ask that."

"Then listen. This is important. There's something you're not telling me. I can tell. I can sense it. So trust me. Please—"

Zoe hesitated, then weakened. "Mariana, listen—"

But then, glancing over Mariana's shoulder, Zoe saw something—something that silenced her. A strange, fearful look flashed into Zoe's eyes for a second—and then it was gone. She turned back to Mariana and shook her head. "There's—nothing. Honest."

Mariana turned to see what Zoe had seen. And there, standing by the chapel entrance, were Professor Fosca and his entourage—the beautiful girls in white dresses, deep in whispered conversation.

Fosca was lighting a cigarette. His eyes met Mariana's through the smoke—and they stared at each other for a second.

Then the professor left the group and walked over to them, smiling. Mariana heard Zoe sigh slightly under her breath as he approached.

"Hello," he said when he reached them. "I didn't get a chance to introduce myself before. I'm Edward Fosca."

"I'm Mariana—Andros." She hadn't meant to use her maiden name. It just came out like that. "I'm Zoe's aunt."

"I know who you are. Zoe has told me about you. I'm very sorry about your husband."

"Oh," said Mariana, taken aback. "Thank you."

"And I'm sorry for Zoe," he said, glancing at her. "Having lost her uncle, and now having to grieve all over again for Tara."

Zoe didn't answer; she just shrugged, evading Fosca's eyes.

There was something not being said by Zoe here—something being avoided. *She's afraid of him,* Mariana suddenly thought. *Why?*

Mariana didn't find Fosca remotely threatening. To her, he seemed completely genuine, and sympathetic. He gave her a heartfelt look. "I'm so sorry for all the students," he said. "This will devastate the whole year—if not the entire college."

Zoe turned abruptly to Mariana. "I have to go—I'm meeting some friends for a drink. Do you want to come?"

Mariana shook her head. "I said I'd pop in to see Clarissa. I'll find you later."

Zoe nodded, and started walking off.

Mariana turned back to where Fosca had been—but to her surprise, he had already gone, striding away across the courtyard.

There was just a lingering trace of cigarette smoke where he had been standing, twisting and turning before it vanished in the air.

19

"Tell me about Professor Fosca," said Mariana.

Clarissa gave her a curious look as she poured amber-colored tea from a silver teapot into two delicate china cups. She handed Mariana the cup and saucer.

"Professor Fosca? What makes you ask about him?"

Mariana decided it might be best not to go into detail. "No reason," she said. "Zoe mentioned him."

Clarissa shrugged. "I don't know him terribly well—he's only been with us a couple of years. First-class mind. American. Did his doctorate under Robertson at Harvard."

She sat down opposite Mariana, in the faded lime-green arm-chair by the window. She smiled at Mariana fondly. Professor Clarissa Miller was in her late seventies, with an ageless face hidden under a mop of messy gray hair. She was wearing a white silk shirt and a tweed skirt, with a loose-knit green cardigan that was probably considerably older than most of her students.

Clarissa had been Mariana's director of studies when she was a student. Most of the teaching at St. Christopher's was done on a one-to-one basis, between fellow and student, usually taking place in the fellow's rooms. At any time after midday, or even earlier, at the discretion of the fellow concerned, alcohol was invariably served—an excellent Beaujolais, in Clarissa's case, brought up from the labyrinthine wine cellars beneath college—providing an education in drinking as well as literature.

It also meant that tutorials took on a more personal flavor, and lines between teacher and pupil became blurred—confidences were given, and intimacies exchanged. Clarissa had been touched, and perhaps intrigued, by this lonely motherless Greek girl. She kept a maternal eye on Mariana during her time at St. Christopher's. And for her part, Mariana was inspired by Clarissa—not just by the professor's remarkable academic achievements in a field dominated by men, but also by her knowledge, and enthusiasm for imparting that knowledge. And Clarissa's patience and kindness— and occasional irascibility—meant Mariana retained much more from her than from any other tutor she encountered.

They stayed in touch after Mariana graduated, through occasional notes and postcards, until one day an unexpected email came from Clarissa, announcing that against all odds she had joined the internet age. She sent Mariana a beautiful and heartfelt email after Sebastian died, which Mariana found so moving, she saved and reread it several times.

"I hear Professor Fosca taught Tara?" Mariana said.

Clarissa nodded. "That's right, yes, he did. Poor girl . . . I know he was quite concerned about her."

"Was he?"

"Yes, he said Tara was barely scraping through, academically. She was quite troubled, he said." She sighed, and shook her head. "Terrible business. Terrible."

"Yes. Yes, it is."

Mariana sipped some tea, and watched Clarissa pack her pipe with tobacco. It was a handsome thing, made of dark cherrywood.

Pipe smoking was a habit Clarissa had picked up from her late husband. Her rooms smelled of smoke and spicy, pungent pipe tobacco; over the years, the odor had seeped into the walls, into the paper in the books, into Clarissa herself. It was overpowering at times, and Mariana knew that students in the past had objected to

Clarissa smoking during supervisions—until Clarissa was eventually forced to comply with changing health-and-safety standards and no longer allowed to inflict her habit on her students.

But Mariana didn't mind; in fact, sitting here now, she realized how much she'd missed this smell. On the rare occasions she encountered a pipe being smoked in the outside world, she would immediately feel reassured, associating the smelly, dark, billowing smoke with wisdom and learning—and kindness.

Clarissa lit the pipe and puffed away on it, disappearing behind clouds of smoke. "It's a struggle to make sense of it," she said. "I feel quite at a loss, you know. It reminds me what sheltered lives we live here in the cloister—naive, perhaps even willfully ignorant of the horrors of the outside world."

Privately, Mariana agreed. Reading about life was no preparation for living it; she had learned this the hard way. But she didn't say so. She just nodded.

"Such violence is horrifying. It's hard for anyone to comprehend."

Clarissa pointed the pipe at Mariana. She often used her pipe as a prop, sending tobacco flying and leaving blackened holes on the rugs where burning embers had landed. "The Greeks had a word for it, you know. For that kind of anger."

Mariana was intrigued. "Did they?"

"*Menis.* There's no real equivalent in English. You remember, Homer begins *The Iliad* with 'μῆνιν ἄειδε θεὰ Πηληϊάδεω Ἀχιλῆος'— 'Sing to me, O goddess, of the *menis* of Achilles.'"

"Ah. What does it mean, exactly?"

Clarissa mused for a second. "I suppose the closest translation is a kind of uncontrollable anger—terrifying rage—a *frenzy*."

Mariana nodded. "A frenzy, yes . . . It was frenzied."

Clarissa placed the pipe in a small silver ashtray. She gave Mariana a small smile. "I'm so glad you're here, my dear. You'll be such a help."

"I'm only staying tonight—I'm just here for Zoe."

Clarissa looked disappointed. "Is that all?"

"Well, I have to get back to London. I have my patients—"

"Of course, but . . ." Clarissa shrugged. "Might you not consider staying a few days? For the sake of the college?"

"I don't see how I can help. I'm a psychotherapist, not a detective."

"I'm aware of that. You're a psychotherapist who specializes in groups . . . And what is this if not a group concern?"

"Yes, but—"

"You were also a student at St. Christopher's—which gives you a level of insight and understanding which the police, however well-intentioned, simply do not possess."

Mariana shook her head. She felt a little annoyed at once again being put on the spot. "I'm not a criminologist. This really isn't my field."

Clarissa looked disappointed, but she didn't comment. Instead, she watched Mariana for a moment. She spoke in a softer tone.

"Forgive me, my dear. It occurs to me I've not once asked you how it feels."

"What?"

"Being here—without Sebastian."

This was the first reference Clarissa had made to him. Mariana was a little thrown by it. She didn't know what to say.

"I don't know how it feels."

"It must be *odd*?"

Mariana nodded. "'Odd' is a good word."

"It was odd for me, after Timmy died. He was always there— and then, suddenly, he wasn't. I kept expecting him to jump out from behind a column and surprise me . . . I still do."

Clarissa had been married to Professor Timothy Miller for thirty years. Two famous Cambridge eccentrics, they were often seen charging around town together, books under their arms, with uncombed hair, wearing occasional odd socks, deep in conversation. One of the happiest couples Mariana had ever encountered, until Timmy died ten years ago.

"It will get easier," Clarissa said.

"Will it?"

"It's important to keep looking ahead. You mustn't forever look back, over your shoulder. Think about the future."

Mariana shook her head. "To be honest, I can't really see a future . . . I can't see much. It's all . . ." She searched for the words. Then she remembered: "Behind a veil. Where's that from? 'Behind the veil, behind the veil—'"

"Tennyson." Clarissa spoke without hesitation. "*In Memoriam*— stanza fifty-six, if I'm not mistaken."

Mariana smiled. Most fellows had an encyclopedia for a brain; Clarissa had an entire library. The professor closed her eyes and proceeded to recite it from memory.

"'O life as futile, then, as frail! / O for thy voice to soothe and bless! / What hope of answer, or redress? / *Behind the veil, behind the veil* . . .'"

Mariana nodded sadly. "Yes . . . Yes, that's it."

"Rather underrated these days, I'm afraid, Tennyson." Clarissa smiled, and then glanced at her watch. "If you're staying tonight, we must find you a room. Let me call the porter's lodge."

"Thank you."

"Wait a moment."

The old woman heaved herself to her feet, and went to the bookcase. She ran her finger along the spines until she located a book. She pulled it off the shelf, and pressed it into Mariana's hands.

"Here. I found this such a source of solace after Timmy died."

It was a slim black leather-bound volume. *IN MEMORIAM A.H.H. by Alfred Tennyson* was embossed on the cover in faded gold lettering.

Clarissa gave Mariana a firm look. "Read it."

20

Mr. Morris found Mariana a room. He was the head porter.

Mariana was surprised to meet him at the porter's lodge. She remembered old Mr. Morris well: he was an elderly, avuncular man, popular around college, famously lenient with undergraduates.

But this Mr. Morris was young, under thirty, tall and powerfully built. He had a strong jaw and dark brown hair, parted on one side and slicked down. He was dressed in a dark suit, a blue-and-green college tie, and black bowler hat.

He smiled at Mariana's look of surprise.

"You look like you were expecting someone else, miss."

Mariana nodded, embarrassed. "I was, actually—Mr. Morris—"

"He was my grandpa. He passed away a few years ago."

"Oh, I see, I'm sorry—"

"Don't worry. Happens all the time—I'm a pale copy, so the other porters often remind me." He winked and tipped his hat. "This way, miss. Follow me."

His polite, formal manners seemed to belong to a different age, Mariana thought. A better one, perhaps.

He insisted on carrying her bag, despite her protestations. "That's the way we do things, here. You know that. St. Christopher's is one place where time stands still."

He smiled at her. He seemed entirely at ease, with an air of total assurance, very much lord of his domain—which was true of all college porters, in Mariana's experience, and rightly so: without them to run the college on a day-to-day basis, everything would quickly fall apart.

Mariana followed Morris to a room in Gabriel Court. It was the same courtyard where she had lived as a student in her final year. She glanced at her old staircase as they passed it—at the stone steps she and Sebastian had run up and down a million times.

She followed Morris to the corner of the courtyard—to an octagonal turret built from slabs of weathered, stained granite; it housed a staircase leading to the college guest rooms. They went inside, and up the oak-paneled circular stairs—up to the second floor.

Morris unlocked a door, opened it, and gave Mariana the key.

"There you go, miss."

"Thank you."

She walked in and looked around. It was a small room—with a bay window, a fireplace, and a four-poster oak bed with twisted barley-sugar bedposts. The bed had a heavy chintz canopy and curtains all the way around. It looked a little suffocating, she thought.

"It's one of the nicer rooms we have available for old students," said Morris. "A little on the small side, perhaps." He placed Mariana's bag on the floor by the bed. "I hope you'll be comfortable."

"Thank you, you're very kind."

They hadn't discussed the murder, but she felt she needed to acknowledge it in some way—mainly because it was constantly in her thoughts.

"It's a terrible thing that's happened."

Morris nodded. "Isn't it?"

"It must be extremely upsetting for everyone in college."

"Yes, it is. I'm glad my old grandpa didn't live to see it. Would have finished him off."

"Did you know her?"

"Tara?" Morris shook his head. "Only by reputation. She was . . . well-known, let's say. Her and her friends."

"Her friends?"

"That's right. Quite a . . . provocative group of young women."

"'Provocative'? That's an interesting choice of word."

"Is it, miss?"

He was being deliberately coy, and Mariana wondered why.

"What do you mean by it?"

Morris smiled. "Just that they're a little . . . boisterous, if you take my meaning. We had to keep a firm eye on them, and their parties. I had to shut them down a few times. All sorts of goings-on."

"I see."

It was hard to read his expression. Mariana wondered what lay beneath his good manners and genial demeanor. What was he really thinking?

Morris smiled. "If you're curious about Tara, I'd talk to a bedder. They always seem to know what's going on in college. All the gossip."

"I'll bear that in mind, thank you."

"If that's all, miss, I'll leave you in peace. Good night."

Morris walked to the door and slipped out. He closed it silently behind him.

Mariana was alone at last—after a long and exhausting day. She sat on the bed, drained.

She looked at her watch. Nine o'clock. She should just go to bed—but she knew she wouldn't be able to sleep. She was too agitated, too upset.

And then, as she unpacked her overnight bag, she found the slim volume of poetry Clarissa had given her.

In Memoriam.

She sat on the bed and opened it. The years had dehydrated the pages, warping and stiffening them, leaving ripples and waves. She cracked open the book and stroked the rough pages with her fingertips.

What had Clarissa said about it? That she would have a different perspective on it now. Why? Because of Sebastian?

Mariana remembered reading the poem as a student. Like most

people, she was put off by its immense length. It was over three thousand lines long, and she'd felt a huge sense of achievement just to have got through it. She didn't respond to it at the time—but she was younger then, happy and in love, and in no need of sad poetry.

In the introduction by an old scholar, Mariana read that Alfred Tennyson had an unhappy childhood—the "black blood" of the Tennysons was infamous. His father was a drunk and a drug addict, and violently abusive—Tennyson's siblings suffered from depression and mental illness, and were either institutionalized or committed suicide. Alfred fled home at the age of eighteen. And like Mariana, he stumbled into a world of freedom and beauty in Cambridge. And he also found love. Whether the relationship between Arthur Henry Hallam and Tennyson was sexual or not, it was obviously deeply romantic: from the day they met, at the end of their first year, they spent every waking moment together. They were often seen walking hand in hand—until, a few years later, in 1833 . . . Hallam suddenly died from an aneurysm.

It was arguable that Tennyson never fully recovered from the loss of Hallam. Depressed, disheveled, unwashed, Tennyson gave in to his grief. He fell apart. For the next seventeen years, he grieved, writing only scraps of poetry—lines, verses, elegies—all of it about Hallam. Finally, these verses were collected together as one enormous poem. It was published as *In Memoriam A.H.H.* and quickly recognized as one of the greatest poems ever written in the English language.

Mariana perched on the bed and began to read. She soon discovered how painfully authentic and familiar his voice sounded— she had the strange, out-of-body sensation this was *her* voice, not Tennyson's; that he was articulating her inexpressible feelings for her: "I sometimes hold it half a sin / To put in words the grief I feel; / For words, like Nature, half reveal / And half conceal the Soul within." Just like Mariana, a year after Hallam's death, Tennyson made the trip back to Cambridge. He walked the same streets he had walked with Hallam; he found it "felt the same, but not the same"—he stood outside Hallam's room, seeing "another name was on the door."

And then Mariana stumbled on those lines that had become so famous they passed into the English language itself—coming across them here, buried among so much other verse, they retained their ability to sneak up behind her, take her by surprise, and leave her breathless:

I hold it true, whate'er befall;
I feel it when I sorrow most;
'Tis better to have loved and lost
Than never to have loved at all . . .

Mariana's eyes filled with tears. She lowered the book and looked out of the window. But it was dark outside, and her face was reflected back at her. She stared at herself as the tears streamed down her cheeks.

Where now? she thought. *Where are you going?*

What are you doing?

Zoe was right—she was running away. But where? Back to London? Back to that haunted house in Primrose Hill? It was no longer a home—just a hole for her to hide in.

Zoe needed her here, whether she admitted it or not; Mariana simply couldn't abandon her—that was out of the question.

She suddenly remembered what Zoe had said outside the chapel—that Sebastian would tell Mariana to stay. Zoe was right.

Sebastian would want Mariana to stand her ground, and fight.

Well, then?

Her mind went back to Professor Fosca's performance in the courtyard. Perhaps "performance" was a good word. Was there something a little too polished about his delivery, a little *rehearsed*? Even so, he had an alibi. And unless he had persuaded his students to lie for him, which seemed unlikely, he must be innocent . . .

And yet—?

Something didn't add up. Something didn't make sense.

Tara accused Fosca of threatening to kill her. Then . . . a few hours later, Tara was dead.

It wouldn't hurt to stay for a few days in Cambridge, and ask a few questions about Tara's relationship with the professor. Professor Fosca could certainly bear some investigating.

And if the police weren't going to pursue him, then perhaps Mariana—as a debt of honor to Zoe's friend—could listen to this young woman's story . . . and take her seriously.

If only because no one else did.

Part Two

My argument with so much of psychoanalysis is the precon-
ception that suffering is a mistake, or a sign of weakness, or a
sign even of illness. When in fact, possibly the greatest truths
we know have come out of people's suffering.

—ARTHUR MILLER

The Lestrygonians and the Cyclops,
And the fierce Poseidon you will never encounter,
If you do not carry them within your soul,
If your soul does not set them up before you.

—C. P. CAVAFY, "Ithaca"

I

I couldn't sleep again tonight. Too energized, too wound up. Overexcited, my mother would say.

So I gave up trying—and went for a walk.

As I wandered the deserted streets of the city, I encountered a fox. He hadn't heard me coming and looked up, startled.

It was the closest I've ever been to one. What a magnificent creature!—that coat, that tail—and those dark eyes, staring right back at me.

I gazed into them and . . . what did I see?

It's hard to describe—I saw all the wonder of creation, the wonder of the universe, there in that animal's eyes, in that second. It was like seeing God. And—for a second—I had a strange feeling. A kind of presence. As if God was there, on the street, next to me, holding my hand.

I felt safe, suddenly. I felt calm, and at peace—as if a raging fever had abated, a delirium burned itself out. I felt the other part of me, the good part, rising with the dawn . . .

But then—the fox vanished. It disappeared into the shadows, and the sun came up . . . God was gone. I was alone, and split in two.

I don't want to be two people. I want to be one person. I want to be whole. But I have no choice, it seems.

And as I stood there on the street, as the sun came up, I had a horrible feeling of recollection—another dawn, years ago. Another morning—just like this.

That same yellow light. That same feeling of being split in two.

But where?

When?

I know I can remember if I try. But do I want to? I have a feeling it's something I tried very hard to forget. What is it I'm so afraid of? Is it my father? Do I still believe he will emerge from a trapdoor like a pantomime villain, and strike me down?

Or is it the police? Do I fear a sudden hand on my shoulder, an arrest, and punishment—retribution for my crimes?

Why am I so afraid?

The answer must be there somewhere.

And I know where I must look.

2

Early next morning, Mariana went to see Zoe.

Zoe had just woken up, and was groggy, clutching Zebra with one hand and pushing away the eye mask from her face with the other.

She blinked at Mariana, who pulled back the curtains to let in the daylight. Zoe didn't look good—her eyes were bloodshot, and she looked exhausted.

"Sorry, I didn't sleep well. Kept having bad dreams."

Mariana handed Zoe a mug of coffee. "About Tara? I think I did too."

Zoe nodded and sipped her coffee. "This all feels like a nightmare. I can't believe she's really—gone."

"I know."

Tears welled up in Zoe's eyes. Mariana didn't know whether to comfort her or distract her. She decided on the latter. She picked up the pile of books on the desk, and looked at the titles—*The Duchess of Malfi, The Revenger's Tragedy, The Spanish Tragedy.*

"Let me guess. Tragedy this term?"

"*Revenge* tragedy," Zoe said with a small groan. "So dumb."

"You're not enjoying it?"

"*The Duchess of Malfi* is okay . . . it's funny—I mean, it's so insane."

"I remember. Poisoned Bibles and werewolves. But some-how—it still works, doesn't it? At least, I always thought so." Mariana looked at *The Duchess of Malfi*. "I've not read it in years."

"They're staging it at the ADC Theatre this term. Come and see it."

"I will. It's a good part. Why don't you audition?"

"I did. Didn't get it." Zoe sighed. "Story of my life."

Mariana smiled. Then this little pretense that nothing was wrong collapsed. Zoe stared at her, a deepening frown on her face.

"Are you leaving? Are you saying goodbye?"

"No. I'm not leaving. I've decided to stay, at least for a few days—and ask some questions. See if I can help."

"Really?" Zoe's eyes lit up, and her frown melted away. "That's amazing. Thank you." She hesitated. "Listen. What I said yesterday—about wishing Sebastian was here instead—I'm sorry."

Mariana shook her head—she understood. Zoe and Sebastian had always had a special bond. When she was very small, it was to Sebastian that Zoe would invariably run if she grazed a knee or cut herself, or needed comforting. Mariana didn't mind—she knew how important it was to have a father. And Sebastian was the closest to a father Zoe ever had since the loss of her parents. She smiled.

"You don't have to apologize. Sebastian always was much better in a crisis than me."

"I guess he always looked after us. And now . . ." Zoe shrugged.

Mariana gave an encouraging smile. "Now we look after each other. Okay?"

"Okay." Zoe nodded. Then she spoke more firmly, pulling herself together. "Just give me twenty minutes to shower and get ready. We can make a plan—"

"What do you mean? Don't you have lectures today?"

"Yeah, but—"

"No buts," said Mariana firmly. "Go to your lectures. Go to your classes. I'll see you for lunch. We can talk then."

"Oh, Mariana—"

"No. I mean it. It's more important now than ever that you keep busy—and focus on your work. Okay?"

Zoe sighed heavily but didn't protest further. "Okay."

"Good," Mariana said, kissing her cheek. "I'll see you later."

Mariana left Zoe's room and went down to the river.

She passed the college boathouse—and the row of moored punts belonging to St. Christopher's, chained to the bank, swaying in the water.

As she walked, Mariana phoned her patients to cancel her week's sessions.

She didn't tell her patients about what had happened. She merely said she had a family emergency. And the majority of them took the news well—apart from Henry. Mariana didn't expect him to react well, and he didn't.

"Thanks a lot," Henry said sarcastically. "Cheers, mate. Much appreciated."

Mariana tried to explain there had been an emergency, but he wasn't interested. Like a child, Henry could only see his own needs being frustrated, and his only interest was in punishing her.

"Do you care about me? Do you even give a shit?"

"Henry, this is beyond my control—"

"What about me? I need you, Mariana. That's beyond *my* control. Things are happening. I—I'm drowning here—"

"What is it? What's wrong?"

"I can't talk about it on the phone. I need you . . . Why aren't you home?"

Mariana froze. How did he know she wasn't there? He must have been watching the house again.

She felt a sudden alarm bell ringing in her head—this situation with Henry was untenable; she felt angry with herself for having allowed it to happen in the first place. She'd have to deal with it—deal with Henry. But not now. Not today.

"I have to go," she said.

"I know where you are, Mariana. You don't know that, do you? I'm watching. I can see you . . ."

Mariana hung up. She felt unnerved. She looked around the riverbank and the path on either side—but couldn't see Henry anywhere.

Of course she couldn't—he was just trying to scare her. She felt annoyed with herself for rising to the bait.

She shook her head—and kept walking.

3

It was a beautiful morning. All along the river, sunlight shimmered through the willow trees, making the leaves glow a luminous green above Mariana's head. And under her feet, wild cyclamen grew along the path in patches, like tiny pink butterflies. It was hard to reconcile such beauty with her reason for being there, or with her thoughts, which revolved around murder and death.

What the hell am I doing? she thought. *This is crazy.*

It was hard not to dwell on the negative—on everything she didn't know. She had no idea how to catch a murderer. She wasn't a criminologist or forensic psychologist, like Julian. All she had was an instinctive knowledge of human nature and human behavior, derived from years of working with patients. And it would have to do; she had to banish this self-doubt, or it would cripple her. She had to trust her instincts. She thought for a second.

Where to begin?

Well, firstly—and most importantly—she needed to understand Tara: who she was as a person, who she loved, who she hated— and who she feared. Mariana suspected that Julian was right: Tara knew her killer. So Mariana needed to discover her secrets. It shouldn't be too difficult. In groups like these, in small cloistered communities, gossip was rife and people had intimate knowledge of one another's private lives. If there was any truth to the affair Tara alleged she was having with Edward Fosca, for instance, there was bound to be some gossip. A great deal could be learned from what others in college had to say. This was where Mariana would begin—by asking questions.

And, more important, by listening.

She had reached a busier part of the river, by Mill Lane. Up ahead, people were walking, running, biking. Mariana contemplated them. The killer could be any one of these people. He could be standing here right now.

He could be watching her.

How would she recognize him? Well, the simple answer was she couldn't. And despite all of Julian's claims of expertise, he couldn't either. Mariana knew that, if asked about psychopathy, Julian would point to frontal or temporal lobe damage in the brain; or quote a series of meaningless labels—antisocial personality disorder, malignant narcissism—along with a glib set of characteristics like high intelligence, superficial charm, grandiosity, pathological lying, a contempt for morality—all of which explained very little. It didn't explain how—or why—a person might end up like this: as a merciless monster, using other human beings as if they were broken toys to be smashed to bits.

A long time ago, psychopathy used to be called simply "evil." People who were evil—who took a delight in hurting or killing others—were written about ever since Medea took an axe to her children, and probably long before that. The word "psychopath" was coined by a German psychiatrist in 1888—the same year Jack the Ripper terrorized London—from the German word *psychopastiche,* literally meaning "suffering soul." For Mariana this was the clue—the *suffering*—the sense that these monsters were also in pain. Thinking about them as victims allowed her to be more rational in her approach, and more compassionate. Psychopathy or sadism never appeared from nowhere. It was not a virus, infecting someone out of the blue. It had a long prehistory in childhood.

Mariana believed that childhood was a reactive experience,

meaning that in order to experience empathy for another human being, we must first be *shown* empathy—by our parents or caregivers. The man who killed Tara was once a little boy—a boy who was shown no empathy, no kindness. He had suffered—and suffered horribly.

Yet many children grow up in terribly abusive environments—and they don't end up as murderers. Why? Well, as Mariana's old supervisor used to say: "It doesn't take much to save a childhood." A little kindness, some understanding or validation: someone to recognize and acknowledge a child's reality—and save his sanity.

In this case, Mariana suspected there had been no one—no kindly grandmother, no favorite uncle, no well-meaning neighbor or teacher to see his pain, name it, and make it real. The only reality belonged to his abuser, and the small child's feelings of shame, fear, and anger were too dangerous to process alone—he didn't know how—so he didn't process these feelings; he didn't feel them. He sacrificed his true self, all that unfelt pain and anger, to the Underworld, to the murky world of the unconscious.

He lost touch with who he really was. And the man who lured Tara to that isolated spot was a stranger as much from himself as he was from everyone else. He was, Mariana suspected, a brilliant performer: impeccably polite, genial, and charming. But Tara provoked him somehow—and the terrified child inside him lashed out, and reached for a knife.

But what had triggered him?

That was the question. If only Mariana could see into his mind and read his thoughts—wherever he was.

"Hello there."

The voice behind her made Mariana jump. She quickly turned around.

"Sorry," he said. "I didn't mean to scare you."

It was Fred, the young man she'd met on the train. He was pushing a bicycle, with a stash of papers under his arm, eating an apple. He grinned.

"Remember me?"

"Yes, I remember."

"Said we'd meet again, didn't I? I predicted it. Told you, I'm a bit psychic."

Mariana smiled. "Cambridge is a small place. It's a coincidence."

"Take it from me. As a physicist. No such thing as coincidence. This paper I'm writing here actually proves it."

Fred nodded at his stack of papers, which slipped out from under his arm—and pages of mathematical equations cascaded all over the path.

"Bugger."

He threw down his bike to the ground, and ran around trying to retrieve the pages. Mariana knelt down to help.

"Thanks," he said as they collected the last of the pages.

He was inches away from her face, staring into her eyes. They looked at each other for a second. He had nice eyes, she thought, before banishing the thought. She stood up.

"I'm glad you're still here," he said. "Will you be staying long?"

Mariana shrugged. "I don't know. I'm here for my niece— she—she's had some bad news."

"You mean the murder? Your niece is at St. Christopher's, right?"

Mariana blinked, confused. "I—don't remember telling you that."

"Oh—well, you did." Fred went on quickly. "Everyone's talking about it—about what happened. I've been thinking about it a lot. I have a few theories."

"What kind of theories?"

"About Conrad." Fred glanced at his watch. "I've got to run right now, but I don't suppose you fancy having a drink? Say— tonight? We could talk." He looked at her hopefully. "I mean, only if you want to—obviously, no pressure—no big deal . . ."

He was tying himself into knots; Mariana was about to refuse and put him out of his misery. But something stopped her. What did he know about Conrad? Perhaps Mariana could pick his brains—he might know something useful. It was a worth a shot.

"Okay," she said.

Fred looked surprised and excited. "Really? Fantastic. How about nine o'clock? The Eagle? Let me give you my number."

"I don't need your number. I'll be there."

"Okay," he said with a grin. "It's a date."

"It's not a date."

"No, of course not. I don't know why I said that. Okay . . . See you later."

He got on his bike.

Mariana watched Fred cycle away along the river path. Then she turned and started walking back to college.

Time to begin. Time to roll up her sleeves and get to work.

4

Mariana hurried across Main Court, toward a group of middle-aged women, all sipping tea from steaming mugs, sharing biscuits, and gossiping. These were the bedders—on their tea break.

"Bedder" was a term peculiar to the university, and something of an institution—for hundreds of years, armies of local women had been employed at the colleges to make beds, empty rubbish bins, and clean rooms—although, it must be said, the bedders' daily contact with the students meant the role often crossed over from domestic service to pastoral care. Mariana's bedder was sometimes the only person she spoke to every day, until she met Sebastian.

The bedders were a formidable bunch. Mariana felt a little intimidated as she approached them. She wondered—not for the first time—what they really thought of the students; these working-class women who had none of the advantages of these privileged, often spoiled young people.

Perhaps they hate us all, Mariana suddenly thought. She wouldn't blame them if they did.

"Good morning, ladies," she said.

Their conversations faded to silence. The women gave Mariana a curious and slightly suspicious look. She smiled.

"I wonder if you might be able to help me. I'm looking for Tara Hampton's bedder."

Several heads turned toward one woman who was standing at the back, lighting a cigarette.

The woman was in her late sixties, possibly older. She was wearing a blue smock, and carrying a bucket of various cleaning products and a feather duster. She was not plump, but stolid and moonfaced. Her hair was dyed red, white at the roots, and her eyebrows were painted on daily; today she had drawn them high on her forehead, making her look rather startled. She seemed a little irritated to have been singled out. She gave Mariana a strained smile.

"That'll be me, dear. I'm Elsie. How can I help?"

"My name's Mariana. I was a student here. And I . . ." she went on, improvising, "I'm a psychotherapist. The dean has asked me to talk to various members of college about the impact of Tara's death. I was wondering if we might . . . have a little chat."

She finished lamely, and didn't hold out much hope that Elsie would take the bait. She was right.

Elsie pursed her lips. "I don't need a therapist, dear. Nothing wrong with my head, thank you very much."

"I didn't mean that—it's for my own benefit, really. It's—I'm conducting some research."

"Well, I really don't have the time—"

"It won't take long. Perhaps I can buy you a cup of tea? A slice of cake?"

At the mention of cake, a glint appeared in Elsie's eye. Her manner softened. She shrugged, and took a drag of her cigarette.

"Very well. We'll have to be quick. I've another staircase to do before lunch."

Elsie stubbed out her cigarette on the cobbles, then pulled off her apron and thrust it at another bedder, who took it wordlessly.

Then she walked over to Mariana.

"Follow me, dear," she said. "I know the best spot."

Elsie marched off. Mariana followed, and the moment her back was turned, she could hear the other women whispering to one another furiously.

5

Mariana followed Elsie along King's Parade. They passed Market Square, with its green and white marquees and stalls selling flowers, books, and clothes; and the Senate House, gleaming white behind shiny black railings. They walked past the fudge shop—and from its open doors flooded out an overwhelmingly sweet smell of sugar and hot fudge.

Elsie stopped outside the red-and-white awning of the Copper Kettle. "This is my local," she said.

Mariana nodded. She remembered the tearoom from her student days. "After you."

She followed Elsie inside. It was busy with a mix of students and tourists, all talking in different languages.

Elsie went straight up to the glass counter with all the cakes. She perused the selection of brownies, chocolate cake, coconut slices, apple pie, and lemon meringue. "I shouldn't, really," she said. "Well . . . perhaps just one."

She turned to the elderly, white-haired waitress behind the counter. "A slice of the chocolate cake. And a pot of English breakfast." She nodded at Mariana. "She's paying."

Mariana ordered some tea, and they sat down at a table by the window.

There was a pause. Mariana smiled. "I'm wondering if you know my niece, Zoe? She was Tara's friend."

Elsie grunted. She didn't look impressed. "Oh, she's your niece, is she? Yes, I look after her. Quite the little madam, she is."

"Zoe? What do you mean?"

"She's been very rude to me—on several occasions."

"Oh—I'm sorry to hear that. That doesn't sound like her. I'll have a word with her."

"Do, dear."

There was a moment's awkwardness.

They were interrupted by the appearance of a waitress—young, pretty, Eastern European—bearing tea and cake. Elsie's face brightened considerably.

"Paulina. How are you?"

"I'm good, Elsie. You?"

"Haven't you heard?" Her eyes widened and a tremor of mock emotion crept into her voice. "One of Elsie's little ones got butchered—cut to bits by the river."

"Yes, yes, I heard. I'm sorry."

"Mind you watch how you go now. It's not safe—a pretty girl like you, outdoors at night."

"I'll be careful."

"Good." Elsie smiled and watched the waitress walk away. Then she turned her attention to the cake, which she attacked with relish. "Not bad," she said between bites. There were traces of chocolate around her mouth. "Fancy some?"

Mariana shook her head. "I'm fine, thanks."

The cake did the trick, improving Elsie's mood. She watched Mariana thoughtfully as she chewed. "Now, dear," she said, "I hope you don't expect me to believe any of that nonsense about psychotherapy. Research, indeed."

"You're very perceptive, Elsie."

Elsie chuckled and dropped a sugar cube into her tea. "Elsie doesn't miss much."

Elsie had rather a disconcerting habit of referring to herself in the third person. She gave Mariana a piercing look. "Come on then—what's this really about?"

"I just want to ask you some questions about Tara . . ." She adopted a confidential tone. "You were close to Tara, weren't you?"

Elsie gave her a slightly wary look. "Who told you that? Zoe?"

"No—I just presumed that, as her bedder, you saw a lot of her. I was very fond of my bedder."

"Were you, dear? That's nice."

"Well, it's such an important service you provide . . . I'm not sure you're always appreciated."

Elsie nodded with enthusiasm. "You're right about that. People think being a bedder is just a matter of wiping down a few surfaces and emptying the odd bin. But the little ones are away from home for the first time—they can't be left to fend for themselves—they need looking after." She smiled sweetly. "It's Elsie who looks after them. It's Elsie who checks on them every day—and wakes them up every morning—or finds them dead, if they've hanged themselves in the night."

Mariana hesitated, taken aback. "When was the last time you saw her?"

"The day she died, of course . . . I'll never forget it. I saw the poor girl walk to her death."

"What do you mean?"

"Well, I was in the courtyard, waiting for a couple of the other ladies—we always get the bus home together. And I saw Tara leave her room. She looked awfully upset. I waved to her and called to her—but she didn't hear me for some reason. I saw her walk off— and she never came back . . ."

"What time was that? Do you remember?"

"Quarter to eight exactly. I remember it because I was checking my watch—we were in danger of missing the bus." Elsie tutted. "Not that it's ever on time anymore."

Mariana poured Elsie some more tea from the pot.

"You know, I was wondering about her friends. What's your impression of them?"

Elsie raised an eyebrow. "Oh, you mean *them*, do you?"

"'Them'?"

Elsie smiled, but didn't reply. Mariana went on, cautiously.

"When I spoke to Conrad, he called them 'witches.'"

"Did he, indeed?" Elsie chuckled. "'Bitches' is more like it, dear."

"You don't like them?"

Elsie shrugged. "They weren't her friends, not really. Tara hated them. Your niece was the only one who was nice to her."

"And the others?"

"Oh, they bullied her, poor love. Used to cry on my shoulder about it, she did. 'You're my only friend, Elsie,' she'd say. 'I love you so, Elsie.'"

Elsie wiped away an imaginary tear. Mariana felt nauseated: this performance was as sickly sweet as the chocolate cake Elsie had just devoured—and Mariana didn't believe a word of it. Elsie was either a fantasist or just an old-fashioned liar. In either case, Mariana was feeling increasingly uncomfortable in her company. Nonetheless, she persevered.

"Why did they bully Tara? I don't understand."

"They were jealous, weren't they? Because she was so beautiful."

"I see . . . I wonder if there might be more to it than that . . ."

"Well—you'd best ask Zoe about *that,* hadn't you?"

"Zoe?" Mariana was taken aback. "What do you mean? What's Zoe got to do with it?"

Elsie gave her a cryptic smile in response. "Now, that's a question, isn't it, dear?"

She didn't elaborate further. Mariana felt annoyed. "And what about Professor Fosca?"

"What about him?"

"Conrad said he had a crush on Tara."

Elsie looked unimpressed and unsurprised. "The professor's a man, isn't he?—like all the rest."

"Meaning?"

Elsie sniffed but didn't comment. Mariana had the sense that the conversation was coming to an end, and to probe any further would only be met with stony disapproval. So, as casually as she could, she slipped in the real reason she had brought Elsie here and bribed her with flattery and cake.

"Elsie. Do you think . . . I might see Tara's room?"

"Her room?" Elsie looked as if she were going to refuse. But then she shrugged. "Can't do any harm, I suppose. The police have been all over it—I was going to give it a good clean tomorrow . . . Tell you what. Let me finish this cuppa, and we can walk over together."

Mariana smiled, pleased. "Thank you, Elsie."

6

Elsie unlocked the door to Tara's room. She went inside and turned on the light. Mariana followed her.

It was like any other teenager's bedroom, messier than most. The police had gone through her things invisibly—it felt as if Tara had just stepped out and might return any second. There was still a trace of her perfume in the air and the musky scent of marijuana clinging to the furnishings.

Mariana didn't know what she was looking for. She was searching for *something* that the police had missed—but what? They had taken away all the devices Zoe had been pinning her hopes on to provide some kind of clue—Tara's computer, phone, and iPad were all missing. Her clothes remained, in the wardrobe and strewn over the armchair, in piles on the floor—expensive clothes treated like rags. Books were similarly disrespected, discarded mid-read, open on the floor, spines cracked.

"Was she always this messy?"

"Oh, yes, dear." Elsie tutted and gave an indulgent chuckle. "Hopeless. I don't know what she would have done without me to look after her."

Elsie sat on the bed. She had apparently taken Mariana into her confidence. And her conversation was no longer guarded; quite the contrary.

"Her parents are boxing up her things today," she said. "I offered to do it. Save them the bother. They didn't want me to, for some reason. No pleasing some people. I'm not surprised. I know what Tara thought of them. She told me. That Lady Hampton is a right stuck-up bitch—and *no lady,* let me tell you that. As for her husband . . ."

Mariana was only half listening, wishing Elsie would go away so she could focus. She went over to a small dressing table. She looked at it. There was a mirror with some photos stuck in the edges of the frame. One of the photographs was of Tara and her parents. Tara was incredibly beautiful, luminously so. She had long red hair, and exquisite features—the face of a Greek goddess.

Mariana considered the rest of the objects on the dressing table. A couple of perfume bottles, some makeup, and a hairbrush. She looked at the hairbrush. A strand of red hair was caught in it.

"She had lovely hair," said Elsie, watching her. "I used to brush it for her. She loved me doing that."

Mariana smiled politely. She picked up a small soft toy—a fluffy rabbit that was propped up against the mirror. Unlike Zoe's old Zebra, battered and beaten up from years of abuse, this toy looked strangely new—almost untouched.

Elsie quickly solved the mystery.

"I bought her that. She was so lonely when she first got here. Needed something soft to cuddle. So I got her the bunny."

"That was nice of you."

"Elsie's all heart. I got her the hot-water bottle too. It gets awfully cold in here at night. That blanket they give them is no use—thin as cardboard." She yawned, looking a little bored. "Do you think you'll be much longer, dear? Only I really ought to be getting on. I've another staircase to do."

"I don't want to keep you. Perhaps . . . perhaps I could let myself out in a few minutes?"

Elsie deliberated for a second. "All right. I'll pop out and have a ciggie and get back to work. Pull the door closed when you leave."

"Thanks."

Elsie left the room, shutting the door behind her. Mariana let out a sigh. Thank God for that. She looked around. She hadn't found it yet, whatever it was she was seeking. She hoped she would recognize it when she saw it. Some kind of clue—an insight into Tara's state of mind. Something that would help Mariana understand—but what was it?

She went over to the chest of drawers. She opened each drawer, examining the contents. A depressing, morbid task. It felt surgical, as if she were cutting open Tara's body and picking through her internal organs. Mariana looked through all her most intimate possessions—her underwear, makeup, hair products, passport, driver's license, credit cards, childhood photographs, snapshots of herself as a baby, little reminders and notes she had written to herself, old shopping receipts, loose tampons, empty cocaine vials, loose tobacco, and traces of marijuana.

It was strange; Tara had vanished, just like Sebastian—leaving all her things behind. *After we die,* Mariana thought, *all that remains of us is a mystery; and our possessions, of course, to be picked over by strangers.*

She decided to give up. Whatever she was looking for wasn't here. Perhaps it had never existed in the first place. She closed the last drawer, and went to leave the room.

Then, as she reached the door, something made her stop . . . and turn back. She glanced around the room one more time.

Her eyes rested on the corkboard on the wall above the desk. Notices, flyers, postcards, a couple of photos stuck into it.

One of the postcards was an image Mariana knew: a painting by Titian—*Tarquin and Lucretia.* Mariana stopped. She looked at it more closely.

Lucretia was in her bedroom, on the bed, naked and defenseless; Tarquin was standing above her—raising a dagger that was glinting in the light, and poised to strike. It was beautiful, but deeply unsettling.

Mariana pulled the postcard away from the board. She turned it over.

There, on the back, was a handwritten quotation in black ink. Four lines, in Ancient Greek:

ἓν δὲ πᾶσι γνῶμα ταὐτὸν ἐμπρέπει:
σφάξαι κελεύουσίν με παρθένον κόρη
Δήμητρος, ἥτις ἐστὶ πατρὸς εὐγενοῦς,
τροπαῖά τ᾽ ἐχθρῶν καὶ πόλει σωτήριαν.

Mariana stared at it, puzzled.

7

Mariana found Clarissa sitting in her armchair by the window, pipe in hand, surrounded by clouds of smoke, correcting a pile of papers on her lap.

"May I have a word?" said Mariana, hovering by the door.

"Oh, Mariana? Are you still here? Come in, come in." Clarissa waved her into the room. "Sit."

"I'm not interrupting?"

"Anything that takes me away from marking undergraduate essays is a truly welcome reprieve." Clarissa smiled and put down the papers. She gave Mariana a curious look as she sat on the sofa. "You've decided to stay?"

"Just for a few days. Zoe needs me."

"Good. Very good. I'm so pleased." Clarissa relit her pipe and puffed away for a moment. "Now, what can I do for you?"

Mariana reached into her pocket and pulled out the postcard. She handed it to Clarissa. "I found this in Tara's room. I was wondering what you make of it."

Clarissa glanced at the picture for a moment, then turned it over. She raised an eyebrow and read the quotation out. "ἓν δὲ πᾶσι γνῶμα ταὐτὸν ἐμπρέπει: / σφάξαι κελεύουσίν με παρθένον κόρῃ /

Δήμητρος, ἥτις ἐστὶ πατρὸς εὐγενοῦς, / τροπαῖά τ᾽ ἐχθρῶν καὶ πόλει σωτήριαν."

"What is it?" asked Mariana. "Do you recognize it?"

"I think . . . it's Euripides. *The Children of Heracles,* if I'm not mistaken. You're familiar with it?"

Mariana felt a flicker of shame that she'd never even heard of the play, let alone read it. "Remind me?"

"It's set in Athens," Clarissa said, reaching for her pipe. "King Demophon is preparing for war, to protect the city against the Mycenaeans." She wedged the pipe in the corner of her mouth, struck a match, and relit it. She spoke between puffs. "Demophon consults the oracle . . . to find out his chances of success . . . The quotation comes from that part of the play."

"I see."

"Does that help you?"

"Not really."

"No?" Clarissa waved away a cloud of smoke. "Where's your difficulty?"

Mariana smiled at the question. Sometimes Clarissa's brilliance made her a bit obtuse. "My Ancient Greek is a little rusty, I'm afraid."

"Ah . . . yes. Of course, forgive me—" Clarissa glanced at the postcard, and translated it. "Roughly speaking, it says . . . 'The oracles agree: in order to defeat the enemy and save the city . . . a maiden must be sacrificed—a maiden of noble birth—'"

Mariana blinked in surprise. "Noble birth? It says that?"

Clarissa nodded. "The daughter of πατρὸς εὐγενοῦς—a nobleman . . . must be sacrificed to κόρη Δήμητρος . . ."

"'Δήμητρος'?"

"The goddess Demeter. And 'κόρη,' of course, means—"

"'Daughter.'"

"That's right." Clarissa nodded. "A noble maiden must be sacrificed to the daughter of Demeter—to Persephone, that is."

Mariana felt her heart beating fast. *It's just a coincidence,* she thought. *It doesn't mean anything.*

Clarissa gave her the postcard with a smile. "Persephone was rather a vengeful goddess, as I'm sure you know."

Mariana didn't trust herself to speak. She nodded.

Clarissa peered at her. "Are you all right, my dear? You look a little—"

"I'm fine . . . it's just—"

For a second she considered trying to explain her feelings to Clarissa. But what could she say? That she had a superstitious fantasy this vengeful goddess had a hand in her husband's death? How could she possibly say that out loud without sounding completely insane? Instead, she shrugged, and said, "It's a little ironic, that's all."

"What? Oh, you mean Tara being of *noble birth*—and being *sacrificed,* so to speak? Indeed, a most unpleasant irony."

"And you don't think it could be more than that?"

"Meaning what?"

"I don't know. Except . . . why was it there? In her room? Where did the postcard come from?"

Clarissa waved the pipe dismissively. "Oh, that's easy . . . Tara was doing the Greek tragedy paper this term. It's hardly beyond the realms of possibility for her to have copied a quotation from one of the plays, is it?"

"No . . . I suppose not."

"It is a little out of character, I grant you that . . . As I'm sure Professor Fosca would attest."

Mariana blinked. "Professor Fosca?"

"He taught her Greek tragedy."

"I see." Mariana tried to sound casual. "Did he?"

"Oh, yes. He is the expert, after all. He's quite brilliant. You should see him lecture while you're here. Very impressive. Do you know his lectures are by far the best attended in the faculty—students queue from downstairs to get in, sitting on the floor if they run out of seats. Have you ever heard of such a thing?" Clarissa laughed, then added quickly, "Of course, one's own lectures have always been very well attended. I've been very fortunate in that regard. But not to that degree, I must admit . . . You know, if you're curious about Fosca, you should really talk to Zoe. She knows him best."

"Zoe?" Mariana was taken aback by this. "Does she? Why?"

"Well, he is her director of studies, after all."

"Oh—I see." Mariana nodded thoughtfully. "Yes, of course."

8

Mariana took Zoe out for lunch. They went to a nearby French brasserie that had recently opened. It was popular with starving students who had visiting relatives.

It was a good deal more sophisticated than the restaurants Mariana remembered from her days as a student. It was busy, and there was the sound of conversation and laughter, and cutlery chiming on plates. It smelled enticingly of garlic and wine and sizzling meat. An elegant waiter, in a waistcoat and tie, directed Mariana and Zoe to a booth in the corner, which had a white tablecloth and black leather seats.

Somewhat extravagantly, Mariana began by ordering half a bottle of rosé champagne. This was unlike her, and Zoe raised an eyebrow.

"Well, why not?" said Mariana with a shrug. "We could use cheering up."

"I'm not complaining," said Zoe.

When the champagne arrived, the pink bubbles, fizzing and sparkling in thick crystal glasses, lifted their spirits considerably. They didn't discuss Tara or the murder at first. They jumped around from topic to topic, catching up. They spoke about Zoe's studies at St. Christopher's, and how she felt about entering her third year—and her frustrating lack of clarity about her life and what she wanted to do.

And then they spoke about love. Mariana asked Zoe if she was seeing anyone.

"Of course not. They're such *boys* here." She shook her head. "I'm totally happy being self-partnered. I'll never fall in love."

Mariana smiled. She sounded so young, she thought, when she talked like that. *Still waters*. She suspected that despite Zoe's protestations, when she did fall, it would be hard and deep.

"One day," Mariana said, "you'll see. It'll happen."

"No." Zoe shook her head. "No, thanks. As far as I can see, love only brings sorrow."

Mariana had to laugh. "That's a little pessimistic."

"Don't you mean *realistic*?"

"Hardly."

"What about you and Sebastian?"

Mariana was unprepared for this blow, decidedly below the belt, and delivered so casually. It took her a second to find her voice.

"Sebastian brought me a lot more than sorrow."

Zoe was immediately apologetic. "Sorry. I didn't mean to upset you—I—"

"I'm not upset. It's okay."

But it wasn't okay. Being here, in this lovely restaurant, drinking champagne, it allowed them to pretend for a while—to escape the murder and all the unpleasantness—and exist happily in a little bubble of the present moment. But now Zoe had punctured that bubble, and Mariana felt all her sadness, worry, and fear flood back.

They ate in silence for a moment. Then Mariana said in a low voice:

"Zoe. How are you doing . . . ? About Tara?"

Zoe didn't reply for a second. She shrugged. She didn't look up.

"Okay. Not great. I can't stop thinking about it—the way she died, I mean. I can't—get it out of my head."

Zoe looked at Mariana. And Mariana felt an ache of frustrated empathy; she wanted to make it all okay, take away Zoe's pain, the way she used to when she was a little girl—put a bandage on the wound and kiss it better—but she knew she couldn't. She reached across the table and squeezed her hand.

"I know it's hard to believe right now—but it will get easier."

"Will it?" Zoe shrugged. "It's been over a year since Sebastian died—and it's not any easier. It still hurts."

"I know." Mariana nodded, unable to bring herself to contradict Zoe. She was right, so there was no point. "All we can do," she said, "is try and honor their memory—the best way we can."

Zoe held her gaze and nodded. "Okay."

Mariana went on: "And the best way to honor Tara . . ."

"Is to catch him?"

"Yes. And we will."

Zoe seemed comforted by the thought. She nodded. "So, have you made any progress?"

"I have, as a matter of fact." Mariana smiled. "I spoke to Tara's bedder, Elsie. And she said—"

"Oh God." Zoe rolled her eyes. "Just so you know, Elsie is a sociopath. And Tara *hated* her."

"Oh, really? Elsie said they were very close . . . Elsie also said that you were rude to her."

"Because she's a *psycho,* that's why. She gives me the creeps."

"Psycho" wasn't the word Mariana would have used, but she didn't entirely disagree with Zoe's impression. "All the same, it's not like you to be rude." She hesitated. "Elsie also implied that you know more about this than you're telling me."

She watched Zoe carefully. But Zoe just shrugged it off.

"Whatever. Did she also tell you Tara banned her from her room? Because Elsie kept coming in without knocking, trying to catch her coming out of the shower? She was practically stalking her."

"I see." Mariana thought for a moment, and reached into her pocket. "And what do you think about this?"

She pulled out the postcard she had found in Tara's room. She translated the quotation, and asked Zoe what she thought. "Do you think it's possible that Tara might have written it?"

Zoe shook her head. "I doubt it."

"Why do you say that?"

"Well, Tara didn't really give a shit about Greek tragedy, to be honest."

Mariana couldn't help but smile. "Any ideas about who might have sent it?"

"Not really. It's such a weird thing to do. Such a creepy quote."

"What about Professor Fosca?"

"What about him?"

"Do you think it might be him?"

Zoe shrugged. She didn't look convinced. "I mean, maybe—but why send a message in Ancient Greek? And why that message?"

"Why, indeed?" Mariana nodded to herself. She eyed Zoe for a moment. "Tell me about him. About the professor."

"What about him?"

"Well, what's he like?"

Zoe shrugged, as a slight frown appeared on her face. "You know, Mariana. I did tell you all about him, when he first started teaching me. I told you and Sebastian."

"Did you?" Mariana nodded as it came back to her. "Oh, yes— the American professor. That's it. I remember now."

"Do you?"

"Yes, it stuck in my head for some reason. I remember Sebastian wondered if you had a crush on him."

Zoe pulled a face. "Well, he was wrong. I didn't."

Zoe said this with such defensiveness, such surprising ve-hemence, that Mariana suddenly wondered if Zoe *did* have a crush—and what if she did? It was hardly unusual for students to have crushes on tutors—particularly when they were as charismatic and handsome as Edward Fosca.

But then, she might be reading Zoe wrong . . . She might be picking up on something else entirely.

She decided to let it go, for the moment.

9

After lunch, they walked back to college along the river.

Zoe bought a chocolate ice cream, and was engrossed in eating it. They walked in companionable silence for a moment.

All the time, Mariana was conscious of a kind of double image—another faint picture projected onto this one: a memory of Zoe as a little girl, walking on this exact same pathway of broken, cracked-up stones, eating another ice cream. It was on that visit, when Mariana was a student, that little Zoe first met Sebastian. She remembered Zoe's shyness—and how Sebastian got over it with a little magic trick, conjuring up a pound coin from behind Zoe's ear, a trick that continued to delight her for years.

And now Sebastian was walking with them too, of course, another ghostly image projected on the present.

Funny, the things you remember. Mariana glanced at an old weathered wooden bench as they passed it. They had sat there, on that bench—she and Sebastian—after Mariana's final exams, celebrating with prosecco mixed with crème de cassis, and smoking blue Gauloises cigarettes, stolen by Sebastian from a party the night before. She remembered kissing him, and how sweet his kisses tasted, with the faint trace of liqueur mingled with tobacco on his lips.

Zoe glanced at her. "You're being very quiet. You okay?"

Mariana nodded. "Can we sit down for a second?" And then, quickly, "Not this bench." She pointed at another bench, farther along. "That one."

They walked over to the bench and sat down.

It was a peaceful spot, in the dappled shade of a willow tree, right by the water's edge. The willow's branches moved in the breeze, and the ends were trailing lazily in the water. Mariana watched a punt drift by under the bridge.

Then a swan glided past, and her eyes followed it.

The swan had an orange beak, with black markings around its eyes. It looked a little worse for wear. Its once-gleaming feathers were dirty and discolored around the neck, stained green from the river. Nonetheless, it was an impressive creature—ragged but serene, and highly imperious. It turned its long neck, and looked in Mariana's direction.

Was it her imagination—or was it staring directly at her?

For a second, the swan held her in its gaze. Its black eyes seemed to be sizing her up, with a cool intelligence.

And then the appraisal was over. It turned its head, and Mariana was dismissed—forgotten. She watched it disappear under the bridge.

"Tell me," she said, glancing at Zoe. "You don't like him, do you?"

"Professor Fosca? I never said that."

"It's just an impression I have. Do you?"

Zoe shrugged. "I don't know . . . The professor—he *dazzles* me, I suppose."

Mariana was surprised by this, and not entirely clear what she meant. "And you don't like being dazzled?"

"Of course not." Zoe shook her head. "I like to see where I'm going. And there's something about him—I don't know how to describe it—it's like he's *acting*—like he's not who he pretends to be. Like he doesn't want you to see who he really is. But maybe I'm wrong . . . Everyone else thinks he's amazing."

"Yes, Clarissa said he's very popular."

"You've no idea. It's like a cult. The girls, especially."

Mariana suddenly thought of the girls in white, gathered around Fosca at the service for Tara. "You mean Tara's friends? That group of girls? Aren't they your friends too?"

Zoe shook her head forcefully. "No way. I avoid them like the plague."

"I see. They don't seem very popular."

Zoe gave her a pointed look. "Depends on who you ask."

"Meaning?"

"Well, they're Professor Fosca's favorites . . . His *fan club*."

"What do you mean, fan club?"

Zoe shrugged. "They're in his private study group. A secret society."

"Why secret?"

"It's only for *them*—his 'special' students." Zoe rolled her eyes. "He calls them the Maidens. Isn't that the dumbest thing you've ever heard?"

"The Maidens?" Mariana frowned. "Are they all girls?"

"Uh-huh."

"I see."

And Mariana did see—or was beginning to, at least, have an inkling where all this might be leading, and why Zoe had been so reticent.

"And was Tara one of the Maidens?"

"Yeah." Zoe nodded. "She was."

"I see. And the others? Can I meet them?"

Zoe pulled a face. "Do you want to? They're not exactly friendly."

"Where are they now?"

"Now?" Zoe looked at her watch. "Well, Professor Fosca is lecturing in a half an hour. Everyone will be there."

Mariana nodded. "Then so will we."

10

Mariana and Zoe arrived at the English Faculty with only a few moments to spare.

They looked at the board outside the lecture-theater building and consulted the schedule for the day. The afternoon lecture by Professor Fosca was in the biggest room upstairs. They made their way up there.

The lecture theater was a large, well-lit space, with rows of dark wooden desks descending to the stage at the bottom, where there was a podium and a microphone.

Clarissa was right about the popularity of Fosca's lectures—the auditorium was packed. They found a couple of remaining seats high up at the back. There was a palpable sense of anticipation as the audience waited, more akin to a concert or theater performance than a lecture on Greek tragedy, Mariana thought.

And then, Professor Fosca entered.

He was dressed in a smart black suit, and his hair was pulled back and tied in a tight knot. He was holding a folder of notes, and walked across the stage, up to the podium. He adjusted the microphone, surveyed the room for a moment, then bowed his head.

There was a ripple of excitement in the audience. All talking faded to a hush. Mariana couldn't help but feel a little skeptical—her background in group theory told her, as a rule, to be suspicious of any group in love with a teacher; those situations rarely ended well. To Mariana, Fosca looked more like a brooding pop star than a lecturer, and she half expected him to burst into song. But when he looked up, he didn't sing. To her surprise, his eyes were full of tears.

"Today," Fosca said, "I want to talk about Tara."

Mariana heard whispering around her and saw heads turning, looks being exchanged; this was what the students had been hoping for. She even noticed a couple of them starting to cry.

Fosca's own tears spilled out of his eyes and fell down his cheeks, without him brushing them away. He refused to react to them, and his voice remained calm and steady. He projected so well, Mariana thought, he didn't really need the mike.

What had Zoe said? He was always performing? If so, the performance was so good that Mariana—like the rest of the audience—couldn't help being affected.

"As many of you know," Fosca said, "Tara was one of my students. And I'm standing here in a state of—heartbreak. I nearly said 'despair.' I wanted to cancel today's lecture. But what I loved most about Tara was her strength, her fearlessness—and she wouldn't want us to give in to despair, and be defeated by hate. We must go on. That is our only defense against evil . . . and the best way to honor our friend. I'm here today for Tara. And so are you."

There was thunderous applause, and cheers from the audience. He acknowledged it with a bow of the head. He collected his notes and looked up again. "And now, ladies and gentlemen—to work."

Professor Fosca was an impressive speaker. He rarely consulted his notes—and gave the impression of improvising the entire lecture. He was animated, engaging, witty, impassioned—and, most important, present; he seemed to be communicating directly with each member of his audience.

"Today," he said, "I thought it would be a good idea to talk about, among other things, the *liminal* in Greek tragedy. What does that mean? Well, think of Antigone, pushed to a choice between death and dishonor; or Iphigenia, preparing herself to die for Greece; or Oedipus, deciding to blind himself and wander the highways. The *liminal* is between two worlds—on the very edge of what it means to be human—where everything is stripped away from you; where you transcend this life, and experience something beyond it. And when the tragedies are working, they give us a glimpse of what that feels like."

Then, Fosca showed a slide, projected onto the large screen behind him. It was a marble relief of two women, standing on either side of a nude male youth, each with her right hand extended toward him.

"Anyone recognize these two ladies?"

A sea of shaking heads. Mariana had a slight inkling of who they might be, and she very much hoped she was wrong.

"These two goddesses," he said, "are about to initiate a young man into the secret cult of Eleusis. They are, of course, Demeter and her daughter, Persephone."

Mariana caught her breath. She did her best not to be distracted. She tried to focus.

"This is the Eleusinian cult," Fosca said. "The secret rite of Eleusis—that gives you exactly that liminal experience of being between life and death—and of transcending death. What was this cult? Well, Eleusis is the story of Persephone—the Maiden, as she was known—the goddess of death, queen of the Underworld . . ."

As Fosca was speaking, for a second he caught Mariana's eye. He smiled, ever so slightly.

He knows, she thought. *He knows what happened to Sebastian—and that's why he's doing this. To torment me.*

But how—how could he know? He couldn't know. It wasn't possible. She had told no one, not even Zoe. It was just a coincidence—that's all; it meant *nothing*. She forced herself to calm down, and concentrate on what he was saying.

"When she lost her daughter at Eleusis, Demeter plunged the world into wintry darkness, until Zeus was forced to intervene.

He allowed Persephone to return from the dead, every year, for six months, which is our spring and summer. And then, for the six months she resides in the Underworld, we have fall and winter. Light and dark—life and death. This journey Persephone goes on—from life to death and back again—gave birth to the cult of Eleusis. And there, at Eleusis, at the entry point to the Underworld, *you too* could take part in this secret rite—that gives you the same experience as the goddess."

He lowered his voice, and Mariana could see heads leaning forward, necks craning to catch every word. He had them in the palm of his hand.

"The exact nature of the rites at Eleusis have remained secret for thousands of years," he said. "The rites, the mysteries, they were 'unspeakable'—because they were an attempt to initiate us into something beyond words. People who experienced them were never the same again. There were stories of visions and ghostly visitations and journeys to the afterlife. As the rites were open to everyone—men, women, slaves, or children—you didn't even have to be Greek. The only requirement was that you *understood* Greek, so you could understand what was being said to you. In preparation, you had a drink called *kykeon*—which was made of barley. And on this particular barley there was a black fungus called ergot, which had hallucinogenic properties; thousands of years later, LSD would be made from it. Whether the Greeks knew it or not, they were all tripping slightly. Which might account for some of the visions."

Fosca said this with a wink, and it got a laugh. He let the laughter subside, and went on in a more serious tone.

"Imagine it. Just for a second. Imagine being there—imagine the excitement and the apprehension. All those people meeting at midnight by the Oracle of the Dead—and being led by the priests into the chambers of the rock—into the caves within. The only lights were torches carried by the priests. How dark and smoky it must have been. Cold, wet stone, going deeper and deeper underground, into a vast chamber—a *liminal* space, on the very border of the Underworld. The Telesterion, where the mysteries took place. It was huge—forty-two towering marble columns—a forest made of stone. It could accommodate thousands of initiates at one time and was big enough to house another temple—the Anaktoron, the sacred space where only the priests themselves could enter—where the relics of the Maiden were kept."

Fosca's black eyes sparkled as he spoke. He was seeing it all before him, as he conjured it up with his words, as if casting a spell.

"We'll never know exactly what happened there—the mystery of Eleusis remains, after all, a *mystery*—but at dawn, the initiates emerged into the light, having undergone an experience of death and rebirth—and with a new understanding of what it means to be human—to be alive."

He paused, and stared at the audience for a moment. He spoke in a different tone, now—quiet, impassioned, emotional.

"Let me tell you something—*this* is what those old Greek plays are about. What it means to be human. What it means to be alive. And if you miss that when you read them—if all you see is a bunch of dead words—then you're missing the whole damn thing. I don't just mean in the plays—I mean in your lives, right *now*. If you're not aware of the transcendent, if you're not awake to the glorious mystery of life and death that you're lucky enough to be part of—if that doesn't fill you with joy and strike you with awe . . . you might as well not be alive. That's the message of the tragedies. Participate in the wonder. For your sake—for Tara's sake—*live it*."

You could have heard a pin drop. And then—sudden, loud, emotional, spontaneous applause.

The applause went on for some time.

11

Zoe and Mariana queued on the stairs to exit the lecture theater.

"Well?" Zoe said, giving her a curious look. "What did you think?"

Mariana laughed. "You know, 'dazzling' is a good word."

Zoe smiled. "Told you so."

They emerged into the sunlight. Mariana considered the crowds of students milling around. "Are they here? The Maidens?"

Zoe nodded. "Over there."

She pointed at six young women gathered around a bench, talking. Four of them were standing, two were sitting; a couple were smoking.

Unlike the other students milling around the faculty, these girls weren't scruffy or eccentrically dressed. Their clothes were elegant and looked expensive. They all took care of themselves, and were made-up, well-groomed, manicured. Most distinctive of all was the way they held themselves: with an obvious air of confidence, even superiority.

Mariana considered them for a moment. "They don't look friendly; you're right."

"They're not. They're such snobs. They think they're so 'important.' I guess they are—but still . . ."

"Why do you say that? Why are they important?"

Zoe shrugged. "Well . . ." She pointed at a tall blonde perched on the armrest of the bench. "For instance—that's Carla Clarke. Her dad is *Cassian Clarke*."

"Who?"

"Oh, Mariana. He's an actor. He's really famous."

Mariana smiled. "I see. Okay. And the others?"

Zoe proceeded to discreetly point out the other members of the group. "The one on the left, the pretty one with the short dark hair? That's Natasha. She's Russian. Her dad's an oligarch or something—he owns half of Russia . . . Diya is an Indian princess—she got the highest first in the university last year. She's practically a genius—she's talking to Veronica—her dad is a senator—I think he ran for president—" She glanced at Mariana. "Get the idea . . . ?"

"I do. You mean they're intelligent—and highly privileged."

Zoe nodded. "Just hearing about their holidays is enough to make you throw up. It's always yachts and private islands and ski chalets . . ."

Mariana smiled. "I can imagine."

"No wonder everyone hates them."

Mariana glanced at her. "Does everyone hate them?"

Zoe shrugged. "Well, everyone's jealous, anyway."

Mariana thought for a second. "Okay. Let's give it a shot."

"What do you mean?"

"Let's talk to them—about Tara, and Fosca."

"Now?" Zoe shook her head. "No way. That'll never work."

"Why not?"

"They don't know you, so they'll clam up—or turn on you—particularly if you mention the professor. Trust me, don't."

"Sounds like you're afraid of them."

Zoe nodded. "I am. Terrified."

Before Mariana could respond, she saw Professor Fosca walk out of the lecture-theater building. He went up to the girls, and they gathered closely around him, whispering intimately.

"Come on," said Mariana.

"What? No, Mariana, don't—"

But she ignored Zoe, and marched over to Fosca and the students.

He looked up as Mariana approached. He smiled.

"Good afternoon, Mariana," Fosca said. "I thought I saw you in the lecture theater."

"That's right."

"I hope you enjoyed it."

Mariana searched for the right words. "It was very . . . informative. Very impressive."

"Thank you."

Mariana looked at the young women gathered around the professor. "Are these your students?"

Fosca glanced at the young women with a slight smile. "Some of them. Some of the more interesting ones."

Mariana smiled at the students. They returned her gaze stonily, a blank wall.

"I'm Mariana," she said. "Zoe's aunt."

She looked around, but Zoe hadn't followed her over and was nowhere to be seen. Mariana turned back to the others, smiling.

"You know, I couldn't help but notice you at the service for Tara. You all stood out, wearing white." She gave them a smile. "I'm curious why."

There was a slight hesitation. Then one of them, Diya, glanced at Fosca, and said, "It was my idea. In India, we always wear white at burials. And white was Tara's favorite color, so . . ."

She shrugged, and another girl completed the sentence for her.

"So we wore white in her honor."

"She hated black," said another.

"I see," said Mariana, nodding. "That's interesting."

She smiled again at the girls. They didn't smile back.

There was a slight pause. Mariana glanced at Fosca. "Professor. I have a favor to ask."

"Go ahead."

"Well, the dean has asked me, as a psychotherapist, to have a few informal chats with the pupils, see how they are coping with what's happened." She glanced at the girls. "Can I borrow some of your students?"

Mariana said this as innocently as she could, but now, as she kept looking at the girls, she could feel Fosca's laser-like eyes on her—staring at her, trying to size her up. She could imagine him thinking, wondering if she were genuine—or secretly trying to check up on him. He glanced at his watch.

"We're about to have a class," he said. "But I daresay I can spare a couple of them." He nodded at two of the girls. "Veronica? Serena? How about it?"

The two young women glanced at Mariana. It was impossible to read their feelings.

"Sure," said Veronica with a shrug. She spoke with an American accent. "I mean, I've already got a shrink . . . But I'll have a drink if she's buying."

Serena nodded. "I will too."

"Okay, then. A drink, it is." Mariana smiled at Fosca. "Thank you."

Fosca's dark eyes fixed on Mariana's face. He smiled back at her.

"A pleasure, Mariana. I sincerely hope you get everything you want."

12

Mariana found Zoe skulking by the entrance as she left the English Faculty. She asked Zoe to join them—and the offer of a drink made her cautiously accept. They made their way to a St. Christopher's College bar that was located in a corner of Main Court.

The college bar was entirely made of wood—old, warped, and knotted floorboards, oak-paneled walls, and a large wooden bar. Mariana and the three young women sat together at the large oak table by the window, which overlooked an ivy-covered wall outside. Mariana sat next to Zoe, opposite Veronica and Serena.

Mariana had recognized Veronica as the young woman who gave an emotional Bible reading at Tara's service. Her name was Veronica Drake, and she came from a wealthy American political family—her father was a senator in Washington.

Veronica was striking, and knew it. She had long blond hair, which she had a habit of tossing and playing with as she spoke. Her makeup was heavy, emphasizing her mouth and her big blue eyes. She had a great figure, which she showed off in tight jeans. And she carried herself with confidence, with the unselfconscious sense of authority of someone who has known every advantage since birth.

Veronica ordered a pint of Guinness, which she drank quickly.

She spoke a lot. There was something ever so slightly stilted about her speech. Mariana wondered if she'd had elocution lessons. When Veronica revealed that, after graduation, she intended to be an actress, Mariana wasn't surprised. She thought that beneath the makeup, deportment, and elocution, there was another person entirely, but Mariana had no idea who that was, and suspected Veronica might not either.

It was Veronica's twentieth birthday in a week's time. She was trying to organize a party, despite the current grim circumstances in college.

"Life must go on, right? It's what Tara would have wanted. Anyway, I'm hiring out a private room at the Groucho Club in London. Zoe, you must come," she added, somewhat unconvincingly.

Zoe grunted and focused on her drink.

Mariana glanced at the other girl—Serena Lewis, silently sipping white wine. Serena had a slim, petite build, and the way she sat there reminded Mariana of a little perching bird, watching everything but saying nothing.

Unlike Veronica, Serena wore no makeup—not that she needed to; she had a clear and flawless complexion. Her long dark hair was tightly plaited, and she wore a pale pink blouse and a skirt that went below the knee.

Serena was from Singapore, but had been brought up in a series of English boarding schools. She had a soft voice, with a distinctly upper-class English accent. Serena was as reserved as Veronica was forward. She kept checking her phone; her hand was drawn to it like a magnet.

"Tell me about Professor Fosca," said Mariana.

"What about him?"

"I heard he and Tara were quite close."

"I don't know where you heard that. They weren't close *at all*." Veronica turned to Serena. "Were they?"

On cue, Serena looked up from texting on her phone. She shook her head. "No, not at all. The professor was kind to Tara—but she just used him."

"Used him?" Mariana said. "How did she use him?"

"Serena didn't mean that," Veronica said, interrupting. "She means Tara wasted his time and energy. Professor Fosca puts a lot of work into us, you know. He's the best tutor you could find."

Serena nodded. "He is the most wonderful teacher in the whole world. The most brilliant. And—"

Mariana cut short the eulogy. "I was wondering about the night of the murder."

Veronica shrugged. "We were with Professor Fosca all evening. He was giving us a private tutorial in his rooms. Tara was meant to be there, but she didn't show up."

"And what time was this?"

Veronica glanced at Serena. "It started at eight, right? And we went on until, what? Ten?"

"Yeah, I think so. Ten or just after."

"And Professor Fosca was with you the entire time?"

Both girls answered at once.

"Yeah," said Veronica.

"No," said Serena.

There was a flash of irritation in Veronica's eyes. She gave Serena an accusing look. "What are you talking about?"

Serena looked flustered. "Oh, I—nothing. I mean, he only left for a couple of minutes, that's all. Just to have a cigarette outside."

Veronica backed down. "Yeah, he did. I forgot. He was only gone a minute."

Serena nodded. "He doesn't smoke inside when I'm there because I have asthma. He's really considerate."

Her phone suddenly beeped as a text came through. She pounced on it. Her face lit up as she read the message.

"I've got to go," Serena said. "I have to meet someone."

"Oh, what?" Veronica rolled her eyes. "The mystery man?"

Serena glared at her. "Stop it."

Veronica laughed, and said in a singsong voice, "*Serena has a secret boyfriend.*"

"He's not my boyfriend."

"But he is a secret—she won't tell us who he is. Even *me*." She gave a knowing wink. "I wonder . . . is he *married*?"

"No, he's not married," said Serena, going red. "He's not *anything*—just a friend. I have to go."

"Actually, so do I," said Veronica. "I have a rehearsal." She smiled sweetly at Zoe. "It's such a shame you didn't get into *The Duchess of Malfi*. It's going to be an amazing production. Nikos, the director, is a genius. He's going to be really famous one day." Veronica glanced triumphantly at Mariana. "*I'm* playing the Duchess."

"Of course you are. Well, thank you for talking to me, Veronica."

"No problem."

Veronica gave Mariana a sly look; then she left the bar, followed by Serena.

"Ugh . . ." Zoe pushed away her empty glass and gave a long sigh. "Told you. Totally toxic."

Mariana didn't disagree. She didn't like them much either.

More important, Mariana had the feeling, honed from years of working with patients, that Veronica and Serena had both been lying to her.

But about what—and why?

13

For years, I was afraid even to open the cupboard that contained it.

But today I found myself standing on a chair, reaching up and taking hold of the small wicker box—this collection of things I wanted to forget.

I sat by the light, and opened it. I sifted through the contents: the sad, lonely love letters I wrote to a couple of girls but never sent—a couple of childish stories about farm life—some bad poems I had forgotten about.

But the last thing in this Pandora's box was something I remembered all too well. The brown leather journal I kept that summer, when I was twelve—the summer I lost my mother.

I opened the journal and flicked through the pages—long entries written in immature, childish handwriting. It looked so trivial. But if it weren't for the contents of these pages, my life would be very different.

Sometimes it was hard to decipher the writing. It was erratic and scrawled, particularly toward the end, as if written in some haste, in a fit of madness—or sanity. As I sat there, it was as if a fog started to lift.

A path appeared, leading all the way back to that summer. Back to my youth.

It's a familiar journey. I make it often enough in my dreams: turning onto the winding dirt road, heading toward the farmhouse.

I don't want to go back.

I don't want to remember . . .

And yet—I need to. Because this is more than just a confession. This is a search for what was lost, for all the vanished hopes and forgotten questions. It's a quest for explanation: for the terrible secrets hinted at in that child's journal—which I now consult like a fortune-teller, peering into a crystal ball.

Except I don't seek the future.

I seek the past.

14

At nine o'clock, Mariana went to meet Fred at the Eagle.

The Eagle was the oldest pub in Cambridge, as popular now as it had been in the 1600s. It was a collection of small, interconnecting wood-paneled rooms. It was lit by candlelight, and smelled of roast lamb, rosemary, and beer.

The main room was known as the RAF bar. Several pillars held up the uneven ceiling, which was covered with graffiti from World War II. As Mariana waited at the bar, she became conscious of the messages from dead men above her head. British and American pilots used pens, candles, and cigarette lighters to inscribe their names and squadron numbers on the ceiling, and they scribbled drawings—like cartoons of naked women in lipstick.

Mariana got the attention of the baby-faced barman, wearing a green-and-black-checked shirt. He smiled as he removed a steaming tray of glasses from a dishwasher. "What can I get you, love?"

"A glass of sauvignon blanc, please."

"Coming up."

He poured her a glass of white. Mariana paid for it, then looked for somewhere to sit.

There were young couples everywhere, holding hands and

having romantic conversations. She refused to let herself look at the corner table, where she and Sebastian always used to sit.

She checked her watch. Ten minutes past nine.

Fred was late—perhaps he wasn't coming. She felt hopeful at the thought. She would wait ten minutes, then go.

She gave in and glanced at the corner table. It was empty. And she went over and sat down.

She sat there, stroking the cracks in the wooden table with her fingertips, just like she used to. Sitting here, sipping the cold wine and shutting her eyes, listening to the timeless sound of chatter and laughter all around, she could imagine herself transported back into the past—as long she kept her eyes shut, she could be there, nineteen years old, waiting for Sebastian to appear in his white T-shirt and his faded blue jeans with the rip across the knee.

"Hello," he said.

But it was the wrong voice—not Sebastian's—and Mariana felt a split second of confusion before she opened her eyes. And the spell was broken.

The voice belonged to Fred, who was holding a pint of Guinness and grinning at her. His eyes were bright and he looked flushed.

"Sorry to be late. My supervision ran over, so I cycled as fast as I could. I collided with a lamppost."

"Are you all right?"

"I'm all right. The lamppost got the worst of it. May I?"

Mariana nodded, and he sat down—in Sebastian's chair. For a second Mariana thought about asking if they could move to another table. But she stopped herself. How did Clarissa put it? She had to stop looking over her shoulder. She had to focus on the present.

Fred grinned. He produced a small packet of nuts from his pocket. He offered them to Mariana. She shook her head.

He tossed a couple of cashews into his mouth and crunched on them, keeping his eyes on Mariana. There was an awkward pause, as she waited for him to say something. She was feeling annoyed with herself. What was she doing here with this earnest young man?

What a stupid idea it was. She decided to be uncharacteristically blunt. After all, she had nothing to lose.

"Listen," she said. "Nothing is going to happen between us. You understand? Ever."

Fred choked on a cashew nut, and started coughing. He gulped some beer and managed to catch his breath. "Sorry," he said, looking embarrassed. "I—I wasn't expecting that. Message received. You're out of my league, obviously."

"Don't be silly." Mariana shook her head. "That's not it."

"Then why?"

She shrugged, uncomfortable. "A million reasons."

"Name one."

"You're much too young for me."

"What?" Fred's face colored. He looked indignant and embarrassed. "That's *ridiculous*."

"How old are you?"

"Not that young—I'm nearly twenty-nine."

Mariana laughed. "*That's* ridiculous."

"Why? How old are you?"

"Old enough not to round my age up. I'm thirty-six."

"So what?" Fred shrugged. "Age doesn't matter. Not when you feel—how you feel." He glanced at her. "You know, when I first saw you, on the train, I had the strongest premonition that, one day, I would ask you to marry me. And you would say yes."

"Well, you were wrong."

"Why? Are you . . . married?"

"Yes—no, I mean—"

"Don't tell me he left you? What an idiot."

"Yes, I think so frequently." Mariana sighed, then spoke quickly to get it over with. "He—died. About a year ago. It's hard—to talk about."

"I'm sorry." Fred looked crestfallen. He didn't speak for a moment. "I feel stupid now."

"Don't be. It's not your fault."

Mariana felt so tired, suddenly, and frustrated with herself. She drained her wine. "I should go."

"No, not yet. I've not told you what I think about the murder. About Conrad. That's why you're here, isn't it?"

"Well?"

Fred looked at her with a sly, sidelong glance. "I think they've got the wrong man."

"Have they? What makes you say that?"

"I've met Conrad. I know him. He's no murderer."

Mariana nodded. "Zoe doesn't think so either. But the police do."

"Well, I've been thinking. I've half a mind to try and solve it myself. I like solving puzzles. I have that kind of brain." Fred smiled at her. "How about it?"

"How about what?"

"You and me," Fred said with a grin. "Teaming up? Solving it together?"

Mariana thought for a second. She could probably use his help, and she wavered—but she knew she'd regret it. She shook her head.

"I don't think so, but thanks."

"Well, let me know you if you change your mind." He took out a pen from his pocket and scrawled his phone number on the back of the beer mat. He handed it to her. "Here. If you need anything—anything at all—call me."

"Thanks—but I'm not staying long."

"You keep saying that, but you're still here." Fred grinned. "I have a good feeling about you, Mariana. A hunch. I'm a big believer in hunches."

As they left the pub, Fred chatted happily to Mariana. "You're from Greece, right?"

She nodded. "Yes. I grew up in Athens."

"Ah, Athens is a lot of fun. I love Greece. Have you been to many islands?"

"A few of them."

"How about Naxos?"

Mariana froze. She stood there awkwardly on the street, suddenly unable to look at him.

"What?" she whispered.

"Naxos? I went last year. I'm a big swimmer—well, diving, mainly—and it's great for that. Have you been? You should really—"

"I have to go."

Mariana turned away before Fred could see the tears in her eyes, and she kept walking off without looking back.

"Oh," she heard him say. He sounded a little shocked. "Okay, then. I'll see you later—"

Mariana didn't reply. *It's just a coincidence,* she told herself. *It doesn't mean anything—forget it, it's nothing. Nothing.*

She tried to banish the mention of the island from her mind, and kept walking.

15

As she left Fred, Mariana hurried back to the college.

It was getting colder in the evening now, and there was a slight chill in the air. Mist was spreading above the river—up ahead, the street disappeared in a cloudy haze, the mist hovering like thick smoke over the ground.

Mariana soon became aware she was being followed.

The same set of footsteps had been behind her soon after she left the Eagle. It was a heavy tread, a man's tread; forceful, hard-soled boots repetitively hitting the cobbles, echoing along the deserted street—and a little way behind her. It was hard to judge just how near the footsteps were, not without turning around. She summoned her courage, and glanced over her shoulder.

There was no one there—not as far as she could see, which wasn't far. Clouds of mist enveloped the street, swallowing it.

Mariana kept going. She turned a corner.

A few seconds later, the footsteps followed her.

She sped up. So did the footsteps.

She looked over her shoulder—and this time, she saw someone.

The shadow of a man, not far behind her. He was walking away from the streetlight, against the wall, keeping in the dark.

Mariana could feel her heart beating fast. She looked around for an escape—and she saw a man and a woman, on the other side of the street, walking arm in arm. She quickly stepped off the curb and walked across the road toward them.

But just as she reached the pavement, they went up some steps to a front door, unlocked it, and disappeared inside.

Mariana kept walking, listening for footsteps. And glancing over her shoulder, there he was—a man wearing dark clothing, his face in shadow—crossing the misty street after her.

Mariana glanced at a narrow alleyway to her left. She made a sudden decision, and turned down the alley. Without looking back, she broke into a run.

She ran along the alley, all the way down to the river. The wooden bridge lay ahead of her. She kept going and hurried over it—across the water, to the other side.

It was darker here, down by the water, with no streetlamps to illuminate the gloom. The mist was thicker, feeling cold and wet against her skin, and it smelled icy, like snow.

Mariana carefully bent back some branches of a tree. Then she stepped around it and hid behind it. She held on to the trunk, feeling its smooth wet bark, and tried to be as still and silent as possible. She tried to slow her breathing down, and quiet it.

And she watched, and waited.

Sure enough, a few seconds later, she glimpsed him—or his shadow—sneak over the bridge and onto the bank.

She lost sight of him, but could still hear his footsteps, on softer ground now, on earth—prowling around, barely a few feet away.

And then, silence. No sound at all. She held her breath.

Where was he? Where did he go?

She waited for what seemed an interminable time, just to make sure. Had he gone? It seemed he had.

She cautiously emerged from behind the tree. It took her a few seconds to find her bearings. Then she realized—the river was there in front of her, gleaming in the darkness. All she had to do was follow it.

She hurried along the riverbank, all the way to the back entrance of St. Christopher's. There, she crossed the stone bridge—and went up to the big wooden gate in the brick wall.

She reached out, gripped the cold brass ring, and pulled. The gate didn't move. It was locked.

Mariana hesitated, unsure what to do—then . . . she heard footsteps.

The same urgent footsteps. The same man.

And he was getting closer.

Mariana looked around—but couldn't see anything—just clouds of mist disappearing into the dark shadows.

But she could hear him approaching, crossing the bridge toward her.

She tried the gate again—but it wouldn't budge. She was trapped. She could feel herself starting to panic.

"Who is it?" she called into the darkness. "Who's there?"

There was no reply. Just footsteps getting closer, closer—

Mariana opened her mouth to cry out—

Then, suddenly, on her left, a little farther along, there was a creaking sound. A small gate opened in the wall. It was partly hidden by a bush, and Mariana hadn't registered it before. It was a third of the size of the main gate, and made of plain, unvarnished wood. The beam of a torch shone from it, out into the darkness. It shone onto her face, blinding her.

"Everything all right, miss?"

She recognized Morris's voice at once, and felt instantly relieved. He moved the light out of her eyes, and she saw him stand up straight, having stooped down to pass through the low gate. Morris was dressed in a black overcoat and black gloves. He peered at her.

"Are you all right?" he said. "Just doing my rounds. The back gate is locked at ten o'clock, you should know that."

"I forgot. Yes—I'm fine."

He shone the torch around the bridge. Mariana followed the light anxiously with her eyes. No sign of anyone.

She listened. Silence. No footsteps.

He had gone.

"Can you let me in?" she said, glancing back at Morris.

"Certainly. Go in this way." He gestured at the small gate behind him. "I often use it as a shortcut. Go along the passage and you'll come out in Main Court."

"Thank you," Mariana said. "I'm so grateful."

"Not at all, miss."

She walked past him, up to the open gate. She bowed her head and stooped slightly, and went inside. The ancient brick passage was very dark and smelled of damp. The gate shut behind her. She heard Morris lock it.

Mariana cautiously made her away along the passage, thinking about what had happened. She had a moment of doubt—had someone really been following her? If so, who? Or was she just being paranoid?

In any case, she was relieved to be back in St. Christopher's.

She emerged into an oak-paneled corridor, part of the building that housed the buttery in Main Court. She was about to exit through the main doorway—when she glanced back. And she stopped.

There were a series of portraits hanging along the dimly lit passage. At the end of the passage, one portrait caught her eye. It occupied a wall to itself. Mariana stared at it. It was a face she recognized.

She blinked a few times, unsure she was seeing correctly—and then she slowly approached it, like a woman in a trance.

She reached it and stood there, her face level with the face in the painting. She stared at it. Yes, it was him.

It was Tennyson.

But it wasn't Tennyson as an old man, with white hair and a long beard, as in other paintings that Mariana had seen. This was Alfred Tennyson as a young man. Just a boy, really.

He couldn't have been more than twenty-nine when it was painted. He looked even younger. But it was unmistakably him.

He had one of the handsomest faces Mariana had ever seen.

And seeing him here, close up, his beauty quite took her breath away. He had a strong angular jaw, sensuous lips, and dark, tousled shoulder-length hair. For a moment she was reminded of Edward Fosca, but she banished him from her mind. For one thing, the eyes were quite different. Fosca's eyes were dark, and Tennyson's were light blue, watery blue.

Hallam had probably been dead around seven years when this was painted, meaning Tennyson had another long decade ahead of him before *In Memoriam* was finally completed. Another ten years of grief.

And yet—this wasn't a face ravished by despair. There was surprisingly little, if any, detectable emotion in this face. No sadness, no hint of melancholia. There was stillness, and glacial beauty. But little else.

Why?

It was, Mariana thought, squinting at the picture, as if Tennyson were looking at something . . . something in the near distance.

Yes, she thought—his pale blue eyes appeared to be staring at something just out of sight, something off to one side, behind Mariana's head.

What was he looking at?

She walked away from the painting feeling rather disappointed— as if she had been personally let down by Tennyson. She didn't know what she had hoped to find in his eyes—a little comfort, perhaps?— solace or strength; even heartbreak would have been preferable.

But not *nothing*.

She banished the portrait from her mind. She hurried back to her room.

Outside her door, something was waiting for her.

A black envelope on the floor.

Mariana picked it up and opened it. Inside, there was a piece of notepaper, folded in half. She unfolded it and read it.

It was a handwritten message in black ink, in elegant, slanted writing:

Dear Mariana,

I hope you are well. I was wondering if you might care to join me for a little chat tomorrow morning? How about ten o'clock in the Fellows' Garden?
Yours,
Edward Fosca

16

If I'd been born in Ancient Greece, there would have been numerous bad omens and horoscopes predicting disaster at my birth. Eclipses, blazing comets, and doom-laden portents—

As it was, there was nothing—and in fact, my birth was characterized by an absence of event. My father, the man who would warp my life and make me into this monster, wasn't even present. He was playing a game of cards with some of the farmhands, smoking cigars and drinking whiskey into the night.

If I try to picture my mother—if I squint—I can just about see her, hazy and out of focus—my beautiful mother, just a girl at nineteen, in a private room in the hospital. She can hear the sound of nurses talking and laughing at the end of the corridor. She is alone, but this is not a problem. Alone, she can find a level of peace—she can think her thoughts without fear of attack. She's looking forward to her baby, she realizes, because babies don't talk.

She knows her husband wants a son—but secretly she prays it's a girl. If it's a boy, he'll grow into a man.

And men are not to be trusted.

She's relieved when the contractions resume. They are a distraction from thinking. She prefers to focus on the physical: the breathing, the counting—the searing pain that wipes all thoughts from her mind, like chalk scrubbed from a blackboard. Then she gives into it, the agony, and loses herself—

Until, at dawn, I was born.

To my mother's dismay, I was not a girl. When my father heard the news, that he had a boy, he was elated. Farmers, like kings, have need of many sons. I was his first.

Preparing to celebrate my birth, he arrived at the hospital with a bottle of cheap sparkling wine.

But was it a celebration?

Or a catastrophe?

Was my fate already decided, even then? Was it too late? Should they have smothered me at birth? Left me to die and rot on the hillside?

I know what my mother would say, if she could read this, my search for culpability, my quest for blame. She would have no patience with it.

No one is responsible, she'd say. *Don't glorify the events of your life and try to give them meaning. There is no meaning. Life means nothing. Death means nothing.*

But she didn't always think that way.

There was more than one of her. There was another person once, who pressed flowers and underlined poetry: a secret past I found hidden in a shoebox, at the back of a cupboard. Old photos, flattened flowers, badly spelled love poems from my father to my mother, written during their courtship. But my father quickly stopped writing poetry. And my mother stopped reading it.

She married a man she barely knew. And he took her away from everyone she had ever known. He took her to a world of discomfort—of cold, early mornings and all-day-long strenuous physical labor: weighing the lambs, shearing them, feeding them. Again, and again. And again.

There were magical moments, of course—like lambing season, when tiny innocent little creatures would pop up like white mushrooms. That was the best of it.

But she never let herself get attached to the lambs. She learned not to.

The worst of it was death. Constant, never-ending death—and all its associated processes: marking the ones to be killed, which were gaining too little weight or too much, or not falling pregnant. And then the butcher would appear, in that horrible bloodstained smock of his. And my father would hover, eager to help. He enjoyed doing the slaughtering. He seemed to relish it.

My mother would always run and hide while it went on, smuggling a bottle of vodka into the bathroom, into the shower, where she thought her tears couldn't be heard. And I would go to the farthest part of the farm, as far away as I could get. I'd cover my ears, but I still heard the screaming.

When I'd return to the farmhouse, the stench of death was everywhere. Bodies, cut up in the open barn, nearest to the kitchen—and gutters running red with blood. There was a stink of flesh, as it was weighed and packaged in our kitchen. Bits of congealed meat stuck to the table, and pools of blood collected on the surfaces, circled by fat flies.

The unwanted parts of the bodies—entrails, guts, and other remains—were buried by my father. He'd throw them in the pit at the back of the farm.

The pit was something I always avoided. It terrified me. My father would threaten to bury me alive in the pit if I disobeyed him, or misbehaved—or betrayed his secrets.

No one will ever find you, he'd say. *No one will ever know.*

I used to imagine being buried alive in the pit—surrounded by the rotting carcasses, writhing with maggots and worms and other gray flesh-eating creatures—and I would shiver with fear.

I still shudder now when I think about it.

17

At ten o'clock the next morning, Mariana went to meet Professor Fosca.

She arrived at the Fellows' Garden as the chapel clock struck ten. The professor was already there. He was wearing a white shirt, unbuttoned around the neck, and a dark-gray corduroy jacket. His hair was down, falling around his shoulders.

"Good morning," he said. "I'm happy to see you. I wasn't sure you'd come."

"I'm here."

"And so punctual. What does that say about you, Mariana, I wonder?"

He smiled. Mariana didn't smile back. She was determined to give away as little as possible.

Fosca opened the wooden gate and gestured into the garden. "Shall we?"

She followed him inside. The Fellows' Garden was only for use by the fellows and their guests—it wasn't permitted for undergraduates to enter. Mariana couldn't recall having been inside before.

She was immediately struck by how peaceful it was, how beautiful. It was a low Tudor sunken garden—surrounded by an old, uneven brick wall. Bloodred valerian flowers were growing in between the bricks, in the cracks, very slowly ripping the wall apart. And colorful plants grew all the way around the perimeter, in pinks and blues and fiery reds.

"It's lovely," she said.

Fosca nodded. "Oh, yes, indeed. I often come here."

They began walking along the path as Fosca mused on the beauty of the garden and Cambridge in general. "There's a kind of magic here. You feel it too, don't you?" He glanced at her. "I'm sure you felt it from the start—as I did. I can picture you—an undergraduate, fresh off the boat, new to this country—as I was— new to this life. Unsophisticated—lonely . . . Am I right?"

"Are you talking about me or you?"

Fosca smiled. "I suspect we both had very similar experiences."

"I doubt it."

Fosca glanced at her. He studied her for a second, as if he were going to say something—but decided against it. They walked in silence.

Eventually, he said, "You're very quiet. Not at all what I was expecting."

"What were you expecting?"

Fosca shrugged. "I don't know. An inquisition."

"Inquisition?"

"Interrogation, then." He offered her a cigarette. She shook her head.

"I don't smoke."

"No one does anymore—except me. I've tried and failed to quit. No impulse control."

He put a cigarette in his mouth. It was an American brand, with a white filter on the end. He struck a match, lit it—and blew out a long line of smoke. Mariana watched the smoke dance in the air and disappear.

"I asked you here to meet me," he said, "because I felt we should talk. I hear you've been taking an interest in me. Asking my students all kinds of questions . . . By the way," he added, "I checked with the dean. As far as he is aware, he never requested you talk to any students, informally or otherwise. So the question is, Mariana, what the hell are you up to?"

Mariana glanced at him and saw Fosca staring at her, trying to read her mind with his piercing eyes. She evaded his gaze and shrugged. "I'm intrigued, that's all . . ."

"About me in particular?"

"About the Maidens."

"The Maidens?" Fosca looked surprised. "Why is that?"

"It seems odd, having a special set of students. Surely it only fosters rivalries and resentments among the others?"

Fosca smiled and took a drag on his cigarette. "You're a group therapist, aren't you? So, of all people, you should know small groups provide a perfect environment for exceptional minds to flourish . . . That's all I'm doing—creating that space."

"A cocoon—for exceptional minds?"

"Well put."

"Female minds."

Fosca blinked and gave her a cool look. "The most intelligent minds are often female . . . Is that so hard to accept? There's nothing sinister going on. I'm a tame fellow with a generous alcohol allowance, that's all—if anyone is being abused here, it's me."

"Who said anything about abuse?"

"Don't be coy, Mariana. I can see you have cast me as the villain—a predator preying on my vulnerable students. Except now you've met these young ladies, you can see there's nothing vulnerable about them. Nothing untoward happens at these meetings—it's just a small study group, discussing poetry, enjoying wine and intellectual debate."

"Except now one of those girls is dead."

Professor Fosca frowned. There was an unmistakable flash of anger in his eyes. He stared at her. "Do you think you can see inside my soul?"

Mariana looked away, embarrassed by the question. "No, of course not. I didn't mean—"

"Forget it." He took another drag of his cigarette, all anger apparently gone. "The word 'psychotherapist,' as you know, comes from the Greek *psyche,* meaning 'soul,' and *therapeia,* meaning 'healing.' Are you a healer of souls? Will you heal mine?"

"No. Only you can do that."

Fosca dropped his cigarette onto the path. He ground it into the earth with his foot. "You're determined to dislike me. I don't know why."

To Mariana's annoyance, she realized she didn't know why either. "Shall we go back?"

They started walking back to the gate. He kept glancing at Mariana. "I'm intrigued by you," he said. "I find myself wondering what you're thinking."

"I'm not thinking. I'm—listening."

And she was. Mariana might not be a detective, but she was a therapist, and she knew how to listen. To listen not only to what was being said, but also to everything *unsaid,* all the words unspoken—the lies, evasions, projections, transferences, and other psychological phenomena that occurred between two people, and that required a special kind of listening. Mariana had to listen to all the *feelings* Fosca was unconsciously communicating to her. In a therapeutic context, those feelings were called the transference, and would tell her everything she needed to know about this man, who he was—and what he was hiding. As long as she could keep her own emotions out of it, of course—which wasn't easy. She tried to listen to her body as they walked, and could feel a rising tension: a tight jaw, teeth clenched into a bite. She felt a burning sensation in her stomach, a prickling in her skin—which she associated with anger.

But whose anger? Hers?

No—it was *his.*

His anger. Yes, she could feel it. He was silent now as they walked—but underneath the silence, there was fury. He was disowning it, of course, but it was there, bubbling beneath the surface: somehow, Mariana had angered him during this meeting; she had been unpredictable, hard to read, difficult—and had triggered his rage. She suddenly thought, *If he can get this mad, this fast—what happens if I really provoke him?*

She wasn't sure she wanted to find out.

Then, as they reached the gate, Fosca stopped. He glanced at her, weighing something up. He made a decision. "I'm wondering," he said, "if you'd care to continue this conversation . . . over dinner? How about tomorrow night?"

He gazed at her, waiting for her response. Mariana met his gaze without blinking.

"Okay," she said.

Fosca smiled. "Good . . . My rooms, at eight? And one more thing—"

Before she could stop him, he leaned forward—

And he kissed her on the lips.

It only lasted a second. By the time Mariana could react, he had already pulled back.

Fosca turned and went through the open gate. Mariana heard him whistling as he walked away.

She brushed away the kiss with her fist.

How dare he?

She felt as if she had been assaulted—attacked; and that he had won somehow, succeeded in wrong-footing, intimidating her.

As she stood there, feeling hot and cold in the morning sun, burning with anger, she knew one thing for certain.

This time, the rage she was feeling wasn't his.

It was hers.

All hers.

18

After leaving Fosca, Mariana took out the beer mat Fred had given her. She rang his number, and asked if he was free to meet.

Twenty minutes later, she met Fred by St. Christopher's main gate. She watched him chain his bike to the railings. He reached into his bag and pulled out a couple of red apples.

"I'm calling this breakfast. Want one?"

He offered her an apple. She was automatically about to refuse when she realized she was hungry. She nodded.

Fred looked pleased. He selected the better of the two apples, polished it on his sleeve, and handed it to her.

"Thanks." Mariana took it and bit into the apple. It was crisp and sweet.

Fred smiled at her, speaking between mouthfuls. "I was happy you called. Last night . . . you left a bit suddenly—I thought I upset you or something."

Mariana shrugged. "It wasn't you—it was . . . Naxos."

"Naxos?" Fred peered at her, confused.

"It's—where my husband died. He . . . drowned there."

"Oh, Jesus." Fred's eyes widened. "Oh God. I'm so sorry—"

"You didn't know?"

"How could I know? Of course not."

"So it's just a coincidence?" She watched him carefully.

"Well . . . I told you. I'm a little psychic. So maybe I was picking up on it—that's why Naxos popped into my head."

Mariana frowned. "I'm sorry, I don't believe that."

"Well, it's true." There was an awkward pause. Then Fred went on, quickly, "Look, I'm sorry if I hurt your feelings—"

"You didn't, really. It doesn't matter. Forget it."

"Is that why you called me? To tell me this?"

Mariana shook her head. "No."

She wasn't sure why she had called him. It was probably a mistake. She had told herself she needed Fred's help, but in truth this was an excuse—she was probably just lonely, and upset by her meeting with Fosca. She felt annoyed with herself for doing it—but too late, he was here now. They might as well make the best of it. "Come on," she said. "I want to show you something."

They made their way inside the college, and walked across Main Court, and then through the archway, into Eros Court.

As they entered the courtyard, Mariana glanced up at Zoe's room. Zoe wasn't there—she was in a class with Clarissa. Mariana purposely hadn't told her about Fred, because Mariana didn't quite know how to explain him to Zoe, or to herself.

As they neared Tara's staircase, Mariana nodded at the ground-floor window. "This is Tara's room. On the night she died, her bedder saw her leave this room at a quarter to eight exactly."

Fred gestured at the gate at the rear of Eros Court—which led out onto the Backs. "And she went out that way?"

"No." Mariana shook her head. She pointed in the other direction, through the archway. "She went out through Main Court."

"Hmm. That's odd . . . The back gate leads onto the river—the quickest way to Paradise."

"Which suggests . . . she was going somewhere else."

"To meet Conrad, like he said?"

"Possibly." Mariana thought for a moment. "There's something else—Morris, the porter, saw Tara leave by the front gate at eight o'clock. So if she left her room at a quarter to eight—?"

She left the question hanging. Fred finished it.

"Why did it take her fifteen minutes to walk a distance that takes a minute or two at most? I see . . . Well, it could be anything. She could have been texting someone, or seen a friend, or—"

As he was talking, Mariana looked at the flower bed under Tara's window—a patch of purple and pink foxgloves.

And there, on the earth, was a cigarette butt. She bent down and picked it up. It had a distinctive white filter.

"That's an American brand," said Fred.

Mariana nodded. "Yes . . . like Professor Fosca smokes."

"Fosca?" Fred spoke in a low voice. "I know about him. I've got friends in this college. I've heard the stories."

Mariana glanced at him. "What stories? What are you talking about?"

"Cambridge is a small place. Everybody talks."

"And what do they say?"

"That Fosca's famous—or *infamous* . . . His parties are, anyway."

"What parties? What do you know?"

Fred shrugged. "Not much. They're only for his students. But I mean—I heard they're pretty wild." He stared at her closely, reading her expression. "You think he had something to do with it? With Tara's murder?"

Mariana deliberated, then gave in. "Listen," she said. "I'll tell you."

They walked around the perimeter of the courtyard as she told him all about Tara's accusations against Fosca—and his subsequent denial, his corroborated alibi; and how, despite this, Mariana was unable to let it go. She expected Fred to laugh or scoff, or at the very least disbelieve her—but he didn't. And she felt grateful to him for that. She found herself warming to him, and, for the first time, feeling less alone.

"Unless Veronica and Serena and the others are lying," Mariana finished by saying, "Fosca was with them the whole time—except for a couple of minutes, when he went outside for a cigarette . . ."

"Plenty of time," said Fred, "if he had seen Tara through the window, to go down and meet here, in the court."

"And arrange to meet her in Paradise at ten o'clock?"

"That's right. Why not?"

Mariana shrugged. "He still couldn't have done it. If Tara was murdered at ten, he couldn't have got there in time. It takes twenty minutes to walk there, at least, and probably longer by car . . ."

Fred thought for a second. "Unless he went by water."

Mariana looked at him blankly. "What?"

"Maybe he took a punt."

"A punt?" She almost laughed, it sounded so absurd.

"Why not? No one watches the river—no one would notice a punt—particularly at night. He could arrive and leave invisibly . . . in a couple of minutes."

Mariana thought about it. "Perhaps you're right."

"Can you punt?"

"Not very well."

"I can." Fred grinned. "As it happens, I'm quite good—if I say so myself . . . How about it?"

"How about what?"

"We go to the boathouse, borrow a punt—and test it out? Why not?"

Before Mariana could respond, her phone rang. It was Zoe. She answered immediately.

"Zoe? Are you okay?"

"Where are you?" Zoe's voice had that urgent, anxious quality, telling Mariana that something was wrong.

"I'm in college. Where are you?"

"I'm with Clarissa. The police were just here—"

"Why? What happened?"

There was a pause. Mariana could hear her trying not to cry. Zoe spoke in a low whisper. "It's happened again."

"What—do you mean?"

Mariana knew what Zoe meant. She needed her to spell it out, just the same.

"Another stabbing," Zoe said. "They found another body."

Part Three

The perfect plot, accordingly, must have a single, and not (as some tell us) a double issue; the change in the hero's fortunes must be not from misery to happiness, but on the contrary from happiness to misery; and the cause of it must lie not in any depravity, but in some great error on his part.

—ARISTOTLE, *Poetics*

1

The body had been found in a field, on the edge of Paradise. It was medieval common land, for which farmers had ancient grazing rights, and a farmer, putting his herd of cows out to graze that morning, had made the grisly discovery.

Mariana was anxious about getting there as soon as possible. Despite Zoe's furious protestations, Mariana refused to allow her to accompany her. She was determined to shield Zoe from as much unpleasantness as possible. And this was bound to be unpleasant.

Instead, she set off with Fred. He used the map on his phone to guide them to the field.

As they walked along the river, past the colleges and meadows, Mariana breathed in the smell of grass and earth and the trees—and was transported back to that first autumn, all those years ago, when she had arrived in England, having exchanged the humid heat of Greece for the charcoal skies and wet grass of East Anglia.

Since then, the English countryside had never lost its thrill for Mariana—until today. Today she felt no thrill, just a sick sense of dread. These fields and meadows she loved, these pathways she'd walked with Sebastian, were forever tainted. No longer synonymous with love and happiness—from now on, they would only ever mean blood and death.

They walked mainly in silence. After about twenty minutes, Fred pointed up ahead. "There it is."

In front of them lay a field. At the entry to the field was a line of vehicles—police cars, news vans—parked behind one another along the dirt track. Mariana and Fred walked past the cars until they reached the police cordon, where several officers were keeping the press at bay. There was also a small crowd of onlookers.

Mariana glanced at the onlookers, and suddenly remembered the ghoulish crowd that had gathered on the beach to watch as Sebastian's body was dragged from the water. She remembered those faces—expressions of concern masking prurient excitement. God, she'd hated them—and now, seeing the same expressions here, she felt sick.

"Come on," she said. "Let's go."

But Fred didn't move. He looked a little uncertain. "Where are we going?"

Mariana pointed past the police cordon. "That way."

"How are we going to get in? They'll see us."

Mariana looked around. "How about you go over and distract them—give me the chance to slip past?"

"Sure. I can do that."

"You don't mind not coming?"

Fred shook his head. He didn't meet her eye. "To be honest, I'm a bit squeamish about blood—bodies and things. I'd rather wait here."

"Okay. I won't be long."

"Good luck."

"You too," she said.

He took a moment to summon up his nerve. Then he walked over to the police officers. He started talking to them, asking them questions—and Mariana seized her chance.

She went up to the cordon, lifted it up, and ducked underneath.

Then she straightened up and kept going—but only took a few steps before she heard a voice.

"Hey! What are you doing?"

Mariana turned around. A police officer was charging toward her.

"Stop. Who are you?"

Before Mariana could reply, they were interrupted by Julian. He emerged from a forensic tent, and waved at the officer. "It's all right. She's with me. She's a colleague."

The police officer gave Mariana a mistrustful look, but stepped aside. Mariana watched him depart and she turned to Julian. "Thanks."

Julian smiled. "Not easily discouraged, are you? I like that. Let's hope we don't bump into the inspector." He winked at her. "Do you want to have a look? The pathologist's an old friend of mine."

They walked to the tent. The pathologist was standing in front of it, texting on his phone. He was a man in his forties, tall, completely bald, with piercing blue eyes.

"Kuba," said Julian, "I've brought a colleague, if that's okay."

"By all means." Kuba glanced at Mariana. He spoke with a slight Polish accent. "I warn you, it's not a pretty sight. Worse than last time."

He gestured around the back of the tent with his gloved hand. Mariana took a deep breath and walked around.

And there it was.

It was the most horrible thing Mariana had ever seen. She felt afraid to look at it. It didn't seem real.

The body of a young woman, or the remains of one, was stretched out in the grass. The torso was slashed beyond recognition—all that was left was a mixture of blood and guts, mud and earth. The head was untouched, and the eyes were open, seeing and unseeing—in this gaze, a path led to oblivion.

Mariana kept staring at the eyes, unable to look away; transfixed by this Medusa's look—eyes that had the power to petrify even after death . . .

A line from *The Duchess of Malfi* flashed into her mind—"Cover her face, mine eyes dazzle—she died young."

She did die young. Too young. She was only twenty. It was her birthday next week—she was organizing a party.

Mariana knew this because she recognized her at once.

It was Veronica.

2

Mariana started walking away from the body.

She felt physically sick. She had to put some distance between herself and what she had seen. She wanted to get away, but she knew there was no running away—it was a sight that would haunt her for the rest of her days. The blood, the head, those gaping eyes—

Stop it, she thought. *Stop thinking.*

She kept walking until she reached a rickety wooden fence, forming a boundary between this field and the next. It felt unsteady and liable to collapse; she leaned against it—flimsy support, but better than nothing.

"You all right?"

Julian appeared at her side. He gave her a concerned look.

Mariana nodded. She realized her eyes were full of tears. She brushed them away, embarrassed. "I'm fine."

"When you've seen as many crime scenes as I have, you get used to it. For what it's worth, I think you're brave."

Mariana shook her head. "I'm not, not at all."

"And you were right about Conrad Ellis. He was in custody at the time of the murder, so that lets him off the hook . . ." Julian glanced at Kuba as he approached them. "Unless you don't think they were killed by the same person?"

Kuba shook his head, pulling out a vape from his pocket. "No, it's the same guy. Same MO—I counted twenty-two stab wounds." He took a drag and exhaled clouds of vapor.

Mariana peered at him. "There was something in her hand. What was it?"

"Ah. You noticed that? A pinecone."

"I thought so. How odd."

Julian glanced at her. "Why do you say that?"

Mariana shrugged. "Just there aren't any pine trees around here." She thought for a second. "I'm wondering if there's an inventory of everything found with Tara's body?"

"Funny you say that," Kuba said. "The same thing occurred to me—so I checked. And there was also a pinecone found with Tara's body."

"A pinecone?" said Julian. "How interesting. It must mean something to him . . . But what, I wonder?"

As he said that, Mariana suddenly remembered one of the slides Professor Fosca had showed in his lecture on Eleusis: a marble relief of a pinecone.

Yes, she thought. *It does mean something.*

Julian was looking around, frustrated. He shook his head. "How does he do it? Kills them in the open air—then vanishes, covered in blood, leaving no witnesses, no murder weapon, no discernible evidence . . . nothing."

"Just a glimpse into hell," said Kuba. "But you're wrong about the blood. He wouldn't necessarily be covered in blood. After all, the stabbing takes place postmortem."

"What?" Mariana stared at him. "What do you mean?"

"Exactly that. He cut their throats first."

"Are you sure?"

"Oh, yes." Kuba nodded. "In both cases, the cause of death was a deep incision—severing the tissues all the way to the bone in the neck. Death must have been instantaneous. Judging by the depth of the wound . . . I suspect he struck from behind. If I may?"

He stepped behind Julian, and elegantly demonstrated—using his vape as a knife. Mariana winced as he mimed slashing Julian's throat.

"You see? The arterial spray goes forward. Then, laying the body on the ground, during the stabbing, the blood just trickles downward, into the earth. So he might have no blood on him at all."

Mariana shook her head. "But—that doesn't make any sense."

"Why not?"

"Because that's not—a frenzy. That's not losing control, that's not *rage*—"

Kuba shook his head. "No. The opposite. He's very calm, in control—like he's performing a kind of dance. It's very precise. It's . . . *rytualistyczny* . . ." He searched for the word in English. "Ritualistic . . . ? Is that correct?"

"Ritualistic?"

Mariana stared at him—as a series of images flashed through her mind: Edward Fosca onstage, lecturing about religious rites; the postcard in Tara's room, with an Ancient Greek oracle demanding sacrifice; and—at the back of her mind—the indelible memory of a bright blue sky, with a burning sun and a ruined temple dedicated to a vengeful goddess.

There was something—something she needed to think about. But before she could press Kuba further, there was a voice behind her.

"What's going on here?"

They all turned around. Chief Inspector Sangha was standing there. He did not look happy.

3

"What's she doing here?" said Sangha, frowning.

Julian stepped forward. "Mariana's with me. I thought she might have some insight—and she's been extremely helpful."

Sangha unscrewed the lid from his flask, balanced it precariously on the fence post, and poured some tea. He looked tired, Mariana thought—she didn't envy him his job. His investigation had just doubled in size, and he'd lost his only suspect. She was hesitant to make things worse, but had no choice.

"Chief Inspector," she said, "are you aware the victim is Veronica Drake? She was a student at St. Christopher's."

The inspector stared at her with a slight look of dismay. "Are you sure?"

Mariana nodded. "And are you also aware Professor Fosca taught both victims? They were both part of his special group."

"What special group?"

"I really think you should ask him about it."

Inspector Sangha drained his tea before responding. "I see. Any more tips, Mariana?"

Mariana didn't like his tone, but she smiled politely. "That's it for the moment."

Sangha poured the dregs from the cup onto the ground. He shook the lid and screwed it back on.

"I have already asked you once not to intrude on my investigation. So let me put it like this. If I catch you trespassing on another crime scene, I will arrest you myself. Okay?"

Mariana opened her mouth to reply. But Julian responded first.

"Sorry. Won't happen again. Come on, Mariana."

He guided a reluctant Mariana away from the others, back toward the police cordon.

"I'm afraid Sangha's got it in for you," Julian said. "If I were you, I'd keep out of his way. His bite is infinitely worse than his bark." He winked at her. "Don't worry—I'll keep you informed about any developments."

"Thanks. I'm grateful."

Julian smiled. "Where are you staying? They're putting me up at a hotel by the station."

"I'm staying in college."

"Very nice. Fancy a drink tonight? We can catch up?"

Mariana shook her head. "No—I'm sorry, I can't."

"Oh, why not?" Julian flashed a smile at her—but then he followed her gaze . . . And he saw she was looking at Fred, waving at her from the other side of the cordon.

"Ah." Julian frowned. "I see you already have plans."

"What?" Mariana shook her head. "No. He's just a friend—of Zoe's."

"Sure." Julian gave her a disbelieving smile. "No worries. I'll be seeing you, Mariana."

Julian looked a little annoyed. He turned and walked away.

Mariana was also feeling annoyed—with herself. She ducked under the cordon and walked back toward Fred. She felt increasingly angry. Why tell that stupid lie about Fred being Zoe's friend? Mariana wasn't guilty of anything; she had nothing to hide—so why *lie*?

Unless, of course, she wasn't being honest with herself about her feelings for Fred. Was that possible? If so, it was a deeply unnerving thought.

What else was she lying to herself about?

4

When the news broke that a second student from St. Christopher's College had been murdered—and that she was the daughter of a U.S. senator—the story made headlines around the world.

Senator Drake boarded the next available flight from Washington with his wife, pursued by the U.S. media and followed by the rest of the world's press, which descended on St. Christopher's in a matter of hours.

It reminded Mariana of a medieval siege. Invading hordes of journalists and cameramen held back by a flimsy barrier, several uniformed police officers, and a few college porters; Mr. Morris was at the forefront, sleeves rolled up, ready to defend the college with his fists.

A sprawling media camp was set up on the cobbles outside the main gate, and it spread all the way to King's Parade, where lines of satellite vans were parked. A special press tent was set up by the river, where Senator Drake and his wife gave a television interview, making an emotional appeal for any information that might lead to the capture of their daughter's killer.

At Senator Drake's request, Scotland Yard became involved. Extra police officers were sent up from London—and they erected blockades, made house-to-house calls, and patrolled the streets.

The knowledge they were now dealing with a serial killer meant the whole city was on alert. And in the meantime, Conrad Ellis was released, and all charges dropped.

A nervous, edgy energy was in the air. A monster with a knife was among them, unseen, prowling the streets, apparently able to strike and then melt away invisibly into the darkness . . . His invisibility made him into something more than human, something supernatural: a creature born from myth, a phantom.

Except Mariana knew he wasn't a phantom, or a monster. He was just a man, and he didn't merit being mythologized; he didn't deserve it.

He deserved only—if she could summon it in her heart—*pity* and *fear*. The very qualities, according to Aristotle, that constituted catharsis in tragedy. Well, Mariana didn't know enough about this madman to access pity.

But she did feel fear.

5

My mother often said she didn't want it for me, this life.

She'd tell me that, one day, we would leave, she and I. But it wouldn't be easy.

I don't have an education, she'd say. *I left school at fifteen. Promise me you won't do the same. You need to be educated—that's how to make money. That's how to survive, how to be safe.*

I've never forgotten that. More than anything, I wanted to be safe.

Even now, I still don't feel safe.

My father was a dangerous man, that's why. After a steady flow of whiskeys, a small flame would appear in his eyes. He'd become increasingly argumentative. Avoiding his anger was a minefield.

I was better at it than my mother—better at keeping things steady, staying several steps ahead, keeping the conversation on safe ground, guessing where it was going—outmaneuvering him, if necessary—guiding him away from any subjects that might incur his wrath. Sooner or later, my mother would always fail. Either accidentally—or deliberately, through masochism—she'd say something, do something, disagree with him, criticize him, serve him something he didn't like.

His eyes would glint. His lower lip would droop. He'd bare his teeth. Too late, she'd realize he was in a rage. A table would then be overthrown, a glass smashed. I'd watch, helpless to defend or protect her, as she ran to the bedroom in search of refuge.

She'd frantically try to lock the door . . . but too late—he'd bash it open, and then, then—

I don't understand.

Why didn't she leave? Why didn't she pack our bags and spirit me away in the night? We could have left together. But she didn't make that choice. Why not? Was she too scared? Or did she not want to admit that her family was right—that she'd made a terrible mistake and was running home, tail between her legs?

Or was she in denial, clinging to a hope that things would magically improve? Perhaps that was it. After all, she was highly skilled at ignoring what she didn't want to see—and was staring her in the face.

I learned to do that too.

I also learned, from a young age, that I did not walk on the ground—but on a narrow network of invisible ropes, suspended above the earth. I had to navigate them carefully, trying not to slip or fall. Certain aspects of my personality were offensive, it seemed. I had terrible secrets to hide—even I didn't know what they were.

My father knew, though. He knew my sins.

And he punished me accordingly.

He'd carry me upstairs. He'd take me into the bathroom and lock the door—

And it would begin.

If I picture him now, that frightened little boy—do I feel an ache of sorrow? A pang of empathy? He's just a kid, guilty of none of my crimes— he's terrified, he's in pain. Do I experience a second of compassion? Do I feel for his plight, and all he went through?

No. I don't.

I banish all pity from my heart.

I don't deserve it.

6

Veronica was last seen alive leaving a rehearsal of *The Duchess of Malfi* at the ADC—the Amateur Dramatic Club—Theatre at six o'clock. Then, she apparently disappeared into thin air—until her body was found the next day.

How was this possible?

How did her killer emerge from nowhere, abduct her in broad daylight, leave no witnesses and no trace? Mariana could draw only one conclusion: Veronica went with him willingly. She went to her death quietly and cooperatively—because she knew and trusted the man who took her there.

The next morning, Mariana decided to have a look at where Veronica was last seen. So she made her way to the ADC Theatre on Park Street.

The theater was originally an old coaching inn, converted in the 1850s. The logo was in black letters painted above the entrance.

A large board displayed a poster for the upcoming production, *The Duchess of Malfi,* which Mariana presumed would now not take place—not with Veronica playing the Duchess.

She went up to the main door. She tried it. It was locked. There were no lights on in the foyer.

She thought a moment. Then she turned and walked around

the corner, to the side of the building. Two large black wrought iron gates enclosed a courtyard, which once housed the stables. Mariana tried the gate—and it was unlocked. It swung open easily. So she went inside the courtyard.

The stage door was there. She walked over and tried it, but it was locked.

She was frustrated and about to give up—when she thought of something. She looked at the fire escape. A spiral staircase, leading up to the theater bar on the floor above.

When Mariana was a student, the ADC bar had been famous for staying open late. She and Sebastian would sometimes go for last orders on a Saturday night, dancing and drunkenly kissing in the bar.

She started climbing the steps, going round and round until she reached the top—where she was confronted with the emergency exit.

Without holding out much hope, Mariana reached out and pulled the handle. To her surprise, the door opened.

She hesitated. And went inside.

7

The ADC bar was an old-fashioned theater bar—it had velvet-covered bar stools, and smelled of beer and old cigarette smoke.

The lights were off. It was gloomy, shadowy, and Mariana was distracted for a moment—by a couple of ghosts kissing by the bar.

And then a loud bang made her jump.

Another bang. The whole building seemed to shake with it.

Mariana decided to investigate. It was coming from downstairs. She left the bar and went farther into the building. Trying to be as quiet as possible, she descended the central staircase.

Another bang.

It seemed to be coming from the auditorium itself. She waited at the bottom of the stairs and listened. But there was silence.

She crept over to the auditorium doors. She opened them slightly and looked inside.

The auditorium seemed empty. The set for *The Duchess of Malfi* was onstage—a nightmarish impression of a prison in the German Expressionist style, with slanted walls and bars stretched into distorted angles.

And onstage was a young man.

He was shirtless, and his torso was dripping with sweat. He

seemed to be intent on demolishing the entire set with a hammer. There was a violence to his actions that was quite alarming.

Mariana cautiously made her way down the aisle, passing row after row of empty red seats, until she reached the stage.

He didn't notice her until she was standing just beneath him. He was about six feet tall, with short black hair and a week's worth of stubble. He couldn't have been more than twenty-one, but it was not a youthful nor a friendly face.

"Who are you?" he said, glaring at her.

Mariana decided to lie. "I'm—a psychotherapist—I'm working with the police."

"Uh-huh. They were just here."

"Right." Mariana thought she recognized his accent. "Are you Greek?"

"Why?" He looked at her with a new interest. "Are you?"

Funny that, her split-second instinct to lie. For some reason, she didn't want him knowing anything about her. But she'd get more out of him if she expressed some kind of kinship. "Half," she said with a small smile. Then, in Greek, she said, "I grew up in Athens."

He looked pleased to hear this. He seemed to calm down, and his anger cooled slightly. "And I'm from Thessaloniki. A pleasure to meet you." He smiled, baring his teeth; they were sharp, razor-like. "Let me help you up."

Then, with a sudden, violent movement, he reached down and pulled her up with ease, placing her on the stage. She landed unsteadily on her feet. "Thanks."

"I'm Nikos. Nikos Kouris. And your name?"

"Mariana. You're a student?"

"Yes." Nikos nodded. "I'm responsible for this." He gestured at the ruined set around him. "I'm the director. You're looking at the destruction of my theatrical ambitions." He gave a hollow laugh. "The performance has been canceled."

"Because of Veronica?"

Nikos scowled. "I had an agent coming up from London to see it. I worked all summer, planning it. And it's for nothing . . ."

He pulled down part of the wall with ferocity—it landed with a thud that made the floor shake.

Mariana watched him closely. Everything about him seemed to vibrate with anger; a barely restrained rage, as if he might fly off the handle at any second, lash out indiscriminately—and strike her down instead of the set. He rather frightened her.

"I was wondering," she said, "if I might ask you about Veronica?"

"What about her?"

"I'm curious about when you last saw her?"

"The dress rehearsal. I gave her some critical notes. She didn't like them. She was rather a mediocre actor, if you want the truth. Not nearly as talented as she thought she was."

"I see. What was her mood like?"

"After I gave her the notes? Not good." He smiled, baring his teeth.

"What time did she leave? Do you remember?"

"Around six, I'd say."

"Did she say where she was going?"

"No." Nikos shook his head. "But I think she was going to meet the professor." He turned his attention to stacking up some chairs.

Mariana watched him, her heart beating faster. She sounded a little breathless when she spoke.

"The professor?"

"Yeah." Nikos shrugged. "Can't remember his name. He came to watch the dress rehearsal."

"What did he look like? Can you describe him?"

Nikos thought for a second. "Tall. Beard. American." He glanced at his watch. "What else do you need to know? Because I'm busy."

"That's all, thanks. But can I have a look in the dressing room? Did Veronica leave anything here, do you know?"

"I don't think so. The police took everything. There wasn't much."

"I'd still like to see. If that's okay."

"Go ahead." He pointed into the wings. "Down the stairs, on the left."

"Thanks."

Nikos stared at her for a second, as if contemplating something. But he didn't speak. Mariana hurried into the wings.

It was dark, and it took a few seconds for her eyes to adjust. Something made her look back over her shoulder, back at the stage—and she saw Nikos's face, contorted with rage, as he ripped apart the set. *He hates not getting his own way,* she thought. There was real anger in that young man; she was glad to get away from him.

She turned and hurried down the narrow steps, to the belly of the theater—into the dressing room.

The dressing room was rather a cramped space, shared by all the actors. Rails of costumes competed for space with wigs, makeup, props, books, and dressing tables. She looked at all the clutter—there was no way of telling what had belonged to Veronica.

Mariana doubted she'd find anything useful here. And yet . . .

She looked at the dressing tables. Each had an individual mirror—and the mirrors were decorated with hearts and kisses and good-luck messages scrawled in lipstick. There were some cards and photographs tucked into the mirror frames.

One postcard immediately caught Mariana's eye. It didn't look like any of the others.

She looked at it closely. It was a religious picture—the ikon of a saint. The saint was beautiful, with long blond hair . . . like Veronica. A silver dagger was sticking out of her neck. Even more disturbing, she was holding a tray with two human eyeballs on it.

Mariana felt sick looking at it. Her hand trembled as she reached out. She pulled the postcard from the mirror frame. She turned it over.

And there—as before—was a handwritten quotation, in Ancient Greek:

ἴδεσθε τὰν Ἰλίου
καὶ Φρυγῶν ἐλέπτολιν
στείχουσαν, ἐπὶ κάρα στέφη
βαλουμέναν χερνίβων τε παγάς,
βωμόν γε δαίμονος θεᾶς
ῥανίσιν αἱματορρύτοις
χρανοῦσαν εὐφυῆ τε σώματος δέρην
σφαγεῖσαν.

8

After the second murder, there was a stunned, lifeless atmosphere in St. Christopher's.

It felt as if a kind of pestilence, a plague, were spreading through the college—as in a Greek myth, the sickness that destroyed Thebes; an invisible airborne poison drifting through the courtyards—and these ancient walls, once a refuge from the outside world, no longer offered any protection.

Despite the dean's protestations and assurances of safety, parents were removing their children in increasing numbers. Mariana didn't blame them; nor did she blame the students for wanting to leave. Part of her wished she could scoop up Zoe and take her away to London. But she knew better than to suggest it: it was taken for granted now that Zoe was staying—and so was Mariana.

Veronica's murder in particular had hit Zoe hard. The fact it upset her so much astonished Zoe herself. She said she felt like a hypocrite.

"I mean, I didn't even *like* Veronica—I don't know why I can't stop crying."

Mariana suspected that Zoe was using Veronica's death as a

means of expressing some of her grief for Tara, grief that had been too overwhelming and frightening for her to face. So these tears were a good thing, a healthy thing, and she told Zoe so as she held her, sitting on the bed, rocking back and forth as Zoe wept.

"It's okay, darling. It's okay. You'll feel better, just let it out."

And finally, Zoe's tears subsided. Then Mariana insisted on taking Zoe out for some lunch; she'd barely eaten anything in the past twenty-four hours. And Zoe, red-eyed and weary, agreed. On the way to Hall, they bumped into Clarissa, who suggested they join her at high table.

High table was the part of the dining hall that was reserved exclusively for the fellows and their guests. It was situated at one end of the large hall, on a raised, stagelike dais beneath portraits of past masters on the oak-paneled walls. At the other end of the hall, there was a buffet for the students, operated by the buttery staff, smartly dressed in waistcoats and bow ties. The undergraduates all sat at long tables along the length of the hall.

There weren't many students in Hall. Mariana couldn't help but look at the students who were there, talking in low voices with anxious faces while they picked at their food. None of them looked in much better shape than Zoe.

Zoe and Mariana sat with Clarissa at the far end of high table, away from the other fellows. Clarissa studied the menu with interest. Despite these awful events, her appetite remained undiminished. "I'm going to plump for the pheasant," she said. "And then . . . perhaps pears poached in wine. Or the sticky toffee pudding."

Mariana nodded. "How about you, Zoe?"

Zoe shook her head. "I'm not hungry."

Clarissa gave her a concerned look. "You must eat something, my dear . . . You're not looking well. You need some food to keep your strength up."

"How about the poached salmon and vegetables?" said Mariana. "Okay?"

Zoe shrugged. "Okay."

The waiter came and took their order, and then Mariana showed them the postcard she had found at the ADC Theatre.

Clarissa took the postcard, closely studying the picture. "Ah. St. Lucy, if I'm not mistaken."

"St. Lucy?"

"You're not familiar with her? I suppose she's a little obscure, as saints go. A martyr during Diocletian's scourge of Christians—around 300 AD. Her eyes were gouged out before she was stabbed to death."

"Poor Lucy."

"Quite. Hence patron saint of the blind. She's usually depicted like this, carrying her eyes on a platter." Clarissa turned the postcard over. Her lips moved silently as she read the lines in Greek under her breath. "Well," she said, "this time, it's from *Iphigenia in Aulis,* by Euripides."

"What does it say?"

"It's about Iphigenia being led to her death." Clarissa took a gulp of wine, and translated it: "'Behold the maiden . . . with garlands in her hair, and holy water sprinkled upon her . . . walking to the sacrificial altar of the unspeakable goddess—which will flow with blood'—'αἱματορρύτοις' is the word in Greek—'as her beautiful neck is severed.'"

Mariana felt sick. "Jesus Christ."

"Not very appetizing, I grant you." Clarissa handed the postcard back to Mariana.

Mariana glanced at Zoe. "What do you think? Do you think Fosca might have sent it?"

"Professor Fosca?" said Clarissa, with a startled look, as Zoe studied the postcard. "You're not suggesting—you don't think that the professor—"

"Fosca has a group of favorite students. Did you know that, Clarissa?" Mariana glanced at Zoe for a second. "They meet privately—secretly. He calls them the Maidens."

"The Maidens?" said Clarissa. "First I've heard of it. A play on the Apostles, perhaps?"

"The Apostles?"

"Tennyson's secret literary society—where he met Hallam."

Mariana stared at her. It took her a second to find her voice. She nodded. "Perhaps."

"Of course, the Apostles were all male. Presumably the membership of the Maidens is female?"

"Exactly. And Tara and Veronica were both members. Don't you think that's a strange coincidence? Zoe? What do you think?"

Zoe looked uncomfortable. But she nodded, glancing at Clarissa. "To be honest, I think this *is* the kind of thing he'd do. Sending a postcard like this."

"Why do you say that?"

"The professor is old-fashioned like that—sending postcards, I mean. He often sends handwritten notes. And last term, he gave a lecture on the importance of the letter as an art form . . . I know that doesn't prove anything."

"Doesn't it?" said Mariana. "I'm not so sure about that."

Clarissa tapped the postcard. "What do you think this means? I don't—I don't understand what its purpose is."

"It means . . . it's a game. Announcing his intention like this—it's a challenge—and he's enjoying it." She chose her words carefully. "And there's something else . . . that he might not even be conscious of. There is a reason he chose these quotations; they mean something to him."

"In what sense?"

"I don't know." Mariana shook her head. "I don't understand—and we need to understand. That's the only way we'll stop him."

"And by 'him,' you mean Edward Fosca?"

"Perhaps."

Clarissa looked extremely disturbed by this. She shook her head but didn't comment further. Mariana silently contemplated the postcard in front of her.

Then their food arrived, and Clarissa tucked into her lunch, and Mariana turned her attention to Zoe, making sure she got a little food in her.

Edward Fosca was not mentioned again during the meal. But he remained in Mariana's thoughts—hanging there, in the shadows, like a bat in her head.

9

After lunch, Mariana and Zoe went to the college bar for a drink.

The bar was distinctly quieter than usual. Only a handful of students were there, drinking. Mariana noticed Serena sitting by herself. She didn't notice them.

Zoe ordered a couple of glasses of wine, while Mariana made her way to the end of the bar—where Serena was perched on a stool, finishing a gin and tonic, and texting on her phone.

"Hello," said Mariana.

Serena looked up, and went back to her phone without responding.

"How are you, Serena?"

No response. Mariana glanced at Zoe for help, and Zoe mimed drinking. Mariana nodded.

"Can I get you another drink?"

Serena shook her head. "No. I have to go soon."

Mariana smiled. "Your secret admirer?"

This was clearly the wrong thing to say. Serena turned on Mariana with surprising ferocity.

"What the fuck is your problem?"

"What?"

"What have you got against Professor Fosca? It's like you're obsessed or something. What did you tell the police about him?"

"I don't know what you're talking about."

But Mariana was secretly relieved that Chief Inspector Sangha had taken her seriously enough to question Fosca.

"I didn't accuse him of anything," she said. "I just suggested they ask him some questions."

"Well, they did. They asked him a lot. And me too. Happy now?"

"What did you tell them?"

"The truth. That I was with Professor Fosca when Veronica was killed on Wednesday night—I had a class with him all evening. Okay?"

"And he didn't leave? Not even to have a cigarette?"

"Not even a cigarette."

Serena gave Mariana a cold look, and was distracted by a text message on her phone. She read it and stood up.

"I have to go."

"Wait." Mariana lowered her voice. "Serena. I want you to be very careful, okay?"

"Oh, fuck off." Serena grabbed her bag and walked out.

Mariana sighed. Zoe sat on Serena's empty bar stool.

"That didn't go well."

"No." Mariana shook her head. "It didn't."

"Now what?"

"I don't know."

Zoe shrugged. "If Professor Fosca was with Serena when Veronica was killed, he couldn't have done it."

"Unless Serena is lying."

"You really think she'd lie for him? Twice?" Zoe gave her a dubious look and shrugged. "I don't know, Mariana . . ."

"What?"

Zoe evaded her gaze. She didn't speak for a moment. "It's the way you are about him—it's weird."

"What do you mean, weird?"

"The professor has an alibi for both murders—and you still won't let it go. Is this about him—or *you*?"

"Me?" Mariana couldn't believe her ears. She could feel her cheeks coloring with indignation. "What are you talking about?"

Zoe shook her head. "Forget it."

"If there's something you want to say to me—just say it."

"There's no point. I know the more I try and talk you out of this thing about Professor Fosca, the more you'll dig your heels in. You're so stubborn."

"I'm not stubborn."

Zoe laughed. "Sebastian used to say you were the most stubborn person he ever met."

"He never said that to me."

"Well, he said it to *me*."

"I don't understand what's going on here, Zoe. I don't understand what you're trying to say. What *thing* with Fosca?"

"You tell me."

"What? I'm not attracted to him—if that's what you're suggesting!"

She was aware her voice was raised; a couple of students across the bar heard her and looked over. For the first time in as long as she could remember, she and Zoe were teetering on the edge of an argument. Mariana was feeling irrationally angry. Why was that?

They stared at each other a moment.

Zoe backed down first. "Forget it," she said, shaking her head. "I'm sorry. I'm talking crap."

"I'm sorry too."

Zoe checked her watch. "I have to go. I've got a class on *Paradise Lost*."

"Go on, then."

"See you for dinner?"

"Oh . . ." Mariana hesitated. "I can't. I—I'm seeing—"

She didn't want to tell Zoe about her dinner plans with Professor Fosca—not now; Zoe would read all kinds of things into it that weren't there.

"I—I'm seeing a friend."

"Who?"

"No one you know, an old college friend. You should go, you'll be late."

Zoe nodded. She gave Mariana a quick peck on the cheek. Mariana squeezed her arm. "Zoe. You be careful too. All right?"

"Don't get into any cars with strange men, you mean?"

"Don't be silly. I mean it."

"I can take care of myself, Mariana. I'm not afraid."

It was that note of bravado in Zoe's voice that concerned Mariana the most.

10

After Zoe left, Mariana sat at the bar for a while, nursing the wine in her glass. She kept going over their conversation in her head.

What if Zoe was right? What if Fosca was innocent?

Fosca had an alibi for both murders, and yet, despite this, Mariana had woven a web of suspicion around him, simply by grabbing at a few strands of—what, exactly? Not even facts, nothing that concrete. Small things: that fearful look in Zoe's eyes, the fact he taught Tara and Veronica Greek tragedy, and the fact Mariana was convinced Fosca had sent those postcards.

And her intuition told her that whoever had sent the postcards to these girls also killed them. While that might seem an irrational leap, even delusional, to a man like Chief Inspector Sangha, for a therapist like Mariana, her intuition was often all she had to go on. Although it seemed incredible—that a professor at this university would murder his students, so horribly, so publicly, and hope to get away with it.

And yet . . . if she was right . . .

Then Fosca had got away with it.

But what if she was wrong?

Mariana needed to think clearly—but she couldn't think. Her head was cloudy, and it wasn't the wine. She was feeling overwhelmed, and increasingly unsure of herself. So what now? She had no idea what her next move should be.

Calm down, she thought. *If I were working with a patient and feeling like this—so out of my depth—what would I do?*

The answer came to her immediately. She would ask for help, of course. She would get some supervision.

That wasn't a bad idea.

Seeing her supervisor could only help. And getting out of here—going to London, escaping this college and its poisonous atmosphere, if only for a few hours—it would be an immense relief.

Yes, she thought. *That's what I'll do—I'll call Ruth, and see her in London tomorrow.*

But first, she had an appointment tonight, here in Cambridge.

At eight o'clock she had dinner—with Edward Fosca.

II

At eight o'clock, Mariana made her way to Fosca's rooms.

She stared at the large, imposing door. *Professor Edward Fosca* was painted in white calligraphic writing on a black plaque by the door.

She could hear classical music coming from inside. She knocked. No reply.

She knocked again, louder. No response for a moment, and then—

"It's open," said a distant voice. "Come on up."

Mariana took a breath, steadied herself—and opened the door. She was greeted by an elm staircase: old, narrow, and uneven in places where the wood had warped. She had to watch her step as she climbed up.

The music was louder now. It was Latin, a religious aria or a psalm set to music. She had heard it before, somewhere, but couldn't quite place where. It was beautiful but ominous, with pulsating strings like a heartbeat, ironically mimicking Mariana's own anxious heartbeat as she ascended the stairs.

At the top, the door was ajar. She went inside. The first thing she saw was a large cross hanging in the hallway. It was beautiful—made of dark wood, ornate, Gothic, intricately carved—but its sheer size made it intimidating, and Mariana hurried past it.

She entered the living room. It was hard to see; the only light was from the half-melted, misshapen candles dotted around. It took her eyes a few seconds to adjust to the stygian gloom, thick with burning incense; its black smoke further diffusing the light from the candles, making it harder to see.

It was a large room, with windows overlooking the courtyard. Several doors led off to other rooms. The walls were covered with paintings, and shelves were crammed with books. The wallpaper was dark green and black, a repeating pattern of leaves and foliage with an unsettling effect—it reminded Mariana of being in a jungle.

There were sculptures and ornaments arranged on the mantelpiece and the tables: a human skull glowing in the gloom, and a small statue of Pan—shaggy-haired, clutching a wineskin, with the legs, horns, and tail of a goat. And next to it, a pinecone.

Suddenly, Mariana was sure she was being observed—she felt eyes on the back of her neck. She turned around.

Edward Fosca was standing there. She hadn't heard him enter. Had he been in the shadows the whole time, watching her?

"Good evening," he said.

His dark eyes and white teeth glinted in the candlelight, and his tousled hair was falling around his shoulders. He was wearing a black dinner jacket, crisp white shirt, and black bow tie. He looked extremely handsome, Mariana thought—and immediately felt angry with herself for thinking it.

"I didn't realize we were going to high table," she said.

"We're not."

"But you're dressed—"

"Ah." Fosca glanced at his clothes, and smiled. "I don't often have the opportunity to dine with such a beautiful woman. I thought I'd dress for the occasion. Let me get you a drink."

Without waiting for a reply, he pulled an open bottle of

champagne from the silver ice bucket. He refilled his own glass, then poured one for Mariana. He handed it to her.

"Thank you."

Edward Fosca stood there for a moment, watching her, his dark eyes appraising her.

"To us," he said.

Mariana didn't echo the toast. She raised the glass to her lips and sipped the champagne. It was bubbly and dry, refreshing. It tasted good, and hopefully would settle her nerves. She took another sip.

There was a knock on the door downstairs. Fosca smiled. "Ah. That will be Greg."

"Greg?"

"From the buttery."

There was a flurry of footsteps—and Gregory, a nimbly footed, lithe waiter in waistcoat and tie, appeared with a hot-box in one hand and cold-box in the other. He smiled at Mariana.

"Evening, miss." He glanced at the professor. "Should I—?"

"Absolutely." Fosca nodded. "Go ahead. Set it up. I'll serve us."

"Very good, sir."

He disappeared into the dining room. Mariana gave Fosca a quizzical look. He smiled.

"I wanted us to have more privacy than Hall could afford. But I'm not much of a chef—so I persuaded the buttery to bring Hall to us."

"And how did you do that?"

"By means of a very large tip. I won't flatter you by telling you how much."

"You've gone to a lot of trouble, Professor."

"Please call me Edward. And it's a pleasure, Mariana."

He smiled and stared at her in silence. Mariana felt a little uncomfortable, and looked away. Her eyes drifted to the coffee table . . . and the pinecone.

"What's that?"

Fosca followed her gaze. "The pinecone, you mean? Nothing, just reminds me of home. Why?"

"I seem to remember a slide of a pinecone, in your lecture on Eleusis."

Fosca nodded. "Yes, indeed. That's right. Each initiate into the cult was presented with a pinecone on entry."

"I see. Why a pinecone?"

"Well, it's not really about the pinecone itself. It's what it symbolizes."

"Which is?"

He smiled and stared at her for a moment. "It's the seed—the seed inside the cone. The seed inside us—the spirit within the body. It's about opening your mind to that. A commitment to looking inside and finding your soul."

Fosca picked up the pinecone. He presented it to her.

"I offer this to you. It's yours."

"No, thank you." Mariana shook her head. "I don't want it."

She said that more sharply than she intended.

"I see."

Fosca gave her an amused smile. He replaced the pinecone on the table. There was a pause. A moment later, Greg emerged.

"All done, sir. And the pudding is in the fridge."

"Thank you."

"Good night." He nodded at Mariana and left the room. Mariana heard him descending the steps and closing the door.

They were alone.

There was a pause, a tension between them as they stared at each other. Mariana, at any rate, felt it; she didn't know what Fosca was feeling—what lay beneath that cool, charming manner of his. He was almost impossible to read.

He gestured into the next room.

"Shall we?"

12

In the dark, wood-paneled dining room, the long table was covered with a white linen tablecloth. Tall candles burned in silver candlesticks. And a bottle of red wine had been decanted and was sitting on the sideboard.

Behind the table, out through the window, the oak tree that grew in the center of the courtyard was visible against a darkening sky; stars were twinkling through the branches. In any other situation, thought Mariana, eating in this beautiful old room would be incredibly romantic. But not now.

"Sit down," Fosca said.

Mariana went to the table. Two places had been set opposite each other. She sat, and Fosca walked to the sideboard, where the food had been laid out—a leg of lamb, roast potatoes, and a green salad.

"Smells good," he said. "Trust me—this will be much better than if I attempted to cook something myself. I've a fairly sophisticated palate, but I'm pretty basic in the kitchen. Only the usual pasta recipes taught by an Italian mother to her son."

He smiled at Mariana and picked up a large carving knife. It glinted in the candlelight. She watched as he quickly and deftly used the knife to carve the lamb.

"You're Italian?" she said.

Fosca nodded. "Second generation. My grandparents came over on the boat from Sicily."

"You grew up in New York?"

"Not really. New York State. A farm, in the middle of nowhere."

Fosca served Mariana with several slices of lamb, a few potatoes, and some salad. He prepared a similar plate for himself.

"And you grew up in Athens?"

"I did." She nodded. "Just outside."

"How exotic. I'm jealous."

Mariana smiled. "I could say the same about a farm in New York."

"Not if you went there. It was a dump. I couldn't wait to get the hell out." His smile faded as he said this, and he looked quite different somehow. Harder, and older. He placed the plate in front of her. Then he took his own plate to the other side of the table and sat down. "I like it rare. I hope that's okay."

"That's fine."

"Bon appétit."

Mariana looked at the plate in front of her. The slices of razor-thin lamb were so rare, so raw, that a shiny red puddle of blood was oozing out and spreading across the white china plate. She felt sick looking at it.

"Thank you for agreeing to have dinner with me, Mariana. As I said in the Fellows' Garden—you intrigue me. It's always intriguing when someone takes an interest in me. And you've certainly done that." He chuckled. "This evening is my opportunity to return the favor."

Mariana picked up her fork. But she couldn't bring herself to eat the meat. Instead, she focused on the potatoes and salad, moving the green leaves away from the expanding pool of blood.

She could feel Fosca's eyes on her. How chilly his gaze was—like a basilisk.

"You've not tried the lamb. Won't you?"

Mariana nodded. She cut up a little piece of meat and slipped a red sliver into her mouth. It tasted wet, metallic, of blood. It took all her effort to chew and swallow it.

Fosca smiled. "Good."

Mariana reached for her glass. She washed away the taste of blood with the remains of her champagne.

Noticing her glass was empty, Fosca stood up. "Let's have some wine, shall we?"

He went to the sideboard and poured two glasses of dark red Bordeaux. He returned and handed a glass to Mariana. She brought the wine to her lips, and drank. It was earthy, gravelly, and full-bodied. She was already feeling the effects of the champagne on an empty stomach; she should stop drinking, or she'd soon be drunk. But she didn't stop.

Fosca sat down again, watching her, smiling. "Tell me about your husband."

Mariana shook her head. No.

He looked surprised. "No? Why not?"

"I don't want to."

"Not even his name?"

Mariana spoke in a low voice. "Sebastian."

And somehow, just by uttering his name, she conjured him up for a second—her guardian angel—and she felt safer, calmer; and Sebastian whispered in her ear, *Don't be scared, love, stand up for yourself. Don't be afraid—*

She decided to take his advice. Mariana looked up and met Fosca's gaze without blinking. "Tell me about yourself, Professor."

"Edward. What would you like to know?"

"Tell me about your childhood."

"My childhood?"

"What was your mother like? Were you fond of her?"

Fosca laughed. "My mother? Are you going to psychoanalyze me over dinner?"

Mariana said, "I'm just curious. I wonder what else she taught you besides pasta recipes?"

Fosca shook his head. "My mother taught me very little, unfortunately. How about you? What was your mother like?"

"I never knew my mother."

"Ah." Fosca nodded. "I don't think I really knew mine either."

He appraised Mariana for a moment, thinking. She could see his mind turning—he had a truly brilliant mind, she thought. Sharp as a knife. She'd have to be careful. She adopted a casual tone. "Was it a happy childhood?"

"I can see you're determined to make this into a therapy session."

"Not a therapy session—just a conversation."

"Conversations go both ways, Mariana."

Fosca smiled, and waited. Seeing she had no choice, she rose to the challenge.

"I didn't have a particularly happy childhood," she said. "Sometimes, perhaps. I loved my father very much, but . . ."

"But what . . . ?"

Mariana shrugged. "There was too much death."

They held each other's gaze for a moment. Fosca slowly nodded. "Yes, I can see it in your eyes. There's a great sadness there. You know, you remind me of a Tennysonian heroine—*Mariana of the Moated Grange*: 'He cometh not,' she said. 'I am aweary, aweary. I would that I were dead.'"

He smiled. Mariana looked away, feeling exposed and irritated. She reached for her wine. She drained the glass. Then she faced him.

"Your turn, Professor."

"Very well." Fosca sipped some wine. "Was I a happy child?" He shook his head. "No. I was not."

"Why was that?"

He didn't reply immediately. He got up, and went to fetch the wine. He refilled Mariana's glass as he spoke.

"Truthfully? My father was a very violent man. I lived in fear of my life, and my mother's life. I watched him brutalize my mother on many occasions."

Mariana wasn't expecting such a frank admission. And certainly, the words had the ring of truth, and yet they were entirely disconnected from any emotion. It was as if he felt nothing.

"I'm sorry," she said. "That's terrible."

He shrugged. He didn't reply for a moment. He sat down again. "You have a way of getting things out of people, Mariana. You're a good therapist, I can tell. Despite my intention not to reveal myself to you, you have ended up getting me on your couch." He smiled. "Therapeutically speaking."

Mariana hesitated. "Have you ever been married?"

Fosca laughed. "That's following a train of thought. Are we moving from the couch to bed?" He smiled and drank some more wine. "I have not been married, no. I never met the right woman." He stared at her. "Not yet."

Mariana didn't reply. He kept staring. His gaze was heavy, intense, lingering. She felt like a rabbit in headlights. She thought of the word Zoe used—"dazzling." Finally, unable to bear it, she looked away, which seemed to amuse him.

"You're a beautiful woman," she heard him say, "but you have more than beauty. You have a certain quality—a stillness. Like the stillness in the depths of the ocean, far beneath the waves, where nothing moves. Very still . . . and very sad."

Mariana didn't say anything. She didn't like where this was going—she sensed she was losing the upper hand, if she'd ever had it. She was also a little drunk, and unprepared for Fosca's sudden switch from romance to murder.

"This morning," he said, "I received a visit from Chief Inspector Sangha. He wanted to know where I was when Veronica was murdered."

He looked at Mariana, perhaps hoping for a reaction. She didn't give him one. "And what did you say?"

"The truth. That I was giving a private tutorial to Serena in my rooms. I suggested he check with her if he didn't believe me."

"I see."

"The inspector asked me a lot of questions—the last of which was about you. You know what he asked?"

Mariana shook her head. "I have no idea."

"He wondered why you were so prejudiced against me. What I had done to deserve it."

"And what did you say?"

"I said I had no idea—but that I would ask you." He smiled. "So I'm asking you. What's going on, Mariana? You've been orchestrating a campaign against me since Tara's murder. What if I told you I'm an innocent man? I'd love to oblige and be your scapegoat, but—"

"You're not my scapegoat."

"No? An outsider—a blue-collar American in the elitist world of English academia? I stick out like a sore thumb."

"Hardly." Mariana shook her head. "I'd say you fit in extremely well."

"Well, naturally I've done my best to blend in, but the bottom line is that although the English may be infinitely more subtle than Americans in their xenophobia, I will always be a foreigner—and therefore viewed with suspicion." He fixed his eyes on Mariana intensely. "As are you—you don't belong here either."

"We're not talking about me."

"Oh, but we are—we're one and the same."

She frowned. "We're not. Not at all."

"Oh, Mariana." He laughed. "You don't seriously believe I'm murdering my students? It's absurd. That's not to say a few don't deserve it." He laughed again—and his laugh sent a shiver down Mariana's spine.

She stared at him—feeling she had just glimpsed who he really was: callous, sadistic, entirely uncaring. She was getting into dangerous territory, she knew, but the wine had made her bold and reckless, and she might never get this chance again. She chose her words carefully.

"I'd like to know, then, exactly what kind of person you think killed them?"

Fosca looked at her, as if he were surprised by the question. But he nodded. "I've given it some thought, as it happens."

"I'm sure you have."

"And," he said, "the first thing that strikes me is that it's religious in nature. That's clear. He's a spiritual man. In his eyes, anyway."

Mariana remembered the cross in his hallway. *Like you,* she thought.

Fosca sipped some wine and went on. "The killings are not just random attacks. I don't think the police have worked that out yet. The murders are a sacrificial act."

Mariana looked up sharply. "A sacrificial act?"

"That's right—it's a ritual—of rebirth and resurrection."

"I don't see any resurrection here. Just death."

"It depends entirely on how you look at it." He smiled. "And I'll tell you something else. He's a showman. He loves to perform."

Like you, she thought.

"The murders remind me of a Jacobean tragedy," he said. "Violence and horror—to shock and entertain."

"Entertain?"

"Theatrically speaking."

He smiled. And Mariana was filled with a sudden desire to get as far away from him as possible. She pushed away her plate. "I'm finished."

"Are you sure you don't want anymore?"

She nodded. "I've had enough."

13

Professor Fosca suggested they have coffee and dessert in the sitting room, and Mariana reluctantly followed him into the next room. He gestured at the large dark sofa by the fireplace. "Why don't you sit down?"

Mariana felt unwilling to sit next to him and be that close to him—it made her feel unsafe, somehow. And a thought occurred to her—if *she* felt this uneasy being alone with him, how might an eighteen-year-old girl feel?

She shook her head. "I'm tired. I think I'll skip dessert."

"Don't go, not yet. Let me make some coffee."

Before she could object, Fosca left the room, disappearing into the kitchen.

Mariana fought an impulse to run, to get the hell out of there. She felt woozy and frustrated—and annoyed with herself. Nothing had been accomplished. She'd learned nothing new, nothing she didn't know already. She should just go before he came back and she was forced to fight off his amorous advances, or worse.

As she deliberated what to do, her eyes wandered around the room. Her gaze came to rest on a small stack of books on the coffee table. She stared at the first book on the pile. She tilted her head to read the title.

The Collected Works of Euripides.

Mariana glanced over her shoulder toward the kitchen. No sign of him. She hurried over to the book.

She reached out and picked it up. A red leather bookmark was poking out from inside.

She opened it at the bookmarked page. It was inserted into the middle of a scene from *Iphigenia in Aulis.* The text was in English on one side of the page, and in the original Ancient Greek on the other.

Several lines had been underlined. Mariana recognized them immediately. They were the same lines on the postcard that had been sent to Veronica:

ἴδεσθε τὰν Ἰλίου
καὶ Φρυγῶν ἐλέπτολιν
στείχουσαν, ἐπὶ κάρα στέφη
βαλουμέναν χερνίβων τε παγάς,
βωμόν γε δαίμονος θεᾶς
ῥανίσιν αἱματορρύτοις
χρανοῦσαν εὐφυῆ τε σώματος δέρην
σφαγεῖσαν.

"What are you looking at?"

Mariana jumped—his voice was right behind her. She slammed the book shut. She turned to face him with a forced smile. "Nothing, just looking."

Fosca handed her a small cup of espresso. "Here."

"Thank you."

He glanced at the book. "Euripides, as you may have gathered, is a favorite of mine. I think of him as an old friend."

"Do you?"

"Oh, yes. He's the only tragedian who speaks the truth."

"The truth? About what?"

"Everything. Life. Death. The unbelievable cruelty of man. He tells it like it is."

Fosca sipped some coffee, staring at her. And as she looked into his black eyes, Mariana no longer had any doubts. She was absolutely certain:

She was looking into the eyes of a murderer.

Part Four

And so, when a man comes along and talks like one's own father and acts like him, even adults . . . will submit to this man, will acclaim him, allow themselves to be manipulated by him, and put their trust in him, finally surrendering entirely to him without even being aware of their enslavement. One is not normally aware of something that is a continuation of one's own childhood.

—ALICE MILLER, *For Your Own Good*

The childhood shows the man,
As morning shows the day.

—JOHN MILTON, *Paradise Regained*

I

Death, and what happens next, has always been a big interest of mine.

Ever since Rex, I suppose.

Rex was my earliest memory. A beautiful creature—a black-and-white sheepdog. The best kind of animal. He put up with me pulling his ears and trying to sit on him, and all the abuses a toddler is capable of, but still he wagged his tail when he saw me coming, greeting me with love. It was a lesson in forgiveness—not just once, but again and again.

He taught me more than forgiveness. He taught me about death.

When I was nearly twelve, Rex was getting old, and finding it hard to keep up with the sheep. My mother suggested retiring him, getting a younger dog to take his place.

I knew my father didn't like Rex—sometimes I suspected he hated him. Or was it my mother he hated? She loved Rex—even more than I did. She loved him for his unconditional affection—and his lack of speech. He was her constant companion, working with her all day, and she cooked and cared for him with more devotion than she ever showed her husband, I remember my father saying, during a fight.

I remember what he said when my mother proposed getting another dog. We were in the kitchen. I was on the floor, stroking Rex. My mother was cooking at the stove. My father was pouring himself a whiskey. Not his first.

I'm not paying to feed two dogs, he said. *I'll shoot this one first.*

It took a few seconds for his words to sink in, for me to understand exactly what he meant. My mother shook her head.

No, she said. For once, she meant it. *If you touch that dog, I will—*

What? said my father. *Are you threatening me?*

I knew what was coming. You need real guts to take a bullet for someone. That's what she did when she stood up for Rex that day.

My father went crazy, of course. A crash of glass told me I was too late—I should have run for cover, like Rex, who had leaped out of my arms and was halfway out the door. I had no option but to sit there on the floor, trapped, as my father threw over the table, missing me by inches. My mother retaliated by throwing plates at him.

He charged through the broken dishes toward her. His fists were up. She was backed up against the counter. She was trapped. And then . . .

She held up a knife. A large knife—used for cutting up the lambs. She held it up, pointing it at my father's chest. At his heart.

I'll kill you, dammit, she said. *I mean it.*

There was silence for a moment.

I realized it was entirely possible she might stab him. To my disappointment, she didn't.

My father didn't say another word. He just turned and walked out. The kitchen door slammed after him.

My mother didn't move for a second. Then she started to cry. It's horrible watching your mother cry. You feel so impotent, so powerless.

I'll kill him for you, I said.

But that just made her cry harder.

And then . . . we heard a gunshot.

And then another.

I don't remember leaving the house—or stumbling into the yard. All I remember is seeing Rex's limp, bleeding body on the ground, and my father marching off, holding his rifle.

I watched the life drain out of Rex. His eyes became glassy and unseeing. His tongue went blue. His limbs slowly turned stiff. I couldn't stop staring at him. I had a sense—even then, at that young age—that the sight of this dead animal had stained my life forever.

The soft, wet fur. The broken body. The blood. I shut my eyes, but I could still see it.

The blood.

And later on, when my mother and I carried Rex to the pit and threw him in, down into the depths, to rot with the other unwanted carcasses, I knew that part of me went down with him. The good part.

I tried to summon up some tears for him, but I couldn't cry. That poor animal never did me any harm—he showed me only love, only kindness.

And yet I couldn't cry for him.

Instead, I was learning how to hate.

A cold, hard kernel of hatred was forming in my heart, like a diamond in a dark piece of coal.

I swore I would never forgive my father. And one day, I'd have my revenge. But until then, until I grew up, I was trapped.

So I retreated into my imagination. In my fantasies, my father suffered.

And so did I.

In the bathroom, with the door locked, or in the hayloft, or at the back of the barn, unobserved, I would escape—from this body . . . from this mind.

I would act out cruel, horribly violent death scenes: agonized poisonings, brutal stabbings—butchery and disembowelment. I would be drawn and quartered, tortured to death. I would bleed.

I would stand on my bed and prepare to be sacrificed by pagan priests. They'd grab hold of me and hurl me from the cliff, down, down into the sea, into the depths—where the sea-monsters were circling, waiting to devour me.

I'd shut my eyes and jump off the bed.

And I would be torn to shreds.

2

Mariana left Professor Fosca's rooms feeling unsteady on her feet.

This wasn't from the wine and the champagne—even though she had drunk more than she should. It was the shock of what she had just seen—the Greek quotation underlined in his book. It was strange, she thought, how moments of extreme clarity often had the same texture as drunkenness.

She couldn't keep this to herself. She had to talk to someone. But who?

She paused in the courtyard to think this over. No point in going to find Zoe—not now, not after their last conversation; Zoe simply wouldn't take her seriously. She needed a sympathetic ear. She thought of Clarissa, but she wasn't sure Clarissa would want to believe her.

So that left only one person.

She pulled out her phone and rang Fred. He said he was more than happy to talk to her, and suggested they meet at Gardies in about ten minutes.

The Gardenia, known and beloved by generations of students as Gardies, was a Greek diner in the heart of Cambridge, serving late-night fast food. Mariana walked there, along the curved, pedestrianized alley, smelling Gardies before she saw it—greeted by the smell of chips sizzling in hot oil and frying fish.

Gardies was a tiny place—barely a handful of customers could fit inside at once—so people would congregate outside, eating in the alley. Fred was waiting outside the entrance, under the green awning and the sign reading, *Have a break the Greek way.*

Fred grinned at Mariana as she approached.

"Hello there. Fancy some chips? My treat."

The smell of frying had reminded Mariana she was hungry—she had barely touched that bloody dinner at Fosca's. She nodded gratefully.

"I'd love some."

"Coming right up, miss."

Fred bounded into the entrance, tripping on the step—and colliding with another customer, who swore at him. Mariana had to smile—he really was one of the clumsiest people she had ever met. He soon emerged again, holding two white paper bags, bulging with steaming chips.

"There you go," he said. "Ketchup? Or mayo?"

Mariana shook her head. "Neither, thanks." She blew on the chips to cool them for a minute. Then she tried one. It was salty and sharp, a little too sharp, with vinegar. She coughed, and Fred gave her an anxious look.

"Too much vinegar? Sorry. My hand slipped."

"It's okay." Mariana smiled and shook her head. "They're great."

"Good."

They stood there for a moment, silently eating their chips. As she ate, Mariana glanced at him. The soft lamplight made his boyish features seem even younger. He was just a kid, she thought. An eager boy scout. She felt a genuine fondness for him in that moment.

Fred caught her looking at him. He gave her a timid smile. He spoke between mouthfuls. "I'll regret saying this, I'm sure. But I'm very happy you called me. It means you must have missed me, even if just a tiny bit—" Fred saw her expression, and his smile faded. "Ah. I see I'm wrong. That's not why you called."

"I called because something happened—and I want to talk to you about it."

Fred looked a little more hopeful. "So you did want to talk to me?"

"Oh, Fred." Mariana rolled her eyes. "Just listen."

"Go ahead."

Fred ate his chips as Mariana told him what happened—about finding the postcards, and discovering the same quotation underlined in Fosca's book.

He remained silent after she finished. Finally, he said, "What are you going to do?"

Mariana shook her head. "I don't know."

Fred brushed the crumbs from his mouth, crumpled up the paper bag, and threw it in the bin. She watched him, trying to read his expression.

"You don't think I'm—imagining it?"

"No." Fred shook his head. "I don't."

"Even though he has an alibi—for both murders?"

He shrugged. "One of the girls who gave him an alibi is dead."

"Yes."

"And Serena could be lying."

"Yes."

"And there's another possibility, of course—"

"Which is?"

"He's working with someone. An accomplice."

Mariana peered at him. "I hadn't thought of that."

"Why not? It explains how he can be in two places at once."

"Possibly."

"You don't look convinced."

Mariana shrugged. "He doesn't strike me as the kind of person to have a partner. He's very much a lone wolf."

"Perhaps." Fred thought for a second. "Anyway, we need some *proof*—you know, something concrete—or no one will ever believe us."

"And how do we get that?"

"We'll think of something. Let's meet first thing tomorrow and make a plan."

"I can't tomorrow—I have to go to London. But I'll call you when I get back."

"Okay." He lowered his voice. "But Mariana. Listen. Fosca must know you're on to him, so . . ."

He didn't finish the sentence, just left it hanging. Mariana nodded.

"Don't worry. I'm being careful."

"Good." Fred paused. "There's only one more thing to say." He grinned. "You look incredibly, stunningly beautiful tonight . . . Will you do me the honor of becoming my wife?"

"No." Mariana shook her head. "I won't. But thanks very much for the chips."

"You're welcome."

"Good night."

They smiled at each other. Then Mariana turned and walked away. At the end of the street, still smiling, she glanced back—but Fred had gone.

Funny, that—he seemed to have vanished.

As she made her way back to college, Mariana's phone rang. She pulled it out of her pocket. She glanced at it—the caller's number was withheld.

She hesitated, then answered. "Hello?"

No reply.

"Hello?"

There was silence—and then a whispering voice.

"Hello, Mariana."

She froze. "Who is this?"

"I can see you, Mariana. I'm watching you—"

"Henry?" She was sure it was him—she recognized his voice. "Henry, is that you—?"

The line went dead. Mariana stood there, staring at the phone for a second. She felt deeply uneasy. She looked around—but the street was deserted.

3

The next morning, Mariana got up early to go to London.

As she left her room, walking across Main Court, she glanced through the archway into Angel Court.

And there he was—Edward Fosca—standing outside his staircase, smoking.

But he wasn't alone. He was talking to someone—a college porter who had his back to Mariana. It was obvious, from the sheer size and height of the man, it was Morris.

Mariana hurried over to the archway. She hid behind it, and then cautiously peered around the wall.

Something had told her this was worth investigating, something about the expression on Fosca's face. A look of sustained annoyance that she hadn't seen before. What Fred had said popped into her mind—about Fosca working with someone.

Could it possibly be Morris?

She saw Fosca slip something into Morris's hand. It looked like a bulky envelope. An envelope stuffed with what? Money?

Mariana could feel her imagination running away with her. She let it run. Was Morris blackmailing Fosca—was that it? Was he being paid to keep quiet?

Could this be it—what she needed—some kind of concrete proof?

Morris abruptly turned around. He started walking away from Fosca—and in Mariana's direction.

She pulled back and flattened herself against the wall. Morris marched through the archway, passing by without even noticing her. Mariana watched him cross Main Court and go out the gate.

She quickly followed him.

4

Mariana hurried out the gate, and kept a safe distance from Morris on the street. He seemed to have no sense he was being followed. He sauntered along, whistling to himself, enjoying the walk and in no apparent hurry.

He strolled past Emmanuel College and the terraced houses all the way along the street, past the bikes chained up to the railings. Then he turned left, into a lane, and disappeared.

Mariana hurried to the lane. She peered into it. It was a narrow street, with a row of houses on either side.

It came to a dead end—an abrupt halt. A wall cut across the road: an old redbrick wall, with ivy crawling all over it.

To Mariana's surprise, Morris kept walking, right up to the wall.

He reached it. He dug his fingers into a space left by one of the looser bricks, grabbed hold, and pulled himself up. Then he scaled the wall with ease, climbed over it—and vanished over the other side.

Damn, she thought. Mariana deliberated for a moment.

Then she hurried over to the wall. She considered it. She wasn't sure she could manage it. She scanned the bricks—and saw a space to grip.

She reached up and grabbed hold—but the brick came away from the wall in her hand. She fell back.

She threw the brick aside. She tried again.

This time, Mariana managed to pull herself up. With difficulty, she climbed over the top of the wall—and then fell down the other side . . .

She landed in a different world.

5

On the other side of the wall, there was no road. No houses. Just wild grass, conifer trees, and overgrown blackberry bushes. It took Mariana a few seconds to realize where she was.

This was the abandoned cemetery on Mill Road.

Mariana had been here once before, nearly twenty years ago, when she had explored it with Sebastian one sultry summer afternoon. She hadn't liked the cemetery then; she thought it was sinister, desolate.

She didn't like it now either.

She pulled herself up. She looked around. No sign of Morris. She listened: it was quiet, no sound of footsteps—or even birdsong. Just deathly silence.

She looked at the interconnecting paths up ahead, between a sea of graves overgrown with moss and massive holly bushes. Many of the headstones had toppled over, or snapped in two—throwing dark, jagged shadows onto the wild grass. All the names and dates on the headstones had long since been erased by time and bad weather. All these unremembered people—these forgotten lives. There was such a sense of loss, of futility. Mariana couldn't wait to get out of there.

She made her way along the path nearest the wall. She had no intention of losing her bearings, not now.

She stopped, and listened—but again, no sound of footsteps.

Nothing. No sound.

She had lost him.

Perhaps he had seen her and deliberately given her the slip? There was no point in going on.

She was about to turn back when a large statue caught her eye: a male angel, mounted on a cross, arms outstretched, with large, chipped wings. Mariana stared at the angel for a moment, mesmerized. The statue was tarnished and broken, but still beautiful—he looked a bit like Sebastian.

And then Mariana noticed something—just beyond the statue, through the foliage—a young woman walking on the path. Mariana recognized her at once.

It was Serena.

Serena didn't see Mariana, and she approached a flat-roofed, rectangular stone crypt that once had been white marble but now was speckled gray and mossy green, with wildflowers growing around it.

She sat on it, took out her phone, and looked at it.

Mariana hid behind a nearby tree. She peered through the branches.

She watched as Serena looked up—at a man emerging from the foliage.

It was Morris.

Morris went up to Serena. Neither of them spoke. He took off his bowler hat and balanced it on a headstone. Then he grabbed the back of Serena's head—and with a sudden, violent movement dragged her up, kissing her hard.

Mariana watched as Morris lay Serena down on the marble, still kissing her. He climbed on top of her. They started having sex—aggressive, animalistic sex. Mariana felt repulsed, yet also transfixed—unable to look away. And then—as abruptly as they had begun—they climaxed, and there was silence.

They lay still for a moment. Then Morris got up. He adjusted his clothing. He reached for his bowler and dusted it off.

Mariana thought she had better get out of there. She took a step backward—and a twig snapped beneath her foot.

There was a loud crunch.

Through the branches, she saw Morris look around. He motioned to Serena to keep quiet. Then he moved behind a tree and Mariana lost sight of him.

Mariana turned and hurried back to the path. But which way was the entrance? She decided to go back the way she had come, along the wall. She turned around—

And Morris was standing right behind her.

He stared at her, breathing hard. There was silence for a few seconds.

Morris spoke in a low voice. "What the fuck are you doing?"

"What? Excuse me." She tried to walk past him—but Morris blocked her path. He smiled.

"Enjoy the show, did you?"

Mariana felt her cheeks burning, and looked away.

He laughed. "I see through you. You don't fool me, not for a second. I've had my eye on you, right from the start."

"What's that supposed to mean?"

"It means don't stick your nose in other people's business—as my old grandpa used to say—or it'll get sliced off. Get it?"

"Are you threatening me?"

Mariana sounded braver than she felt. Morris just laughed. He gave her one last look, then turned and sauntered off.

Mariana stood there, shaking, scared, angry, and close to tears. She felt paralyzed, rooted to the spot. Then she looked up and caught sight of the statue—the angel was staring at her, arms outstretched, offering an embrace.

She felt an overwhelming longing for Sebastian at that moment—for him to take her in his arms, hold her, and fight for her. But he was gone.

And Mariana would have to learn to fight for herself.

6

Mariana took the fast train to London.

It didn't stop at any stations on the way, and seemed to be racing to its destination. It felt as if it were going too fast—jolting and bumping madly in the tracks, swinging and swaying out of control. The rails were squealing—a high-pitched wail in Mariana's ears—like someone screaming. And the carriage door didn't close properly. It kept opening and slamming shut, each bang startling and intruding on her thoughts.

There was a lot to think about. She felt deeply unsettled by her confrontation with Morris. She tried to make sense of it. So he was the man Serena was secretly seeing? No wonder they kept it secret—Morris would lose his job if his affair with a student was discovered.

Mariana hoped that's all there was to it. But she doubted it, somehow.

Morris had something to do with Fosca, but what? And how was it related to Serena? Were they blackmailing Fosca together? If so, it was a dangerous game, antagonizing a psychopath—one who had killed twice already.

Mariana had been wrong about Morris, she saw that now; she had fallen for his old-fashioned act—but he was no gentleman.

She thought of the vicious look in his eyes when he threatened her. He wanted to scare her—and he'd succeeded.

Bang—the carriage door slammed, making her jump.

Stop it, she thought. *You're driving yourself crazy.* She had to distract herself, think about something else.

She pulled out the copy of the *British Journal of Psychiatry* that was still in her bag. She flicked through it, and tried to read it but couldn't focus. Something else was bothering her: she couldn't get over the sensation that she was being watched.

She looked over her shoulder, around the carriage—there were a few people in it, but no one she knew, or at least no one she recognized. No one appeared to be watching her.

She couldn't shake it, though—the feeling of being observed. And as the train neared London, an unnerving thought occurred to her.

What if she was wrong about Fosca? What if the killer was some stranger—invisible to her, and sitting right here, in this carriage, watching her now, this very second? Mariana shivered at the thought.

Bang—went the door.

Bang.

Bang.

7

The train soon pulled into King's Cross. As Mariana left the station, she still had that lingering feeling of being observed. The prickling, creeping sensation of eyes on the back of her neck.

Suddenly, convinced someone was right behind her, she spun around—half expecting to see Morris—

But he wasn't there.

And yet the feeling persisted. She arrived at Ruth's house feeling unsettled and paranoid. *Perhaps I'm crazy,* she thought. *Perhaps that's it.*

Crazy or not, there was no one she would rather see than the elderly lady waiting for her at No. 5 Redfern Mews. It felt a relief just to press the doorbell.

Ruth had been Mariana's training therapist when she was a student. And when Mariana qualified, Ruth began acting as her supervisor instead. A supervisor plays an important role in a therapist's life—Mariana would report back to her about her patients, her groups, and Ruth would help Mariana unpack her feelings, distinguishing between her patients' emotions and her own, which wasn't always easy. Without supervision, a therapist might easily get overwhelmed and emotionally swamped by all the distress she had to contain. And she might lose that impartiality that was so important to working effectively.

Following Sebastian's death, Mariana began seeing Ruth more frequently, needing her support more than ever. It was therapy in everything but name—and Ruth suggested she should fully commit: return to therapy, and have Ruth treat her. But Mariana refused. She couldn't explain why exactly, other than she didn't need therapy; she just needed Sebastian. And all the talking in the world couldn't replace him.

"Mariana, my dear," said Ruth, opening the door. She gave her a welcoming smile. "Won't you come in?"

"Hello, Ruth."

It felt so good to go inside, and enter the living room that always smelled of lavender, and hear the silver clock ticking reassuringly on the mantelpiece.

She sat in her usual seat, on the edge of the faded blue couch. Ruth sat opposite her, in the armchair.

"You sounded quite distressed on the phone," Ruth said. "Why don't you tell me about it, Mariana?"

"It's hard to know where to start. I suppose it started when Zoe called me that night, from Cambridge."

Mariana then began telling her story, as clearly and comprehensively as she could. Ruth listened, nodding occasionally but saying very little. When she finished, Ruth remained silent for a moment. She sighed, almost imperceptibly—a sad, weary sigh that echoed Mariana's anguish far more eloquently than any words.

"I can feel the strain it's causing you," she said. "The need to be strong, for Zoe, for the college, for yourself—"

Mariana shook her head. "I don't matter. But Zoe, and those girls . . . I'm so scared—" Her eyes filled with tears. Ruth leaned forward and edged the box of tissues toward her. Mariana took a tissue and wiped her eyes. "Thanks, I'm sorry. I don't even know why I'm crying."

"You're crying because you feel powerless."

Mariana nodded. "I do."

"But that's not true. You know that, don't you?" Ruth gave her an encouraging nod. "You're much more capable than you suppose. The college, after all, is just another group—with sickness at its core. If something of this nature—toxic, malignant, murderous—were operating within one of your groups . . ."

Ruth left the sentence hanging. Mariana pondered it.

"What would I do? That's a good question." She nodded. "I suppose . . . I would talk to them—as a group, I mean."

"Just what I was thinking." There was a twinkle in her eyes as she said this. "Talk to these girls, the Maidens, not *individually*—but as a *group*."

"A therapy group, you mean?"

"Why not? Have a session with them—see what comes up."

Mariana smiled, despite herself. "It's an intriguing idea. I don't quite know how they would respond to that."

"Think about it, that's all. As you know, the best way to treat a group—"

"—is *as* a group." Mariana nodded. "Yes, I see that."

She fell silent for a moment. It was good advice—not easy to achieve, but it touched on something she actually knew about and believed in—and already she felt a little less out of her depth. She smiled gratefully. "Thank you."

Ruth hesitated. "There's something else. Something less easy to say . . . something that strikes me—regarding this man Edward Fosca. I want you to be very careful."

"I am being careful."

"Of *yourself*?"

"What do you mean?"

"Well, presumably this is bringing up all kinds of feelings and associations for you . . . I'm surprised that you've not mentioned your father."

Mariana looked at Ruth in surprise. "What's my father got to do with Fosca?"

"Well, they're both charismatic men, powerful within their

community—and, by the sounds of it, highly narcissistic. I wonder if you feel the same urge to win over this man, Edward Fosca, as you did your father."

"No." Mariana felt annoyed with Ruth for suggesting it. "No," she repeated. "And anyway, I have a very negative transference toward Edward Fosca."

Ruth hesitated. "Your feelings toward your father weren't entirely benign."

"That's different."

"Is it? It's still so hard for you, even now, isn't it?—to criticize him, or acknowledge he let you down in real, fundamental ways. He never once gave you the love you needed. It took a long time for you to be able to see that, and to name it."

Mariana shook her head. "Honestly, Ruth, I don't think my father has anything to do with this."

Ruth looked at her sadly. "It's my feeling that your father is in some way central to this, as far as you're concerned. That might not make much sense right now. But one day, perhaps, it might mean a great deal."

Mariana didn't know how to respond. She shrugged.

"And Sebastian?" said Ruth after a pause. "How are you feeling about him?"

Mariana shook her head. "I don't want to talk about Sebastian. Not today."

She didn't stay for long after that. The mention of her father had cast a pall over the session, which didn't fully disperse until she was in Ruth's hallway.

As Mariana left, she gave the old lady a hug. She felt the warmth and affection in that hug, and tears welled up in her eyes. "Thank you so much, Ruth. For everything."

"Call me if you need me—anytime. I don't want you to think you're alone."

"Thank you."

"You know," Ruth said, after a slight hesitation, "you might find it helpful to talk to Theo."

"Theo?"

"Why not? Psychopathy is, after all, his special subject. He's quite brilliant. Any insights he has are bound to be useful."

Mariana considered it. Theo was a forensic psychotherapist who had trained with her in London. Despite sharing Ruth as a therapist, they hadn't known each other very well.

"I'm not sure," she said. "I mean, I've not seen Theo in a very long time . . . Do you think he'd mind?"

"Not at all. You could try and see him before you go back to Cambridge. Let me give him a ring."

Ruth called him—and Theo said yes, of course he remembered Mariana, and he'd be happy to talk to her. They arranged to meet in a pub in Camden.

And that evening, at six o'clock, Mariana went to meet Theo Faber.

8

Mariana was first to arrive at the Oxford Arms. She got a glass of white wine while she waited.

She was curious to see Theo—but also wary. Sharing Ruth as a therapist made them a little like siblings, each coveting the attention their mother gave the other. Mariana used to feel a little jealous, even resentful, of Theo—she knew Ruth had a soft spot for him. Ruth's voice took on a protective tone whenever she mentioned him, which had led Mariana, quite unreasonably, to concoct a fantasy for herself that Theo was an orphan. It came as a shock when both his parents appeared at their graduation, alive and well.

In truth, Theo did have a waiflike quality that Mariana was picking up on—an otherness. It had nothing to do with his build, but was entirely suggested by his manner: a kind of reticence, a slight distance from others—an awkwardness, something Mariana also recognized in herself.

Theo arrived a few minutes late. He greeted Mariana warmly. He got a Diet Coke at the bar, and joined her at the table.

He looked the same; he hadn't changed at all. He was about forty years old, and had a slim build. He was wearing a battered corduroy jacket and a crumpled white shirt, and he smelled faintly of cigarette smoke. He had a nice face, she thought, a caring face, but there was something—what was the word?—anxious in his eyes, even haunted. And she realized that while she liked him, she wasn't entirely comfortable around him. She wasn't quite sure why.

"Thank you for meeting me," she said. "It was very short notice."

"Not at all. I'm intrigued. I've been following the story, like everyone else. It's fascinating—" Theo quickly corrected himself. "I mean, it's *terrible*, of course. But also fascinating." He smiled. "I'd like to pick your brains about it."

Mariana smiled. "Actually—I was hoping to pick yours."

"Ah." Theo seemed surprised to hear this. "But you're *there*, Mariana, in Cambridge. I'm not. Your insights are much more valuable than anything I can tell you."

"I don't have much experience in this kind of thing—in forensics."

"It makes no difference, really—since every case is completely unique, in my experience."

"That's funny. Julian said exactly the opposite. That every case is always the same."

"Julian? You mean Julian Ashcroft?"

"Yes. He's working with the police."

Theo raised an eyebrow. "I remember Julian from the institute. There was something a bit . . . odd about him, I thought. A little bloodthirsty. And anyway he's wrong—each case is quite different. After all, no one has the same childhood."

"Yes, I agree." Mariana nodded. "But still, you don't think there's anything we can look for?"

Theo sipped his Coke and shrugged. "Look. Say I'm the man you're after. Say I'm extremely unwell, and highly dangerous. It's entirely possible that I can hide all that from you. Not for an extended time, perhaps, or in a therapeutic environment—but on a superficial level, it's very easy to present a false self to the world. Even to people we see every day." He played with his wedding ring for a moment, turning it around on his finger. "Do you want my advice? Forget *who*. Start with *why*."

"Why does he kill, you mean?"

"Yes." Theo nodded. "Something about it doesn't ring true to me. The victims—were they sexually assaulted?"

Mariana shook her head. "No, nothing like that."

"So what does that tell us?"

"That the killing itself, the stabbing and mutilation, provides the gratification? Perhaps. I don't think it's that simple."

Theo nodded. "Neither do I."

"The pathologist said the cause of death was a severed throat—and the stabbing took place postmortem."

"I see," Theo said, looking intrigued. "Which means there is a certain performative aspect to all this. It's staged—for the benefit of the audience."

"And we are the audience?"

"That's right." Theo nodded. "Why is that, do you think? Why does he want us to see this horrific violence?"

Mariana thought for a moment. "I think . . . he wants us to *believe* they were killed in a frenzy—by a serial killer—a madman with a knife. But in fact, he was entirely calm and controlled—and these murders were deliberately and carefully planned."

"Exactly. Which means we're dealing with someone much more intelligent—and much more dangerous."

Mariana thought of Edward Fosca, and nodded. "Yes, I think so."

"Let me ask you something." Theo peered at her. "When you saw the body up close, what's the first thing that came into your mind?"

Mariana blinked—and for a second, she saw Veronica's eyes. She banished the image. "I—don't know . . . that it was horrible."

Theo shook his head. "No. That's not what you thought. Tell me the truth. What was the first thing that came into your mind?"

Mariana shrugged, a little embarrassed. "Funnily enough . . . it was a line from a play."

"Interesting. Go on."

"*The Duchess of Malfi*. 'Cover her face—mine eyes dazzle—'"

"Yes." Theo's eyes lit up suddenly, and he leaned forward, excited. "Yes, that's it."

"I—I'm not sure I understand."

"'Mine eyes *dazzle*.' The bodies are presented like that—to *dazzle* us. To blind us with horror. *Why?*"

"I don't know."

"Think about it. Why is he trying to blind us? *What doesn't he want us to see?* What is he trying to distract us from? Answer that, Mariana—and you'll catch him."

Mariana nodded as she took this in. They sat in contemplative silence for a moment, looking at each other.

Theo smiled. "You have a rare gift for empathy. I can feel it. I can see why Ruth praises you so highly."

"I don't deserve that, but thank you. It's nice to hear."

"Don't be so modest. It's not easy, being so open and receptive to another human being, you're able to feel their feelings . . . It's a poisoned chalice in many ways. I've always thought so." Then he paused, and said in a low voice, "Forgive me. I shouldn't say this . . . but I'm picking up something else in you . . ." He paused. "A kind of—fear. You're afraid of something. And you think it's out there . . ." He gestured into the air. "But it's not—it's in here—" He touched his chest. "Deep within you."

Mariana blinked, feeling exposed and embarrassed. She shook her head.

"I don't—I don't know what you mean."

"Well, my advice is—pay attention to it. Get friendly with it. We should always pay attention when our body tells us something. That's what Ruth says."

He suddenly looked a little awkward, perhaps sensing he had overstepped the mark. He glanced at his watch. "I should go. I have to meet my wife."

"Of course. Thanks so much for seeing me, Theo."

"Not at all. It's been good to see you, Mariana . . . Ruth said you run a private practice now?"

"That's right. And you're at Broadmoor?"

"For my sins." Theo smiled. "I don't know how much longer I can take it, to be honest. I'm not terribly happy there. I'd look for a new job, but, you know—no time."

As he said this, Mariana suddenly thought of something.

"Wait a second," she said.

She reached into her bag. She pulled out the *British Journal of Psychiatry* that she'd been carrying around. She flicked through the pages until she found what she was looking for. She showed Theo the journal, pointing at the advert in the box.

"Look."

It was an advert for the position of forensic psychotherapist at the Grove, a secure psychiatric unit in Edgware.

Mariana glanced at him. "What do you think? I know Professor Diomedes—he runs it. He specializes in group work—he taught me for a while."

"Yes." Theo nodded. "Yes, I know who he is." He studied the advert with obvious interest. "The Grove? Isn't that where they sent Alicia Berenson? After she killed her husband?"

"Alicia Berenson?"

"The painter . . . who won't talk."

"Oh—I remember." Mariana gave him an encouraging smile. "Maybe you should apply for the job? Get her talking again?"

"Perhaps." Theo smiled, and thought about it for a moment. He nodded to himself. "Perhaps I will."

9

The journey back to Cambridge went by in a flash.

Mariana was lost in thought the whole time, going over her conversation with Ruth and her meeting with Theo. His idea that the murders were deliberately horrifying, in order to distract from something, intrigued Mariana—and made emotional sense in a way she couldn't quite explain.

As for Ruth's suggestion she organize a therapy group with the Maidens—well, it wouldn't be easy, and maybe not even possible, but it was definitely worth pursuing.

What Ruth had said about Mariana's father was far more problematic.

She didn't understand why she'd brought him up. What did Ruth say?

It might not mean much now—but one day, it might mean a great deal.

That couldn't be more cryptic. Ruth was obviously hinting at something, but what?

Mariana puzzled over it, staring at the fields whizzing past the window. She thought of her childhood in Athens, and her father: how as a child, she had adored him—this handsome, clever, charismatic man—worshipped and idealized him. It took Mariana a long time to see that her father was not quite the man she thought he was.

The revelation occurred when she was in her early twenties, after she graduated from Cambridge. She was living in London and training to be a teacher. She had begun therapy with Ruth, with the intention of addressing the loss of her mother, but found herself talking mainly about her father.

She felt compelled to convince Ruth what a wonderful man he was: how brilliant, how hardworking, how much he had sacrificed, raising two children on his own—and how much he loved her.

After several months of listening to Mariana, and saying very little . . . one day Ruth finally interrupted.

What she said was simple, direct, and devastating.

Ruth suggested, as gently as she could, that Mariana was in denial about her father. That after everything she had heard, she had to question Mariana's assessment of him as a loving parent. The man Ruth heard described sounded authoritarian, cold, emotionally unavailable, often critical and highly unkind—even cruel. None of these qualities had anything to do with love.

"Love isn't conditional," Ruth said. "It's not dependent on jumping through hoops to please someone—and always failing. You can't love someone if you're afraid of them, Mariana. I know it's hard to hear. It's a kind of blindness—but unless you wake up and see clearly, it will persist throughout your whole life, affecting how you see yourself, and others too."

Mariana shook her head. "You're wrong about my father," she said. "I know he's difficult—but he loves me. And I love him."

"No," said Ruth firmly. "At best, let's call it a desire to be loved. At worst, it's a pathological attachment to a narcissistic man: a melting pot of gratitude, fear, expectation, and dutiful obedience that has nothing to do with love in the true sense of the word. You don't love him. Nor do you know or love yourself."

Ruth was right—this was hard to hear, let alone accept. Mariana stood up and walked out, angry tears streaming down her face. She vowed never to return.

But then, on the street outside Ruth's house, something stopped her. She suddenly thought of Sebastian—of how uncomfortable she would always feel whenever he complimented her.

"You've no idea how beautiful you are," Sebastian used to say.

"Stop it," Mariana would reply, her face coloring with embarrassment, as she batted away the compliment with a wave of her hand. Sebastian was wrong; she wasn't clever or beautiful—that wasn't how she saw herself.

Why not?

Whose eyes was she seeing herself with? Her own eyes?

Or her father's?

Sebastian didn't see with her father's eyes, or anyone else's; he saw with his own eyes. What if Mariana did too? What if, like the Lady of Shalott, she stopped looking at life through a mirror—and turned, and stared at it directly?

And so it began—a crack in the wall of delusion and denial, letting in some light; not much, but enough to see by. This moment proved to be an epiphany for Mariana; it propelled her on a journey of self-discovery she would much rather have forgone. She ended up quitting her teacher-training, and began training as a therapist. Although many years had passed since then, she had never fully resolved her feelings about her father; now that he was dead, presumably she never would.

10

Mariana got off the train at Cambridge station, lost in melancholy thought, and walked back to St. Christopher's, barely aware of her surroundings. When she got back, the first person she saw was Morris. He was standing by the porter's lodge with some police officers. The sight of him brought back all the unpleasantness of their encounter. She felt sick to her stomach.

She refused to look at him—she walked past him, ignoring him. Out of the corner of her eye, she saw him tip his hat at her, as if nothing had happened. He clearly felt he had the upper hand.

Good, she thought, *let him think that.*

For the moment, she decided not to say anything about what had happened—partly because she could imagine Inspector Sangha's reaction: her suggestion Morris was in league with Fosca would only provoke disbelief and ridicule. Like Fred had said, she needed proof. It would serve her better to remain silent, let Morris believe he had got away with it—and give him enough rope to hang himself.

She felt a sudden desire to call Fred, to talk to him—and she stopped herself in her tracks.

What the hell was she thinking? Was it possible she was developing feelings for him? For that *boy*? No—she wouldn't even let herself consider it. It was disloyal—and also frightening. It would be better if she never called Fred again, in fact.

As Mariana reached her room, she saw the door was ajar.

She froze. She listened carefully but couldn't hear a sound.

Very slowly, she reached out and pushed open the door. It creaked as it opened.

Mariana looked inside and what she saw made her gasp. It looked as though someone had torn the room apart: all the drawers and cupboards were thrown open and rifled through, Mariana's possessions strewn around, her clothes torn and ripped to pieces.

She quickly rang down to Morris at the porter's lodge—and asked him to find a police officer.

A few moments later, Morris and a couple of policemen were in her room, inspecting the damage.

"Are you sure nothing's been stolen?" said one officer.

Mariana nodded. "I don't think so."

"We've not seen anyone suspicious leave the college. More likely to be an inside job."

"Looks like the work of a spiteful student," said Morris. He smiled at Mariana. "Been upsetting anyone, miss?"

Mariana ignored him. She thanked the police officers and agreed it probably wasn't a burglary. They offered to check for fingerprints, and Mariana was about to agree—when she saw something that made her change her mind.

A knife, or some sharp instrument, had been used to carve a cross deep into the mahogany desk.

"That won't be necessary," she said. "I won't take this any further."

"Well, if you're sure."

As they left the room, Mariana stroked the grooves of the cross with her fingertips.

She stood there, thinking about Henry.

And for the first time, she felt afraid of him.

II

I was just thinking about time.

About how maybe nothing ever really goes away. It's been here the whole time—my past, I mean—and the reason it's catching up with me is because it never went anywhere.

In some weird way I'll always be there, always twelve years old—trapped in time, on that terrible day, the day after my birthday, when everything changed.

It feels like it's happening to me right now as I write this.

My mother is sitting me down to tell me the news. I know something is wrong because she has brought me into the front sitting room, the one we never use, and sat me down on the uncomfortable wooden chair to break it to me.

I thought she was going to say she was dying, that she was terminally ill—that's what the look on her face led me to believe.

But it was much worse than that.

She said she was leaving. Things with my father had been particularly bad—she was sporting a black eye and split lip to prove it. And she finally had found the courage to leave him.

I felt such a rush of happiness—"joy" is the only word that approximates it.

But my grin quickly faded as I listened to my mother rattle off her immediate plans, involving staying on a cousin's couch, then visiting her parents until she got on her feet—and it became obvious by the way she was avoiding my eye, and by what was not being said, that she was not taking me with her.

I stared at her in a state of shock.

I was unable to feel or think—I don't remember much else of what she said. But she ended with a promise to send for me when she was settled in her new home. Which might as well have been on another planet, for all the reality that held for me. She was leaving me behind. Leaving me here. With him.

I was being sacrificed. Damned to hell.

And then, with that strange crass ineptitude she sometimes had, she mentioned she hadn't yet told my father she was leaving. She wanted to tell me first.

I don't believe she intended to tell him. This was her only goodbye—to me, here and now. Then, if she had any sense at all, she'd pack a bag and flee in the night.

That's what I would have done.

She asked me to keep her secret, and promise not to tell. My beautiful, foolhardy, trusting mother—in many ways I was much older and wiser than she was. I was certainly more devious. All I had to do was tell him. Tell that raging madman of her plan to abandon ship. And then she would be prevented from going. I wouldn't lose her. And I didn't want to lose her.

Did I?

I loved her—didn't I?

Something was happening to me—to my thinking. It began during that conversation with my mother, and the hours afterward—a kind of slow, creeping awareness—a weird epiphany.

I thought she loved me.

But it turns out, there was more than one of her.

And now I started to see this other person, suddenly—I started to see her, there, in the background, watching while my father tortured me. Why didn't she stop him? Why didn't she protect me?

Why didn't she teach me I was worth protecting?

She stood up for Rex—she held a knife to my father's chest and threatened to stab him. But she never did that for me.

I could feel a fire burning—a rising anger, a rage that would not go out. I knew it was wrong—I knew I should curb it before it overwhelmed me. But instead, I fanned the flames. And I burned.

All the horrors I endured—I put up with them for her sake, to keep her safe. But she never put me first. It was every man for himself, it seemed. My father was right—she was selfish, spoiled, thoughtless. Cruel.

She needed to be punished.

I never could have said this to her then. I didn't have the vocabulary. But years later I might have confronted her—in my early twenties, perhaps—when age had made me more articulate. And after one drink too many, after dinner, I'd turn on her, on this old woman, and try to hurt her, as she had once hurt me. I would list my grievances—and then, in my fantasy, she'd break down, prostrate herself and beg my forgiveness. And benevolently, I would bestow it.

What a luxury that would be—to forgive. But I never got that chance.

That night I went to bed, burning, hating . . . It felt like red-hot magma rising in a volcano. I fell asleep . . . and I dreamed I went downstairs, took a large carving knife out of the drawer, and used it to cut off my mother's head. I hacked and sawed through her neck with the knife, until it was severed. Then I hid the head in her red-and-white-striped knitting bag—and put it under my bed, where I knew it would be safe. The body I disposed of—in the pit with the other carcasses—where no one would ever find it.

When I woke up from this dream, in the horrible yellow light of dawn, I felt groggy, disorientated—and afraid, confused about what happened.

I felt unsure enough to go downstairs into the kitchen to check. I opened the drawer where the knives were kept.

I took out the largest knife. I examined it, looking for any traces of blood. There were none. The blade glinted cleanly in the sunlight.

And then I heard some footsteps. I quickly hid the knife behind my back. My mother walked in, alive and unhurt.

Weirdly, seeing my mother with her head intact did nothing to reassure me.

In fact, I was disappointed.

12

The next morning, Mariana met Zoe and Clarissa for breakfast in Hall.

The fellows' buffet was in an alcove to the side of high table. There was a generous selection of breads, pastries, and pots of butter, jams, and marmalades; and large silver terrines containing hot dishes, such as scrambled eggs, bacon, and sausages.

Clarissa was extolling the virtues of a big breakfast as they queued for the buffet. "It sets you up for the day," she said. "Nothing more important, to my mind. Kippers, usually, whenever possible."

She contemplated the various options laid out before them. "But not today. Today, kedgeree, don't you think? Good old-fashioned comfort food. So reassuring. Haddock, eggs, and rice. Can't go wrong with that."

Clarissa's pronouncement was soon proved wrong, once they sat down and she took her first mouthful. She went bright red, choked—and pulled out a large fishbone from her mouth. She peered at it in alarm.

"Good God. It seems the chef is out to kill us. Do be careful, my dears."

Clarissa carefully picked through the rest of her fish with her fork, while Mariana gave them a report of her trip to London—relaying Ruth's suggestion about organizing a group session with the Maidens.

Mariana saw Zoe raise an eyebrow at this. "Zoe? What do you think?"

Zoe shot her a wary look. "I don't have to be there, do I?"

Mariana hid her amusement. "No, you don't have to be there, don't worry."

Zoe looked relieved, and shrugged. "Then go ahead. But I don't think they'll agree, to be honest. Not unless he tells them to."

Mariana nodded. "I think you're probably right about that."

Clarissa nudged her arm. "Speak of the devil."

Mariana and Zoe looked up—as Edward Fosca appeared at high table.

Fosca sat at the other end of the table from the three women. Sensing Mariana's gaze, he looked up, and his eyes lingered on her for a few seconds. Then he turned away.

Abruptly, Mariana stood up. Zoe gave her an alarmed look.

"What are you doing?"

"Only one way to find out."

"Mariana—"

But she ignored Zoe, and walked to the other end of the long table, where Professor Fosca was sitting. He was nursing a black coffee, and reading a slim volume of poetry.

He became conscious of Mariana standing there. He looked up. "Good morning."

"Professor," she said, "I have a request for you."

"Do you?" Fosca gave her a quizzical look. "And what's that, Mariana?"

She met his eyes and held his gaze for a second. "Would you object if I spoke to your students—your special students, I mean? The Maidens?"

"I thought you already had."

"I mean as a group."

"A group?"

"Yes. A therapy group."

"Isn't it up to them, not me?"

"I don't think they'll agree unless you ask them to."

Fosca smiled. "So, in fact, you're asking not for my permission—but my cooperation?"

"I suppose you could put it like that."

Fosca continued to gaze at her, a small smile on his lips. "Have you decided where and when you would like this session to take place?"

Mariana thought for a second. "How about five o'clock to-day . . . in the OCR?"

"You seem to think I have a great deal of influence over them, Mariana. I assure you, that's not the case." He paused. "What, may I ask, is the exact purpose of the group? What do you hope to achieve?"

"I don't hope to achieve anything. That's not really how therapy works. I'm simply aiming to provide a space for these young women to process some of the terrible things they've been through recently."

Fosca sipped some coffee as he pondered this. "And does the invitation extend to me? As a member of the group?"

"I'd prefer if you didn't come. I think your presence might inhibit the girls."

"What if I made it a condition of my agreeing to help?"

Mariana shrugged. "Then I'd have no choice."

"In which case I shall attend."

He smiled at her. She didn't smile back.

"It makes me wonder, Professor," she said, with a slight frown, "what on earth it is that you're so desperate to hide?"

Fosca smiled. "I'm not trying to hide anything. Let's just say I wish to be there, to protect my students."

"Protect them? From what?"

"From you, Mariana," he said. "From you."

13

At five o'clock that afternoon, Mariana waited for the Maidens in the OCR.

She had booked the room from five until six thirty. The OCR—or the Old Combination Room—was a large room used by members of college as a common room: it had several large sofas, low coffee tables, and a long dining table that took up the length of one wall. Old Masters were hanging on the walls; muted, dark paintings against crimson-and-gold flock wallpaper.

A low fire was burning in the marble fireplace—and its flickering firelight was reflected in the gilded furnishings around the room. There was a comforting and containing atmosphere, and Mariana thought it was perfect for the session.

She arranged nine upright chairs in a circle.

Then she sat on one of the chairs, making sure she had a view of the clock on the mantelpiece. It was a couple of minutes after five.

Mariana wondered if they were going to show up or not. She wouldn't be remotely surprised if they didn't.

But then, a moment later, the door opened.

And one by one, the five young women filed in. Judging by their stony expressions, they were there under duress.

"Good afternoon," Mariana said with a smile. "Thank you for coming. Won't you sit down?"

The girls looked at the arrangement of chairs, and then glanced at one another, before apprehensively sitting down. The tall blonde seemed to be the leader; Mariana sensed the others deferring to her. She sat down first, and the others followed suit.

They sat adjacent to one another, leaving empty chairs on either side, and faced Mariana. She felt a little intimidated suddenly, by this wall of unfriendly young faces.

How ridiculous, she thought, to feel intimidated by a handful of twenty-year-olds, no matter how beautiful or intelligent they were. Mariana felt like she was back at school again, an ugly duckling on the fringes of the schoolyard, confronted by a gang of popular girls. The very young part of Mariana felt scared, and she wondered, for a second, what the young parts of these young women were like—if their apparent confidence masked similar feelings of inferiority. Beneath their superior manner, did they feel as small as she did? It was hard to imagine somehow.

Serena was the only one she'd had a conversation with, and she seemed to have difficulty looking Mariana in the eye. Morris must have told her about their confrontation. She kept her head down, eyes on her lap, looking embarrassed.

The others stared at her blankly. They seemed to be waiting for her to speak. She didn't say anything. They sat in silence.

Mariana glanced at the clock; it was now ten minutes past five. Professor Fosca wasn't here—and, with any luck, he had decided not to come.

"I think we should begin," she said eventually.

"What about the professor?" asked the blond girl.

"He must have been held up. We should start without him. Why don't we begin with our names? I'm Mariana."

There was a slight pause. The blond girl shrugged. "Carla."

The others followed suit.

"Natasha."

"Diya."

"Lillian."

Serena was last to speak. She glanced at Mariana and shrugged. "You know my name."

"Yes, Serena, I do."

Mariana composed her thoughts. Then she addressed them as a group.

"I'm wondering how this feels, sitting here together."

This was met with silence. No reaction at all, not even a shrug. Mariana could feel their stone-cold hostility toward her. She went on, undiscouraged.

"I'll tell you how it feels for me. It's strange. My eyes keep being drawn to the empty chairs." She nodded at the three empty chairs in the circle. "The people who should be here but aren't."

"Like the professor," said Carla.

"I didn't just mean the professor. Who else do you think I mean?"

Carla glanced at the empty chairs and rolled her eyes with derision. "Is that who the other chairs are for? Tara and Veronica? That's so stupid."

"Why is that stupid?"

"Because they're not coming. Obviously."

Mariana shrugged. "That doesn't mean they're not still part of the group. We often talk about that in group therapy, you know— even when people are no longer with us, they can remain a powerful presence."

As she said this, she glanced at one of the empty chairs—and saw Sebastian sitting there, looking at her with amusement.

She banished him, and went on.

"It makes me wonder," she said, "what it feels like to be a part of a group like this . . . What it means to you?"

None of the girls responded. They looked at her blankly.

"In group therapy, we often make the group into our family. We assign siblings and parental figures, uncles and aunts. I suppose this is a bit like a family? In a way, you have lost two of your sisters."

No response. She went on, cautiously.

"I suppose Professor Fosca is your 'father'?" A pause. She tried again. "Is he a good father?"

Natasha let out a heavy, irritated sigh. "This is such *bullshit*," she said with a strong Russian accent. "It's obvious what you are doing."

"What's that?"

"You're trying to make us say something bad about the professor. To trick us. To trap him."

"Why do you think I'm trying to trap him?"

Natasha gave a contemptuous sigh and didn't bother to respond.

Carla spoke for her: "Look, Mariana. We know what you think. But the professor had nothing to do with the murders."

"Yes." Natasha nodded forcefully. "We were with him the *whole* time."

There was a sudden passion in her voice, a burning resentment.

"You're very angry, Natasha," she said. "I can feel it."

Natasha laughed. "Good—because it's directed at you."

Mariana nodded. "It's easy to be angry at me. I'm not threatening. It must be harder to be angry with your 'father,'—for letting two of his children perish?"

"For Christ's sake—it's not his fault they're dead," said Lillian, speaking for the first time.

"Then whose fault is it?" said Mariana.

Lillian shrugged. "Theirs."

Mariana stared at her. "What? How is it their fault?"

"They should have been more careful. Tara and Veronica were stupid, both of them."

"That's right," said Diya.

Carla and Natasha nodded in agreement.

Mariana stared at them, momentarily speechless. She knew anger was easier to feel than sadness—but she, who was so sensitively attuned to picking up on emotions, could sense no sadness here. No grief, no remorse or loss. Just disdain. Just contempt.

It was strange—normally when faced with an attack from the

outside, a group like this would close its ranks, come together, unite—but it struck Mariana that the only person at St. Christopher's who had expressed any real emotion over Tara's death, or Veronica's, was Zoe.

Mariana was sharply reminded of Henry's therapy group in London. There was something reminiscent of it here—the way Henry's presence was splitting the group from within, attacking it so it couldn't function normally.

Was that happening in this group too? If so, it meant the group wasn't responding to an outside threat.

It meant the threat was already here.

At that moment, there was a knock at the door. It opened—

And Professor Fosca was standing there.

He smiled. "May I join you?"

14

"Forgive me for being late," Fosca said. "There was something I had to attend to."

Mariana frowned slightly. "I'm afraid we've already started."

"Well, might I still be allowed in?"

"That's not up to me; it's up to the group." She glanced at the others. "Who thinks Professor Fosca should be admitted?"

Before she had even finished speaking, five hands were raised around the circle. All except hers.

Fosca smiled. "You didn't raise your hand, Mariana."

She shook her head. "No, I didn't. But I am overruled."

Mariana felt the energy in the room change as Fosca joined them in the circle. She sensed the girls tense up, and she noticed a quick look was exchanged between Fosca and Carla as he sat down.

Fosca smiled at Mariana. "Please go on."

Mariana left a slight pause, and decided to try a different approach. She smiled innocently.

"You teach the girls Greek tragedy, Professor?"

"That's correct."

"Have you studied *Iphigenia in Aulis*? The story of Agamemnon and Iphigenia?"

She studied the professor closely as she said this—but there was no apparent reaction to the play being mentioned. He nodded.

"We have indeed. As you are aware, Euripides is a favorite of mine."

"That's right. Well, you know, I always found the character of Iphigenia to be rather curious . . . I was wondering what your students think."

"Curious? How so?"

Mariana thought for a second. "Well, it bothers me, I suppose, that she's so passive . . . so submissive."

"Submissive?"

"She doesn't fight for her life. She isn't bound or restrained; she willingly lets her father put her to death."

Fosca smiled, and glanced at the others. "That's an interesting point Mariana makes. Would someone like to respond . . . ? Carla?"

Carla looked pleased to be called on. She smiled at Mariana, as if humoring a child. "The way Iphigenia dies is the *whole point*."

"Meaning?"

"Meaning that's how she achieves her tragic stature—by means of a heroic death."

Carla glanced at Fosca for approval. He gave her a slight smile.

Mariana shook her head. "I'm sorry. But I don't buy that."

"No?" Fosca looked intrigued. "Why not?"

Mariana glanced at the young women around the circle. "I think the best way to answer that . . . is to bring Iphigenia here, into the session—have her join us, on one of these empty chairs? What do you say?"

A couple of the girls exchanged scornful looks.

"That's so dumb," said Natasha.

"Why? She was about your age, wasn't she? A bit younger, perhaps. Sixteen, seventeen? What a brave, remarkable person she was. Imagine what she would have done with her life—if she had survived—what she could have achieved. What might we say to Iphigenia, now, if she were sitting here? What would we tell her?"

"Nothing." Diya looked unimpressed. "What is there to say?"

"Nothing? You wouldn't try to warn her—about her psychopathic father? Help save her?"

"Save her?" Diya gave her a contemptuous look. "From what? Her fate? Tragedy doesn't work like that."

"Anyway, it wasn't Agamemnon's fault," said Carla. "It was Artemis who demanded Iphigenia's death. It was the will of the gods."

"What if there are no gods?" said Mariana. "Just a girl and her father. What then?"

Carla shrugged. "Then it's not a tragedy."

Diya nodded. "Just a fucked-up Greek family."

Throughout all this Fosca had been silent, watching the debate with quiet amusement. But now his curiosity appeared to get the better of him.

"What would *you* say to her, Mariana? To this girl who died to save Greece? She was younger, incidentally, than you think— closer to fourteen, or fifteen. If she were here now—what would you tell her?"

Mariana thought for a moment. "I suppose I'd want to know about her relationship with her father . . . And why she felt compelled to sacrifice herself for him."

"And why do you think that was?"

Mariana shrugged. "I believe that children will do anything to be loved. When they're very young, it's a matter of physical, then psychological survival. They'll do whatever it takes to be cared for." She lowered her voice, speaking not to Fosca but to the young women seated around him. "And some people take advantage of that."

"Meaning what, exactly?" he said.

"Meaning, if I were her therapist, I would try to help Iphigenia see something—something that was *invisible* to her."

"And what was that?" said Carla.

Mariana chose her words carefully. "It was that, at a very young age, Iphigenia mistook abuse for love. And that mistake colored how she saw herself . . . and the world around her. Agamemnon was not a hero—he was a madman, an infanticidal psychopath. Iphigenia did not need to love and honor this man. She did not need to die to please him."

Mariana looked into the girls' eyes. She was desperate to reach them. She hoped it would penetrate . . . but did it? She couldn't tell. She could feel Fosca's eyes on her—and sensed he was about to interrupt. She went on quickly.

"And if Iphigenia stopped lying to herself about her father . . . if she woke up to the terrible, devastating truth—that *this was not love,* that he didn't love her, because he didn't know how—in that very moment, she would cease to be a defenseless maiden with her head on the block. She'd seize the axe from the executioner's hands. She would become the goddess."

Mariana turned and stared at Fosca. She tried to keep the anger out of her voice. But she couldn't quite disguise it.

"But that didn't happen for Iphigenia, did it? Not Tara, nor Veronica. They never had the chance to become goddesses. They never had the chance to grow up."

As she stared at him, across the circle, she could see a spark of anger in his eyes. But like her, Fosca didn't express it.

"I take it you're in some way casting me as the father in this current situation? As Agamemnon? Is that what you're suggesting?"

"It's funny you say that. Before you arrived, we were debating your merits as a 'father' of the group."

"Oh, indeed? And what was the general consensus?"

"We didn't reach one. But I asked the Maidens if they felt less safe in your care—now that two of their number were dead."

As she said this, her eyes drifted to two empty chairs. Fosca's eyes followed her gaze.

"Ah. Now I see," he said. "The empty chairs represent the missing members of the group . . . A chair for Tara, and a chair for Veronica?"

"That's correct."

"In which case," he said, after a slight pause, "isn't there a chair missing?"

"What do you mean?"

"You don't know?"

"Know what?"

"Oh. She hasn't told you. How very interesting." Fosca kept smiling. He looked amused. "Perhaps you should point that powerful analytical lens back at yourself, Mariana? What kind of 'mother' are you?"

"Physician, heal thyself," said Carla, with a laugh.

Fosca chuckled. "Yes, yes, exactly."

He turned and appealed to the others, with a mock-therapeutic air. "What do we make of this deception—as a *group*? What do we think it *means*?"

"Well," said Carla, "I think it says a *lot* about their relationship."

Natasha nodded. "Oh, yes. They're not nearly as close as Mariana thinks."

"She obviously doesn't trust her," Lillian said.

"Why not, I wonder?" murmured Fosca, still smiling.

Mariana could feel her face going red, burning with annoyance at this little game they were playing—it was straight out of the schoolyard; like any bully, Fosca had manipulated the group, making them gang up against her. They were all in on the joke, grinning, mocking her. She hated them, suddenly.

"What are you talking about?" she said.

Fosca looked around the circle. "Well, who's going to do the honors? Serena? How about you?"

Serena nodded and stood up. She left the circle and walked over to the dining table. She picked up another upright chair, brought it back, and wedged it into the space next to Mariana's chair. Then she sat down again.

"Thank you," Fosca said. He glanced at Mariana. "There was a chair missing, you see. For the Maidens' final member."

"And who is that?"

But Mariana had already guessed what Fosca was going to say. He smiled.

"Your niece," he said. "Zoe."

15

After the meeting, Mariana stumbled out into Main Court, feeling stunned.

She needed to talk to Zoe—and hear her side of the story. In its cruel way, the group had made a good point: Mariana needed to look at herself, and Zoe, closely—and understand why Zoe had not confided in her about being a member of the Maidens. Mariana needed to know why.

She found herself walking toward Zoe's room, to find Zoe and confront her. But the moment she reached the archway leading to Eros Court, Mariana paused.

She had to handle this carefully. Not only was Zoe fragile and vulnerable, but also, for whatever reason—and Mariana couldn't help thinking it had to do with Edward Fosca himself—she felt unable to confide the truth to Mariana.

And Fosca had just deliberately betrayed Zoe's confidence—in an attempt to provoke Mariana. So it was imperative Mariana not rise to the bait. She mustn't barge into Zoe's room, and accuse her of lying.

She needed to support Zoe, and think hard about how to proceed.

She decided to sleep on it—and talk to Zoe in the morning

after she had calmed down a bit. Mariana turned around; and, lost in thought, she didn't notice Fred until he stepped out of the shadows.

He stood on the path in front of her.

"Hello, Mariana."

She caught her breath. "Fred. What are you doing here?"

"Looking for you. I wanted to check you're okay."

"Yes, I am, just about."

"You know, you said you'd get in touch when you got back from London."

"I know, I'm sorry. I—I've been busy."

"You sure you're all right? You look—like you could use a drink."

Mariana smiled. "I could, actually."

Fred smiled back. "Well, in that case—how about it?"

Mariana hesitated, unsure. "Oh, well, I—"

Fred went on quickly: "I happen to have a very impressive Burgundy, stolen from a formal hall. I've been saving it for a special occasion . . . What do you say? It's in my room."

What the hell, Mariana thought. She nodded. "Okay. Why not?"

"Really?" Fred's face lit up. "Okay, great. Come on—"

He held out his arm, but Mariana didn't take it. She started walking—and Fred hurried to catch up with her.

16

Fred's room in Trinity was larger than Zoe's, although its furnishings were slightly more threadbare. The first thing Mariana noticed was how tidy it was: no clutter, no mess, apart from paper everywhere—pages and pages of scribbled writing and mathematical formulae. It rather looked like the work of a madman—or a genius—connected by arrows and illegible notes going up and down the sides of the pages.

The only personal items Mariana could see were a couple of framed photographs on the shelf. One of the photos had a slightly faded look, as if it had been taken in the eighties: an attractive young man and woman, presumably Fred's parents, standing in front of a picket fence and a meadow. The other photo was of a small boy with a dog; a little boy with a pudding-bowl haircut, and a serious look on his face.

Mariana glanced at Fred. He still had the same expression now as he concentrated on lighting some candles. He then put on some music—a recording of Bach's *Goldberg Variations*. He gathered up all the papers from the sofa, stacking them in an unsteady pile on his desk. "Sorry it's such a mess."

"Is that your thesis?" she said, nodding at the piles of paper.

"No." Fred shook his head. "It's—just something I'm writing. A kind of . . . book, I suppose." He seemed at a loss as to how to describe it. "Won't you sit?"

He gestured at the sofa. Mariana sat down. She felt a broken spring underneath her, and shifted slightly.

Fred pulled out the bottle of vintage Burgundy. He displayed it proudly. "Not bad, eh? They'd have killed me if they caught me nicking it."

He reached for a corkscrew, and wrestled with opening it. For a second, Mariana thought he'd drop the bottle. But he successfully uncorked it with a loud pop—and poured the dark red wine into two chipped, mismatched wineglasses. He gave Mariana the less damaged of the two.

"Thank you."

He raised his glass. "Cheers."

Mariana sipped some wine—it was excellent, of course. Fred evidently thought so. He sighed happily, a tinge of red wine around his lips.

"Lovely," he said.

They fell into silence for a moment. Mariana listened to the music, losing herself in Bach's rising and falling scales, so elegant, so mathematical in construction; presumably why they appealed to Fred's mathematical brain.

She glanced at the stack of pages on the desk. "This book you're writing . . . What's it about?"

"Honestly?" Fred shrugged. "No idea."

Mariana laughed. "You must have some idea."

"Well . . ." Fred averted his eyes. "In a way, I suppose . . . it's about my mother."

He glanced at her shyly, as if afraid she might laugh.

But Mariana didn't find it funny. She gave him a curious look. "Your mother?"

Fred nodded. "Yeah. She left me . . . when I was a boy . . . She—died."

"I'm sorry," Mariana said. "My mother died too."

"Did she?" Fred's eyes widened. "I didn't know that. Then we're both orphans."

"I wasn't an orphan. I had my father."

"Yeah." Fred nodded and spoke in a low voice. "I did too."

He reached out for the bottle and started refilling Mariana's glass. "That's enough," she said. But he ignored her and filled it to the brim. She didn't mind, really—she was relaxing for the first time in days, and felt grateful to him.

"You see," Fred said, pouring himself more wine, "my mother's death is what drew me to theoretical mathematics—and to parallel universes. That's what my thesis is about."

"I'm not sure I understand."

"Not sure I do either, really. But if there are other universes, identical to ours, it means that somewhere, another universe exists—where my mother didn't die." He shrugged. "So . . . I went looking for her."

He had a sad, faraway expression in his eyes, like a lost little boy. Mariana felt sorry for him.

"Did you find her?" she asked.

He shrugged. "In a way . . . I discovered that time doesn't exist—not really—so she hasn't gone anywhere. She's right here."

As Mariana wrestled with this, Fred put down his wineglass, took off his glasses, and faced her.

"Mariana, listen—"

"Please, don't."

"What? You don't know what I'm going to say."

"You're going to make some kind of romantic declaration— and I don't want to hear it."

"A declaration? No. Just a question. Am I allowed a question?"

"It depends."

"I love you."

Mariana frowned. "That's not a question."

"Will you marry me? That's the question."

"Fred, please shut up—"

"I love you, Mariana—I fell in love with you the first second I saw you, sitting on the train. I want to be with you. I want to take care of you. I want to look after you—"

That was the wrong thing to say. Mariana felt her temperature rise; her cheeks burned with irritation. "Well, I don't want to be *looked after*! I can't think of anything worse. I'm not a damsel in distress, a . . . *maiden* waiting to be rescued. I don't need a knight in shining armor—I want—I want—"

"What? What do you want?"

"I want to be left *alone*."

"No." Fred shook his head. "I don't believe that." And then, quickly, he said, "Remember my premonition: one day, I'll ask you to marry me—and you'll say yes."

Mariana couldn't help laughing. "Sorry, Fred. Not in this universe."

"Well, you know, in some other universe, we're married already."

Before she could protest, Fred leaned forward and gently pressed his lips against hers; she felt the softness of his kiss, its warmth and tenderness. She felt both alarmed and disarmed by it.

It was over as quickly as it began. He pulled back, his eyes searching hers. "I'm sorry. I—I couldn't help it."

Mariana shook her head; she didn't speak. She felt affected in some way she couldn't quite explain.

"I don't want to hurt you, Fred."

"I don't mind. It's okay if you hurt me, you know. After all— 'it's better to have loved and lost, than never to have loved at all.'"

Fred laughed. Then he saw Mariana's face fall, and looked worried. "What? What did I say?"

"It's nothing." She looked at her watch. "It's late, I should go."

Fred looked pained. "Already? Fine. I'll walk you downstairs."

"You don't need to—"

"I want to."

Fred's manner seemed to have changed slightly; he seemed sharper. Some of his warmth had evaporated. He stood up, not looking at her.

"Let's go," he said.

17

Fred and Mariana walked down the steps in silence. They didn't speak again until they were on the street. Mariana glanced at him. "Good night then."

Fred didn't move. "I'm going for a walk."

"Now?"

"I often walk at night. Is that a problem?"

There was a prickliness, a hostility to his tone. He felt rejected—she could tell. Perhaps unfairly, she felt annoyed with him. But his hurt feelings were not her concern. She had more important things to worry about.

"Okay," she said. "Goodbye."

Fred didn't move. He kept looking at her. And then, suddenly, he said, "Wait." He reached into his back pocket and pulled out a few pages of folded paper. "I was going to give you this later, but—take it now."

He held it out to her. She didn't take it.

"What is it?"

"A letter. It's for you—it explains my feelings better than I can in person. Read it. Then you'll understand."

"I don't want it."

He thrust it at her again. "Mariana. Take it."

"No. Stop. I will not be bullied."

"Mariana—"

But she turned and left. As she made her way down the street, she felt anger at first, then a surprising twinge of sadness—then regret. Not at having hurt him, but at having rejected him, having closed the door to this other narrative that might have been.

Was it possible? Could Mariana ever have grown to love him, this serious young man? Could she hold him at night, and tell him her stories? Even as she thought this, she knew it was impossible.

How could she?

She had too much to tell. And it was for Sebastian's ears alone.

When Mariana returned to St. Christopher's, she didn't immediately go to her room. Instead, she drifted through Main Court . . . and into the building that housed the buttery.

She wandered along the darkened passage until she was face-to-face with the painting.

The portrait of Tennyson.

The picture had been on her mind—and she kept thinking about it, without quite knowing why. Sad, handsome Tennyson.

No—not sad—that wasn't the right word to describe the look in his eyes. What was it?

She searched his face, trying to read the expression. Again, she had the strange feeling he was looking past her, just over her shoulder—staring at something . . . something just out of sight.

But what?

And then, suddenly, Mariana understood. She understood what he was looking at; or, rather, *who*.

It was Hallam.

Tennyson was staring at Hallam—at Hallam, standing just beyond the light . . . behind the veil. That was the look in his eyes. The eyes of a man communing with the dead.

Tennyson was lost . . . He was in love with a ghost. He had turned his back on life. Had Mariana?

Once, she thought she had.

And now—?

Now, perhaps . . . she wasn't so sure.

Mariana stood there for a moment longer, thinking. Then, as she turned to walk away . . . she heard some footsteps. She stopped.

A man's hard-soled shoes were slowly walking along the stone floor of the long gloomy passage . . .

And he was getting closer.

At first, Mariana couldn't see anyone. But then . . . as he drew nearer, she saw something moving in the shadows . . . and the glint of a knife.

She stood there, frozen, scarcely daring to breathe, trying to see who it was. And then, slowly . . . Henry emerged from the darkness.

He stared at her.

He had a horrible look in his eyes; not entirely rational, slightly manic. He'd been in a fight, and his nose was bleeding. There was blood smeared on his face and spattered on his shirt. He was holding a knife, about seven or eight inches long.

Mariana tried to sound calm and unafraid. But she couldn't keep a slight tremor out of her voice.

"Henry? Please put down the knife."

He didn't answer. He just stared at her. His eyes were huge, like lamps, and he was clearly high on something.

"What are you doing here?" she said.

Henry didn't reply for a moment. "Needed to see you, didn't I? You won't see me in London, so I had to come all the way here."

"How did you find me?"

"Saw you on the telly. You were standing with the police."

Mariana spoke cautiously. "I don't recall that. I've done my best to avoid being caught on camera."

"You think I'm lying? You think I followed you here?"

"Henry, it was you who broke into my room, wasn't it?"

A hysterical tone crept into his voice. "You abandoned me, Mariana. You—you *sacrificed* me—"

"What?" Mariana stared at him, unnerved. "Why—did you use that word?"

"It's true, isn't it?"

He raised the knife, and took a step toward her. But Mariana held her ground.

"Put down the knife, Henry."

He kept walking. "I can't go on like this. I need to free myself. I need to cut myself free."

"Henry, please stop—"

He held up the knife, as if preparing to strike. Mariana felt her heart racing.

"I'm going to kill myself right now, in front of you," he said. "And you're going to watch."

"Henry—"

Henry raised the knife higher, and then—

"Oi!"

Henry heard the voice behind him and turned around—as Morris charged out of the shadows—and lunged at Henry. They wrestled for the knife—and Morris easily overpowered him, throwing him aside as if he were made of straw. Henry landed in a crumpled heap on the floor.

"Leave him alone," Mariana said to Morris. "Don't hurt him."

She went over to Henry, to help him up—but he shoved away her hand.

"I hate you," he said, sounding like a little boy. His red eyes filled with tears. "I hate you."

Morris called for the police, and Henry was then arrested, but Mariana insisted he needed psychiatric care—and he was taken to the hospital, where he was sectioned. He was prescribed antipsychotic medication and Mariana arranged to speak to the consultant psychiatrist in the morning.

She blamed herself for what had happened, of course.

Henry was right: she had sacrificed him, and the other vulnerable people in her care. If she had been available, as Henry needed her to be, it might not have come to this. That was the truth.

And now Mariana had to make sure this enormous sacrifice was not in vain . . . whatever the cost.

18

It was nearly one in the morning by the time Mariana got back to her room. She was exhausted, but too wide awake to sleep, too anxious and wound up.

The room was cold, so she turned on the old electric heater attached to the wall. It couldn't have been used since the previous winter—as it heated up, there was the heavy smell of burning dust. Mariana sat there, on the hard, upright wooden chair, staring at the electric bar glowing red in the dark, feeling its heat, listening to it hum. She sat there, thinking—thinking about Edward Fosca.

He was so smug, so sure of himself. *He thinks he's got away with it,* she thought. He thought he had won.

But he hadn't. Not yet. And Mariana was determined to outsmart him. She had to. She would sit up all night and think, and work it out.

She sat there for hours, in a vigil, a kind of trance—thinking, thinking—going over everything that had happened since Zoe first called her on Monday night. She went over every event of the story, all the various strands—examining it all from every angle, trying to make sense of it—trying to see clearly.

It must be obvious—the answer must be right there in front of her. But still, she couldn't grasp it—it was like trying to assemble a jigsaw puzzle in the dark.

Fred would say that in some other universe, Mariana had already figured it out. In some other universe, she was smarter.

But not this one, unfortunately.

She sat there until her head hurt. Then, at dawn, exhausted and depressed, she gave up. She crawled into bed, and immediately fell fast asleep.

As Mariana slept, she had a nightmare. She dreamed that she was searching for Sebastian through desolate landscapes, trudging through wind and snow. She finally found him—in a shabby hotel bar, in a remote Alpine mountain hotel, during a snowstorm. She greeted him, overjoyed—but, to her horror, Sebastian didn't recognize her. He said she had changed—that she was a different person. Mariana swore over and over that she was the same: *It's me, it's me,* she cried. But when she tried to kiss him, he pulled away. Sebastian left her, and went out into the snowstorm. Mariana broke down, weeping, inconsolable—and Zoe appeared, wrapping her in a blue blanket. Mariana told Zoe how much she loved Sebastian—more than breathing, more than life. Zoe shook her head, and said that love only brings sorrow, and that Mariana should wake up. "Wake up, Mariana."

"What?"

"Wake up . . . Wake up!"

Then, suddenly, Mariana woke up with a start—in a cold sweat, with her heart racing.

Someone was banging on the door.

19

Mariana sat up in bed, her heart pounding. The banging continued.

"Wait," she called out, "I'm coming."

What time is it? Bright sunlight was creeping around the edges of the curtains. Eight? Nine?

"Who's there?"

There was no reply. The banging got louder—as did the banging in her head. She had a throbbing headache; she must have drunk a lot more than she thought.

"Okay. Just a second."

Mariana pulled herself out of bed. She was disorientated and groggy. She dragged herself to the door. She unlocked and opened it.

Elsie was standing there, poised to knock again. She smiled brightly.

"Good morning, dear."

She had a feather duster under her arm, and was clutching a bucket of cleaning materials. Her eyebrows were painted on in a stern angle that made her look rather frightening—and she had an excited glint in her eye, a glint that struck Mariana as sinister and predatory.

"What time is it, Elsie?"

"Just gone eleven, dear. Didn't wake you, did I?"

She leaned in, past Mariana, peering at the unmade bed. Mariana could smell cigarette smoke on her, and was that alcohol on her breath? Or was it her own breath she was smelling?

"I didn't sleep well," Mariana said. "I had a nightmare."

"Oh, dear." Elsie tutted sympathetically. "I'm not surprised, with all that's going on. I'm afraid I have more bad news, dear. But I thought you should know."

"What?" Mariana stared at her, her eyes wide. She was suddenly fully awake, and felt scared. "What's happened?"

"I'll tell you if you give me a chance. Aren't you going to ask Elsie in?"

Mariana stepped back, and Elsie entered the room. She smiled at Mariana and put down her bucket. "That's better. Best prepare yourself, dear."

"What is it?"

"They found another body."

"What? When?"

"This morning—by the river. Another girl."

It took Mariana a second to find her voice.

"Zoe—where's Zoe?"

Elsie shook her head. "Don't worry your pretty head about Zoe. She's safe enough. Probably still lazing in bed, if I know her." She smiled. "I can see it runs in the family."

"For Christ's sake, Elsie—who is it? Tell me."

Elsie smiled. There was something truly ghoulish in her expression. "It was little Serena."

"Oh God—" Mariana's eyes suddenly filled with tears. She choked back a sob.

Elsie tutted sympathetically. "Poor little Serena. Ah, well, the Lord moves in mysterious ways . . . I'd best get on—no rest for the wicked."

She turned to go—then she stopped. "Goodness me. Nearly forgot . . . This was under your door, dear."

Elsie reached into the bucket and pulled something out. She handed it to Mariana.

"Here—"

It was a postcard.

The image on the postcard was one Mariana recognized—a black-and-white Ancient Greek vase, thousands of years old, depicting the sacrifice of Iphigenia by Agamemnon.

As Mariana turned it over, her hand was trembling. And on the back, as she knew there would be, was a handwritten quotation in Ancient Greek:

τοιγάρ σέ ποτ᾽ οὐρανίδαι
πέμψουσιν θανάτοις: ἦ σὰν
ἔτ᾽ ἔτι φόνιον ὑπὸ δέραν
ὄψομαι αἷμα χυθὲν σιδάρῳ

Mariana had a strange feeling of vertigo, of dizziness, as she stared at the postcard in her hand; as if she were looking down on it from a great height—and in danger of losing her balance, and falling down . . . into a deep, dark abyss.

20

Mariana didn't move for a moment. She felt paralyzed, rooted to the spot. She barely noticed Elsie leave the room.

She kept staring at the postcard in her hands, unable to look away, transfixed; as if the Ancient Greek letters had caught fire in her mind, and were blazing and burning themselves into her brain.

With some effort, she turned the postcard facedown, breaking its spell. She needed to think clearly—she needed to work out what to do.

She had to tell the police, of course. Even if they thought she was crazy, which they probably already did, she couldn't keep these postcards to herself any longer—she had to tell Inspector Sangha.

She had to find him.

She slipped the postcard into her back pocket, and left her room.

It was an overcast morning; the morning sun had yet to penetrate the clouds, and a wispy carpet of mist was still hovering in pools above the ground like smoke. And through the gloom, across the courtyard, Mariana made out the figure of a man.

Edward Fosca was standing there.

What was he doing? Waiting to see Mariana's reaction to the postcard? Getting off on it, relishing her torment? She couldn't see his expression, but she felt sure he was smiling.

And Mariana was suddenly very angry.

It was unlike her to lose control—but now, because she had barely slept, and because she was so upset and scared and angry . . . she let go. It wasn't bravery as much as desperation: a violent expulsion of her anguish—directed at Edward Fosca.

Before she knew it, she was charging across the courtyard toward him. Did he flinch a little? Possibly. It was unexpected, this sudden approach, but he stood his ground—even when she reached him and stopped, inches away from his face, her cheeks flushed, her eyes wild, breathing hard.

She didn't say anything. She just stared at him, with mounting anger.

He gave her an uncertain smile. "Good morning, Mariana."

Mariana held up the postcard. "What does it mean?"

"Hmm?"

Fosca took the postcard. He glanced at the inscription on the back. He murmured in Greek as he read it. There was a flicker of a smile on his lips.

"What does it mean?" she repeated.

"It's from *Electra* by Euripides."

"Tell me what it says."

Fosca smiled, and stared into Mariana's eyes. "It means: 'The gods have willed your death—and soon, from your throat, streams of blood shall gush forth at the sword.'"

As Mariana heard this, her anger erupted—the bubble of burning fury burst forth, and her hands clenched into fists. With all of her strength, she struck him in the face.

Fosca reeled backward. "Jesus—"

But before he could catch his breath, Mariana punched him again. And again.

He raised his hands to protect himself—but she kept hitting him, pummeling him with her fists, shouting.

"You bastard—you sick bastard—"

"Mariana—stop! Stop—"

But Mariana couldn't stop, wouldn't stop—until she felt a pair of hands grab her from behind, pulling her back.

A police officer held on to her, forcibly restraining her.

A crowd of onlookers was gathering. Julian was there, staring at her in disbelief.

Another officer went over to assist Fosca—but the professor waved him away angrily. Fosca's nose was bleeding—blood was spattered all over his crisp white shirt. He looked upset and embarrassed. It was the first time Mariana had seen him lose his cool, and she drew some small satisfaction from that.

Chief Inspector Sangha appeared. He stared at Mariana, stunned—as if he were looking at a crazy person.

"What the hell is going on?"

21

Soon afterward, Mariana found herself in the dean's office, and was asked to explain her actions. She sat across the desk from Chief Inspector Sangha, Julian, the dean—and Edward Fosca.

It was hard to find the right words. The more she said, the more she sensed she was being disbelieved. Telling her story, saying it all aloud, she was aware how implausible it sounded.

Edward Fosca had regained his composure; he kept smiling at her the whole time—as if she were telling a long joke and he were anticipating the punch line.

Mariana had also calmed down, and was making an effort to remain calm. She presented the narrative as simply and clearly as she could, with as little emotion as possible. She explained how, step by step, she had arrived at this incredible deduction—that the professor had murdered three of his students.

The Maidens first made her suspicious, she said. A group of favorites, all young women. No one knew what went on at these meetings. And as a group therapist, and a woman, Mariana could scarcely fail to be concerned. Professor Fosca had a kind of strange, guru-like control over his pupils, Mariana said. She had witnessed this firsthand—even her own niece had expressed a reticence to betray Fosca and the group.

"This is typical of unhealthy group behavior—an urge to conform and submit. Voicing opinions contrary to the group, or the group leader, evokes a great deal of anxiety—if they can be voiced at all. I felt it when Zoe spoke about the professor—something wasn't quite right. I could feel she was *afraid* of him."

Small groups like this, Mariana explained, like the Maidens, were particularly vulnerable to unconscious manipulation, or abuse. Unconsciously the girls might treat the leader of the group the way they treated their father when they were very young—with dependence and acquiescence. "And if you're a damaged young woman," she went on, "in denial about your childhood and the suffering you endured—in order to maintain that denial, you might well collude with another abuser—and pretend to yourself that his behavior is perfectly normal. If you were to open your eyes and condemn him, you would have to condemn others in your life also. I don't know what the childhoods of those girls was like. It's easy to dismiss Tara as a privileged young woman with no problems. But to me, her abuse of alcohol and drugs suggests she was troubled—and vulnerable. Beautiful, fucked-up Tara—she was his favorite."

She maintained eye contact with Fosca as she said this, aware of the rising anger in her voice and doing her best to control it. Fosca stared back at her coolly, a smile on his face. She went on, trying to stay calm.

"I realized I was looking at the murders the wrong way around. This wasn't the work of a madman, a psychopathic killer driven by uncontrollable rage—it was just meant to look that way. These girls were murdered methodically and rationally. The only intended victim was Tara."

"And why do you think that?" said Edward Fosca, speaking for the first time.

Mariana looked him in the eyes. "Because Tara was your lover. And then something happened—she discovered you were sleeping with the others?—and threatened to expose you—and then what? You'd lose your job, and this elitist academic world that you cherish; you'd lose your reputation—you couldn't let that happen. You threatened to kill Tara. And you then carried out that threat. Unfortunately for you, she told Zoe first . . . And Zoe told me."

Fosca stared at her. His dark eyes glinted in the light like black ice. "That's your theory, is it?"

"Yes." Mariana held his gaze. "That's my theory. Along with the others, Veronica and Serena gave you an alibi—they were all sufficiently under your spell to do so—but then what? Did they change their minds—or threaten to? Or did you just want to make sure they never would?"

No one answered this question. There was just silence.

The chief inspector didn't say anything; he poured himself some tea. The dean was staring at Mariana with astonishment, clearly unable to believe his ears. Julian wouldn't meet her eye, and made a pretense of looking through his notes.

Edward Fosca spoke first. He addressed Chief Inspector Sangha.

"Obviously, I deny this. All of it. And I'm happy to answer any questions you may have. But first, Inspector—do I need a lawyer?"

The inspector held up his hand. "I don't think we're quite there yet, Professor. If you'll just wait a second." Sangha fixed his eyes on Mariana. "Do you have any evidence at all to back up these accusations?"

Mariana nodded her head. "Yes—these postcards."

"Ah. The famous postcards." Sangha looked down at the postcards in front of him. He picked them up and shuffled them slowly, dealing them like cards.

"If I understand correctly," he said, "you believe they were sent to each victim before the murder, as a kind of calling card? Announcing his intention to kill?"

"Yes, I do."

"And now that you have received one—presumably you are in imminent danger? Why do you think he has chosen you as a victim?"

Mariana shrugged. "I think—I've become a threat to him. I got too close. I got inside his head."

She didn't look at Fosca; she didn't trust herself to retain her composure.

"You know, Mariana," she heard Fosca say, "anyone can copy out a Greek quotation from a book. You don't need a Harvard degree."

"I'm aware of that, Professor. But when I was in your room, I found the same quotation underlined in your own copy of Euripides. Is that just a coincidence?"

Fosca laughed. "If we were to go to my room right now—and take any book off the shelf—you'll see I underline practically *everything*." He went on before she could speak. "And do you honestly believe, if I killed those girls, I would send them postcards quoting texts that *I* teach them? Do you think I would be that stupid?"

Mariana shook her head. "It's not stupid—you didn't think these messages would be understood, or even noticed by the police, or anyone else. It was your private joke—at the girls' expense. That's what made me sure it was you. Psychologically, it's just the kind of thing you *would* do."

Inspector Sangha responded before Fosca could speak. "Fortunately for Professor Fosca, he was seen in college, at the exact time of Serena's murder—at midnight."

"Who saw him?"

The inspector went to pour more tea, but realized the flask was empty. He frowned. "Morris. The head porter. He encountered the professor smoking outside his room, and they spoke for several minutes."

"He's lying."

"Mariana—"

"Listen to me—"

Before Sangha could stop her, Mariana told him she suspected Morris was blackmailing Fosca—that she had followed him, and seen him and Serena together.

The chief inspector seemed mildly stunned. He leaned forward and stared at her.

"You saw them—in the graveyard? I think you'd better tell me exactly what you've been up to."

So she did, going into more detail, and to her dismay, the more the conversation moved away from Edward Fosca, the more the inspector seemed excited about Morris as a suspect.

Julian agreed. "That explains how the killer could move around invisibly. Who goes unnoticed around college? Who don't we see? A man in a uniform—a man with a perfect right to be there. A porter."

"Exactly." The chief inspector thought for a moment. Then he beckoned over one of the junior officers and told him to bring in Morris for questioning.

Mariana was about to intervene, even though she knew there would be little point. But then, Julian smiled at her. He spoke.

"Listen, Mariana. I'm on your side—so don't get upset about what I'm going to say."

"What?"

"To be honest, I noticed it as soon as I saw you here in Cambridge. It struck me straightaway, that you seemed a little strange—a little paranoid."

Mariana couldn't help but laugh. "What?"

"I know it's hard to hear—but it's obvious you're suffering from persecutory feelings. You're unwell, Mariana. You need help. And I'd like to help you . . . if you'll let me—"

"Fuck you, Julian."

The inspector banged his flask on the desk. "That's enough!"

There was silence. Chief Inspector Sangha spoke firmly. "Mariana. You've repeatedly tested my patience. You've made totally unsubstantiated accusations against Professor Fosca—not to mention physically assaulting him. He's perfectly within his rights to press charges."

She tried to interrupt, but Sangha kept talking. "No, enough— you need to listen to me now. I want you gone by tomorrow morning. Away from this college and Professor Fosca—away from this investigation—away from me. Or I will have you arrested and charged with obstructing justice. Is that clear? Listen to Julian, okay? See your doctor. Get some help."

Mariana opened her mouth—and choked back a scream, a howl of frustration. She swallowed her anger, and sat in silence. There was no point in arguing further. She lowered her head, indignant but defeated.

She had lost.

Part Five

The spring is wound up tight. It will uncoil of itself. That is what is so convenient in tragedy. The least little turn of the wrist will do the job.

—JEAN ANOUILH, *Antigone*

I

An hour later, in order to avoid the press, a police car was driven around the back of the college, by the gate, which opened onto a narrow street. Mariana stood among various students and members of staff who gathered to watch as Morris was arrested, handcuffed, and led to the car. Some of the porters booed and jeered at him as he went by. Morris's face colored slightly, but he didn't react. His jaw was clenched, and he kept his eyes low.

At the last minute, Morris looked up—and Mariana followed his eyes . . . to the window—where Edward Fosca was standing.

Fosca was watching the proceedings with a small smile on his face. *He's laughing at us,* Mariana thought.

And as he made eye contact with Morris, a brief spasm of rage flashed across Morris's face.

Then the police officer pulled off his bowler hat—and Morris was bundled into the police car. Mariana watched it drive off, taking him away—and the gate was closed.

Mariana looked up again at Fosca's window.

But he had gone.

"Thank God," she heard the dean say. "At last, it's over."

He was wrong, of course. It was far from over.

• • •

Almost immediately, the weather changed. As if responding to events in college, summer, having held on for so long, finally withdrew. A chilly wind hissed through the courtyards. It started spitting rain, and in the distance, a thunderstorm could be heard rumbling.

Mariana and Zoe were having a drink with Clarissa in the Fellows' Parlor—a common room for the fellows. This afternoon, it was deserted apart from the three women.

It was a large, shadowy room, furnished with ancient leather armchairs and couches, mahogany writing desks, and tables laden with newspapers and journals. It smelled smoky, of wood and ash from the fireplaces. Outside, the wind was rattling the windowpanes, and the rain was tapping on the glass. It was chilly enough for Clarissa to request a small fire be lit.

The three women sat in low armchairs, around the fire, drinking whiskey. Mariana swirled the whiskey around in her glass, watching the amber liquid glow in the firelight. She felt comforted being here, cocooned by the fire with Clarissa and Zoe. This small group gave her strength—and courage. She needed courage now; they all did.

Zoe had come from a class at the English Faculty. Possibly her last class, said Clarissa; there was talk of an imminent closure of the college, pending a police investigation.

Zoe had been caught in the rain; as she dried herself by the fire, Mariana told them what had happened—and about her confrontation with Edward Fosca. When she finished, Zoe spoke in a low voice.

"That was a mistake. Confronting him like that . . . Now he knows you know."

Mariana glanced at Zoe. "I thought you said he was innocent?"

Zoe met her gaze and shook her head. "I changed my mind."

Clarissa looked from one to the other. "You're quite sure, both of you, then, that he *is* guilty? One doesn't want to believe it."

"I know," said Mariana. "But I believe it."

"So do I," said Zoe.

Clarissa didn't reply. She reached for the decanter and refilled her glass. Mariana noticed her hand was trembling.

"What do we do now?" said Zoe. "You're not going to leave, are you?"

"Of course not." Mariana shook her head. "Let him arrest me, I don't care. I'm not going back to London."

Clarissa looked astonished. "What? Why on earth not?"

"I can't run away. Not anymore. I've been running since Sebastian died. I need to stay—I need to face this, whatever it is. I'm not afraid." The phrase sounded unfamiliar on her tongue. Mariana tried it again. *"I'm not afraid."*

Clarissa tutted. "That's the whiskey talking."

"Perhaps." Mariana smiled. "Dutch courage is better than none." She turned to Zoe. "We keep going. That's what we do. We keep going—and we catch him."

"How? We need some proof."

"Yes."

Zoe hesitated. "What about the murder weapon?"

Something about the way she said this made Mariana look at her. "You mean the knife?"

Zoe nodded. "They've not found it yet, have they? I think—I know where it is."

Mariana stared at her. "How do you know that?"

Zoe avoided her eye for a second. She kept looking away at the fire—a furtive, guilty gesture that Mariana recognized from childhood.

"Zoe?"

"It's a long story, Mariana."

"Now's a good time for it. Don't you think?" She lowered her voice. "You know, when I saw the Maidens, they told me something, Zoe . . . They told me that *you* were part of the group."

Zoe's eyes widened. She shook her head. "That's not true."

"Zoe, don't lie—"

"I'm not! I only went once."

"Well, why didn't you tell me?" said Mariana.

"I don't know." Zoe shook her head. "I was afraid. I felt so ashamed . . . I wanted to tell you for so long, but I . . ."

She fell silent. Mariana reached out and touched her hand. "Tell me now. Tell us both."

Zoe's lip trembled a little, and she nodded. She began to speak, and Mariana steeled herself—

And the very first thing Zoe said made Mariana's blood run cold.

"I suppose," Zoe said, "it begins with Demeter—and Persephone." She glanced at Mariana. "You know them, right?"

It took Mariana a second to find her voice.

"Yes." She nodded. "I know them."

2

Zoe drained her drink. She placed it on the mantelpiece. The fire was smoking slightly, and gray-white smoke swirled around her.

Mariana watched Zoe, with the red-and-gold flames dancing beneath her, and Mariana had a funny campfire-like feeling, as if she were about to be told a ghost story . . . Which in a way, she was.

Zoe began telling the story, tentatively at first, bit by bit, that Professor Fosca was so fond of—the secret rites at Eleusis to honor Persephone: rites that took you on a journey from life to death and back again.

The professor knew the secret, he said—and he shared it with a few special students.

"He made me swear an oath of secrecy. I couldn't talk about what happened with anyone. I know it was weird, but—I was flattered that he thought I was special enough—clever enough. And I was curious too. And then . . . it was my turn to be initiated into the Maidens . . . He told me to meet him at the folly, at midnight, for the ceremony."

"The folly?"

"You know—it's by the river, near Paradise."

Mariana nodded. "Go on."

"Just before twelve, Carla and Diya met me at the boathouse, and escorted me—on the river, in a punt."

"A punt, why?"

"It's the easiest way to get there from here—the path is over-grown with brambles." She paused for a moment. "The others were there when I arrived. Veronica and Serena were standing by the entrance to the folly. They were wearing masks—meant to be Persephone and Demeter."

"Good God," said Clarissa, letting out an involuntary groan of disbelief. She quickly gestured at Zoe to continue.

"Lillian led me into the folly—the professor was waiting there. He put a blindfold on me, and then—I drank the *kykeon*—which he said was just barley water. But he was lying. Tara told me later it was spiked with GHB—he used to buy it from Conrad."

Mariana was feeling unbearably tense—she didn't want to hear anymore. But she knew she had no choice. "Go on."

"And then," Zoe said, "he whispered in my ear . . . that I would die tonight—and be reborn at dawn. And he took out a knife, and he touched my throat with it."

"He did that?" said Mariana.

"He didn't cut me or anything—he said it was just a ritual sacrifice. Then he took off my blindfold . . . And that's when I saw where he put the knife . . . He slid it into a gap in the wall—between two stone slabs."

Zoe shut her eyes for a second. "After that, it's hard to remem-ber. My legs were like jelly, like I was melting . . . And we left the folly. We were in the trees . . . in the woodland. Some of the girls were dancing naked . . . the others were in the river, swimming—but I—I didn't want to take my clothes off . . ." She shook her head. "I don't remember exactly. But I lost them, somehow—and I was alone, and high—and scared—and . . . he was there."

"Edward Fosca?"

"That's right." Zoe seemed unwilling to say his name. "I tried to speak but couldn't. He kept—kissing me . . . touching me—saying he loved me. His eyes were wild . . . I remember his eyes—they

were crazy. I tried to get away . . . But I couldn't. And then—Tara
appeared, and they started kissing—and somehow, I managed to
get away—I ran through the trees—I kept running . . ." She lowered her head, and fell silent for a moment. "I kept running . . . I
got away."

Mariana prompted her. "What happened then, Zoe?"

Zoe shrugged. "Nothing. I never spoke to the girls about it
again—apart from Tara."

"And Professor Fosca?"

"He acted as if it never happened. So I—tried to pretend it
hadn't." She shrugged. "But then Tara found me that night in my
room . . . She told me he had threatened to kill her. I'd never seen
Tara so scared—she was terrified."

Clarissa spoke in a low voice. "Dear girl, you should have alerted
the college. You should have told someone. You should have come
to *me*."

"Would you have believed me, Clarissa? It's such a crazy story—
it's my word against his."

Mariana nodded, feeling close to tears. She wanted to reach out
and pull Zoe into a hug and hold her.

But first, there was something she had to know.

"Zoe—why now? Why are you telling us this now?"

Zoe didn't speak for a moment. She went over to the armchair
where her jacket was hanging, drying by the fire. She reached into
the pocket.

She pulled out a slightly damp, rain-speckled postcard.

Zoe dropped it in Mariana's lap.

"Because I got one too."

3

Mariana stared at the postcard in her lap.

The image was from a murky rococo painting—Iphigenia naked on a bed, with Agamemnon creeping up behind her, brandishing a knife. On the back, there was an inscription in Ancient Greek. Mariana didn't bother to get Clarissa to translate. There was no point.

She needed to be strong for Zoe. She needed to think clearly and think fast. She kept all emotion out of her voice.

"When did you receive this, Zoe?"

"This afternoon. It was under my door."

"I see." Mariana nodded to herself. "This changes things."

"No, it doesn't."

"Yes, it does. We need to get you out of here. Now. We need to go to London."

"Thank goodness for that," said Clarissa.

"No." Zoe shook her head. She had a fiercely stubborn look on her face. "I'm not a child. I'm not going anywhere. I'm staying here, like you said—we're going to fight. We're going to catch him."

As she said this, Mariana thought how vulnerable Zoe looked, how tired and wretched. Recent events had visibly affected and altered her—she looked mentally as well as physically beaten up.

So fragile, yet so determined to keep going. *That's what bravery looks like,* thought Mariana. *This is courage.*

Clarissa also seemed to sense this. She spoke in a quiet voice.

"Zoe, dear child," she said, "your bravery is commendable. But Mariana is right. We must go to the police, tell them everything you've just said . . . And then, you must leave Cambridge—both of you. Tonight."

Zoe pulled a face and shook her head. "No point in telling the police, Clarissa. They'll think Mariana put me up to it. That's a waste of time. We don't have time. We need *evidence.*"

"Zoe—"

"No, listen." She appealed to Mariana. "Let's check the folly—just in case. Where I saw him hide the knife. And if we don't find it, then . . . we go to London, okay?"

Before Mariana could reply, the professor forestalled her.

"Good God," said Clarissa. "Are you trying to get yourselves killed?"

"No." Zoe shook her head. "The murders always happen at night—we still have a few hours." She glanced out the window, and gave Mariana a hopeful look. "And it's stopped raining. It's brightening up."

"Not yet," Mariana said, looking outside. "But it will." She thought for a second. "Go and have a shower, get out of those wet clothes. And I'll meet you in your room in twenty minutes."

"Okay." Zoe nodded, looking pleased.

Mariana watched her gather her things. "Zoe—please be careful."

Zoe nodded, and left the room. The moment the door closed, Clarissa turned on Mariana. She looked worried. "Mariana, I must protest. It's most unsafe for either of you to be venturing to the river like this—"

Mariana shook her head. "I've no intention of letting Zoe go anywhere near the river. I'll make her pack a few things, and we'll leave right away. We'll go to London, like you said."

"Thank heavens." Clarissa looked relieved. "That's the right decision."

"But listen carefully. If anything happens to me—I want you to go to the police, okay? You must tell them all of this—everything that Zoe said. Understand?"

Clarissa nodded. She looked deeply unhappy. "I wish you two would go to the police right now."

"Zoe's right—there's no point. Inspector Sangha won't even listen to me. But he'll listen to you."

Clarissa didn't say anything. She just sighed and stared into the fire.

"I'll call you from London," Mariana said.

No response. Clarissa didn't even seem to hear her.

Mariana felt disappointed. She had expected more. She expected Clarissa to be a tower of strength—but clearly this had all been too much for her. Clarissa seemed to have aged somehow; she seemed shrunken, small, and frail.

She wouldn't be any use, Mariana realized. Whatever terrors she and Zoe had ahead, they'd have to face them alone.

Mariana gently kissed the professor goodbye on the cheek. Then she left her by the fire.

4

As Mariana made her way to Zoe's room across the courtyard, she kept her mind on practicalities. They would pack quickly, and then, without being seen, they would slip out of the college, through the back gate. A cab to the station; the train to King's Cross. And then—and her heart swelled at the thought of it—they would be home, safe and sound in the little yellow house.

She climbed the stone steps to Zoe's room. The room was empty; she must still be in the shower block downstairs.

And then Mariana's phone rang. It was Fred.

She hesitated, but answered. "Hello?"

"Mariana, it's me." Fred sounded anxious. "I need to talk to you. It's important."

"Now isn't a good time. I think we said everything last night."

"This isn't about last night. Listen to me, carefully. I mean it. I had a premonition—about *you*."

"Fred, I don't have time—"

"I know you don't believe it—but it's true. You're in serious danger. Right now, this *second*. Wherever you are—get the hell out of there. Go. Run—"

Mariana hung up, feeling exasperated and very angry. She had enough to worry about without Fred's nonsense. She had already been feeling anxious—now she felt much worse.

What was keeping Zoe?

As Mariana waited, she paced the room restlessly. Her eyes drifted around, touching upon Zoe's belongings: a baby picture in a silver frame; a photo of Zoe as a bridesmaid at Mariana's wedding; various lucky charms and trinkets, stones and crystals collected on holidays abroad; other childhood mementos Zoe had been carrying around since she was a little girl—such as old, battered Zebra, perched precariously on her pillow.

Mariana felt incredibly moved by this jumble of junk. She had a sudden memory of Zoe as a small child, kneeling against the bed, hands clasped in prayer. *God bless Mariana, God bless Sebastian, God bless Grandfather, God bless Zebra*—and so on, including people whose names she didn't even know, like the unhappy woman at the bus stop, or the man in the bookshop with the cold. Mariana would watch this childish ritual fondly, but not for one moment did she ever believe in what Zoe was doing. Mariana didn't believe in a God who could be reached so easily—or whose merciless heart would be swayed by the prayers of a little girl.

But now, suddenly, she felt her knees giving way—buckling, as if pushed from behind by some unseen force. She sank to the floor, clasping her hands together—and bowed her head in prayer.

But Mariana didn't pray to God, or Jesus, or even to Sebastian.

She prayed to a handful of dirty, weather-beaten stone columns on a hill, against a brilliant, birdless sky.

She prayed to the goddess.

"Forgive me," she whispered. "Whatever it is I did—whatever it is I have done—to offend you. You took Sebastian. That's enough. I beg you—don't take Zoe. Please—I won't let you. I—"

She stopped, suddenly self-conscious, embarrassed at the words coming out of her mouth. She felt more than a little crazy—like a demented child bargaining with the universe.

And yet, on some very deep level, Mariana was aware that, at long last, she had reached the moment where all of this had been leading: her much delayed but inevitable confrontation—her reckoning—with the Maiden.

Mariana slowly pulled herself to her feet.

And Zebra toppled off the pillow, fell off the bed, and landed on the floor.

Mariana picked up the toy and repositioned it on the pillow. As she did so, she noticed that the seam across Zebra's belly had come loose; three stitches were missing. And something was poking out from inside the stuffing.

Mariana hesitated—then, without quite knowing what she was doing, she pulled it out. She looked at it. It was some paper, folded and refolded, concealed in the body of the stuffed toy.

Mariana stared at it. She felt disloyal, but also compelled to know what it was. She had to know.

She carefully unfolded it—and it opened out into several pages of notepaper. It looked like a typed letter of some kind.

Mariana sat down on the bed.

And she began to read.

5

And then, one day, my mother left.

I don't remember the exact moment she went, or the final goodbye, but there must have been one. I don't remember my father there either—he must have been in the fields when she made her escape.

She never did send for me, you know, in the end. I never saw her again, in fact.

That night she left, I went upstairs to my room, and sat at my little desk—I wrote for hours in my journal. When I finished, I didn't read what I had written.

And I never wrote in that journal again. I put it in a box and hid it away with other things I wanted to forget.

But today, I took it out for the first time, and read it—all of it.

Well, almost all . . .

You see, there are two pages missing.

Two pages torn out.

They were destroyed because they were dangerous. Why? Because they told a different story.

That's okay, I guess. Every story can stand a little revision.

I wish I could revise the next few years at the farm—revise them, or forget them.

The pain, the fear, the humiliation—every day, I was more determined to escape. *One day, I'll get away. I'll be free. I'll be safe. I'll be happy. I'll be loved.*

I'd repeat this to myself, again and again, under the covers at night. It became my mantra in times of trouble. More than that, it became my vocation.

It led me to you.

I never thought I was capable—of love, I mean. I only knew hate. I'm so afraid I'll hate you too, one day. But before I ever hurt you, I will turn the knife on myself, and plunge it deep into my heart.

I love you, Zoe.

That's why I'm writing this.

I want you to see me as I am. And then? You'll forgive me, won't you? Kiss all my wounds and make them better. You are my destiny, you know that, don't you? Maybe you don't believe it yet. But I've known from the start. I had a premonition—from the very first second I saw you, I knew.

You were so shy at first, so mistrustful. I had to slowly tease your love out of you. But I'm nothing if not patient.

We will be together, I promise, one day, once my plan is complete. My brilliant, beautiful idea.

I must warn you, it involves blood—and sacrifice.

I'll explain, when we are alone. Until then, have faith.

Yours,

forever—

X

6

Mariana lowered the letter to her lap.

She stared at it.

She was finding it hard to think—hard to breathe; as if she had been winded, punched repeatedly in the stomach. She didn't understand what she had read. What did it mean, this monstrous document?

It didn't make sense. She didn't believe it was real—she wouldn't believe it. It couldn't mean what she thought. It couldn't be that. And yet—that was the only conclusion to draw, no matter how unacceptable or nonsensical—or terrifying.

Edward Fosca had written it—this hellish love letter—and he had written it to Zoe.

Mariana shook her head. No—not Zoe, *her* Zoe. She didn't believe it—she didn't believe Zoe could possibly be involved with that *monster* . . .

Then she suddenly remembered that strange look on Zoe's face—staring at Fosca across the courtyard. A look Mariana had taken for fear. What if it was something more complicated?

What if, from the very start, Mariana had been seeing everything from the wrong angle, looking at it from very way up? What if—

Footsteps—coming up the stairs.

Mariana froze. She didn't know what to do—she must say something, do something. But not now, not like this; she had to think first.

She grabbed the letter and stuffed it in her pocket, just as Zoe appeared at the door.

"Sorry, Mariana. I was as quick as I could."

Zoe gave her a smile as she entered the room. Her cheeks were flushed, and her hair was wet. She was in a dressing gown and clutching a couple of towels. "Let me just get dressed. One sec."

Mariana didn't say anything. Zoe put on some clothes, and that quick flash of nakedness—that young, smooth skin—reminded Mariana for a second of the beautiful baby girl she had loved, that beautiful, innocent child. Where had she gone? What happened?

Tears came into her eyes, but not sentimental tears; tears of anguish, of physical pain—as if someone had slapped her face. She turned away so Zoe wouldn't see, and hastily wiped her eyes.

"I'm ready," said Zoe. "Shall we go?"

"Go?" Mariana looked at her blankly. "Where?"

"To the folly, of course. To look for the knife."

"What? Oh . . ."

Zoe looked at her with surprise. "Are you all right?"

Mariana slowly nodded. All hopes of escape, all thoughts of fleeing to London with Zoe, had faded from her mind. There was nowhere to go, nowhere to run. Not anymore.

"Okay," she said.

And like a sleepwalker, Mariana followed Zoe down the stairs and across the courtyard. It had stopped raining; the sky was leaden, and oppressive charcoal clouds swarmed above their heads, twisting and turning in the breeze.

Zoe glanced at her. "We should go by the river. It's the easiest way."

Mariana didn't say anything, just gave a brief nod.

"I can punt," Zoe said. "I'm not as good as Sebastian was, but I'm not bad."

Mariana nodded, and followed her to the river.

Outside the boathouse, seven punts were creaking in the water, chained to the bank. Zoe took one of the poles resting against the boathouse wall. She waited for Mariana to climb into a punt, then loosened the heavy chain securing it to the bank.

Mariana sat on the low wooden seat; it was damp from the rain, but she barely noticed that.

"This won't take long," Zoe said as she pushed them away from the bank with the pole. Then she raised the pole high in the air, plunged it into the water, and began their journey.

They weren't alone; Mariana knew that right from the start. She could sense they were being followed. She resisted the temptation to look over her shoulder. But when she finally did turn her head, just as she expected, she briefly glimpsed the figure of a man in the distance, vanishing behind a tree.

But Mariana decided she must be imagining things. Because it wasn't who she was expecting to see—it wasn't Edward Fosca.

It was Fred.

7

As Zoe had predicted, they made fast progress. They soon left the colleges behind, and were surrounded by open fields on either side of the river—a natural landscape that had survived unchanged for centuries.

On the grassland, there were some black cows grazing. There was a smell of dampness and moldering oak, wet mud. And Mariana could smell smoke from a bonfire somewhere, a musty smell of damp leaves burning.

A thin layer of mist was rising up from the river, and it swirled around Zoe as she punted. She was so beautiful standing there, her hair blowing in the breeze, that faraway look in her eyes. She resembled the Lady of Shalott on her doomed, final journey along the river.

Mariana was trying to think, but she was finding it difficult. And with each muffled thud of the pole on the riverbed, and each sudden rush forward of the punt on the surface of the water, she knew time was running out. Soon they would be at the folly.

And then what?

She could feel the letter burning in her pocket—she knew she needed to make sense of it.

But she must be wrong. She had to be.

"You're being very quiet," Zoe said. "What's on your mind?"

Mariana looked up. She tried to speak, but couldn't find her voice. She shook her head and shrugged. "Nothing."

"We'll be there soon." Zoe pointed toward the bend in the river. Mariana turned and looked. "Oh—"

To her surprise, a swan had appeared in the water. It glided effortlessly toward her, its dirty white feathers rippling gently in the breeze. As it neared the punt, the swan turned its long head and looked directly at her. Its black eyes stared into hers.

And a shiver ran down Mariana's spine. She looked away.

When she looked back, the swan had vanished.

"We're here," Zoe said. "Look."

Mariana saw the folly, on the bank of the river. It wasn't a large structure—four stone columns supporting a sloping roof. Originally white, it had been discolored by two centuries of relentless rain and wind, staining it gold and green with rust and algae.

It was an eerie location for the folly—alone, by the water's edge, surrounded by a woodland and marsh. Zoe and Mariana sailed past it, past the wild irises growing in the water, and the rambling roses covered in thorns, blocking the path.

Zoe guided the punt to the bank. She wedged the pole deep into the mud of the riverbed, mooring the punt, pinning it against the river's edge.

Zoe climbed onto the bank—and held out her hand to help Mariana. But Mariana didn't take her hand. She couldn't bear to touch her.

"Are you sure you're okay?" said Zoe. "You're being so weird."

Mariana didn't reply. She clambered out of the punt, onto the grassy bank, and followed Zoe over to the folly.

She paused outside and looked up at it.

It had a coat of arms above the entrance, carved in stone—the emblem of a swan in a storm.

Mariana froze when she saw that. She stared at it for a second.

But then she kept going.

She followed Zoe inside.

8

Inside the folly, there were two windows in the stone wall, looking out onto the river, and a stone window seat. Zoe pointed through the window, at the green woodland in the near distance.

"They found Tara's body over there—through the trees, by the marsh. I'll show you." Then she knelt down, and looked under the seat. "And this is where he put the knife. In here—"

Zoe slid her arm into a space between two stone slabs. And she smiled.

"Aha."

Zoe withdrew her hand—and she was clutching a knife. It was about eight inches long. It was stained slightly with red rust—or dried blood.

Mariana watched Zoe grip it by the handle; she held it with a sense of familiarity—and then she stood up, turned the knife toward Mariana.

She pointed the blade directly at her. She stared at Mariana without blinking, her blue eyes radiating darkness.

"Come on," she said. "We're going for a walk."

"What?"

"That way—through the trees. Let's go."

"Wait. Stop." Mariana shook her head. "This isn't you."

"What?"

"This isn't you, Zoe. This is *him*."

"What are you talking about?"

"Listen. *I know.* I found the letter."

"What letter?"

In response, Mariana took out the letter from her pocket. She unfolded it and showed it to Zoe.

"This letter."

Zoe didn't speak for a second. She just stared at Mariana. No emotional reaction. Just a blank look.

"You read it?"

"I didn't mean to find it. It was an accident—"

"Did you read it?"

Mariana nodded and whispered, "Yes."

There was a flash of fury in Zoe's eyes. "You had no right!"

Mariana stared at her. "Zoe. I don't understand. It—it doesn't mean—it can't possibly mean—"

"What? What can't it mean?"

Mariana struggled to find the words. "That you had something to do with these murders . . . That *you and he* . . . are somehow *involved*—"

"He loved me. We loved each other—"

"No, Zoe. This is important. I'm saying this because I love you. You are a victim here. Despite whatever you may think, *it wasn't love*—"

Zoe tried to interrupt, but Mariana wouldn't let her. She went on.

"I know you don't want to hear it. I know you think it was deeply romantic, but whatever he gave you, it was not love. Edward Fosca is not capable of love. He's too damaged, too dangerous—"

"Edward Fosca?" Zoe stared at her with a look of astonishment. "You think *Edward Fosca* wrote the letter?—and that's why I kept it safe, hidden in my room?" She shook her head scornfully. *"He* didn't write it."

"Then who did?"

The sun suddenly went behind a cloud, and time seemed to slow to a crawl. Mariana could hear the first drops of rain, tapping at the stone windowsill in the folly, and an owl screeching somewhere in the distance. And in this timeless space, Mariana realized something: she already knew what Zoe was going to say, and perhaps, on some level, she had always known.

Then the sun came out again—time caught up with itself with an abrupt jolt. And Mariana repeated the question.

"Who wrote the letter, Zoe?"

Zoe stared at her, her eyes full of tears. She spoke in a whisper.

"Sebastian, of course."

Part Six

Oft have I heard that grief softens the mind,
And makes it fearful and degenerate;
Think therefore on revenge, and cease to weep.

—WILLIAM SHAKESPEARE, *Henry VI, Part 2*

I

Mariana and Zoe stared at each other in silence.

It was raining now, and Mariana could hear and smell the rain hitting the mud outside. She could see raindrops breaking up the reflections of shivering, shaking trees in the river. Finally, she broke the silence.

"You're lying," she said.

"No." Zoe shook her head. "I'm not. Sebastian wrote the letter. He wrote it to me."

"That's not true. He—" Mariana struggled to find the words. "Sebastian—didn't write this."

"Of course he did. Wake up. You're so blind, Mariana."

Mariana glanced at the letter in her hand. She stared at it helplessly. "You . . . and Sebastian . . ." She couldn't finish the sentence. She looked up at Zoe, desperately, hoping she would take pity on her.

But Zoe only had pity for herself, and her eyes glittered as they brimmed with tears. "I loved him, Mariana. I loved him—"

"No. No—"

"It's true. I've been in love with Sebastian ever since I can remember—ever since I was a little girl. And he loved *me*."

"Zoe, stop. Please—"

"You have to face it, now. Open your eyes. We were lovers. We were lovers ever since that trip to Greece. On my fifteenth birthday, in Athens, remember? Sebastian took me into the olive grove, by the house—he made love to me, there, in the dirt."

"No." Mariana wanted to laugh, but it was too sick to laugh at. It was horrible. "You're lying—"

"No, *you're* lying—to yourself—that's why you're so fucked up—because deep down, you know the truth. It was all bull-shit. Sebastian never loved *you*. It was me he loved—always me. He only married you to be near me . . . And for the *money*, of course . . . you know that, don't you?"

Mariana shook her head. "I'm—I'm not listening to this."

She turned and walked out of the folly. She kept walking.

Then she started to run.

2

"Mariana," Zoe called after her. "Where are you going? You can't run away. Not anymore."

Mariana ignored her and kept going. Zoe followed her.

The dark clouds thundered above, and suddenly, there was a massive streak of lightning. The sky was almost green. Then, the heavens opened. Rain started falling heavily, pummeling the earth, churning up the surface of the river.

Mariana ran into the wood. It was dark and gloomy in the trees. The ground was moist, sticky, and it smelled dank. The interlocking branches of the trees were covered with intricate cobwebs, mummified bluebottles, and other insects, suspended in silken strands above her head.

Zoe followed, taunting her; her voice echoing through the trees.

"One day, Grandfather caught us in the olive grove. He threatened to tell you—so Sebastian had to kill him. He suffocated him right then with those giant hands of his. Then Grandfather left you all that money . . . *So much money*—it dazzled Sebastian—he had to have it. He wanted it for me, for him—for *us*. But you were in the way . . ."

The branches from the trees grabbed at Mariana as she fought her way past, tearing and scratching her hands and her arms.

She could hear Zoe close behind her, crashing through the trees, like an avenging Fury. All the time, she kept talking.

"Sebastian said if anything happened to you, he'd be the first suspect. 'We need a distraction,' he said, *like in a magic trick.*' Remember the tricks he used to do for me when I was little? 'We need to make everyone look at the wrong thing—and in the wrong place.' I told him about Professor Fosca and the Maidens—and that's when he got the idea. It grew in his mind like a beautiful flower, he said—he had such a poetic way of talking—remember? He worked out every detail. And it was beautiful. It was perfect. But then . . . you took him away—and he never came back. Sebastian didn't want to go to Naxos. You made him. It's your fault he's dead."

"No," Mariana whispered. "That's not fair—"

"Yes, it is," Zoe hissed. "You killed him. *And you killed me too.*"

Suddenly, the trees thinned out in front of them—and they found themselves in a clearing. The marsh spread out before them. It was a large pool of limpid green water, overgrown with weeds and brambles. There was a fallen tree, split open and slowly rotting, covered in yellow-green moss and surrounded by spotted toadstools.

And there was a strange smell of decay, a stench of something foul and rotten—was it the stagnant water?

Or was it—death?

Zoe stared at Mariana, breathless, holding the knife. Her eyes were red and full of tears.

"When he died, it was like I'd been stabbed in the guts. I didn't know what to do with all my anger—all my pain . . . Then, one day—I understood—I saw. I had to carry out Sebastian's plan for him, just like he wanted. It was the last thing I'd be able to do for him. To honor him, and his memory—and have my revenge."

Mariana stared at her, incredulous. She was barely able to find her voice. She spoke in a whisper.

"What have you done, Zoe?"

"Not *me. Him*. It was all *Sebastian* . . . I just did what he told me to. It was a labor of love—I copied out the quotes he selected, planted the postcards like he said, underlined the passages in Fosca's books. When I had a supervision, I pretended to go to the bathroom, and planted some hairs from Tara's head in the back of Fosca's wardrobe—I spattered some of her blood there too. The police haven't found it yet. But they will."

"Edward Fosca is innocent? You framed him?"

"No." Zoe shook her head. "*You* framed him, Mariana. Sebastian said all I had to do was make you think I was afraid of Fosca. You did the rest. That was the funniest part of this whole performance: watching you play detective." She smiled. "You're not the detective . . . You're the *victim*."

Mariana stared into Zoe's eyes, as all the pieces came together in her mind, and she finally faced the terrible truth she had wanted to avoid seeing. There was a word for this moment in Greek tragedy: *anagnorisis*—recognition—the moment the hero finally sees the truth and understands his fate—and how it's always been there, the whole time, in front of him. Mariana used to wonder what that moment felt like. Now she knew.

"You killed them—those girls—how could you?"

"The Maidens were never important, Mariana—they were just a distraction. A red herring, that's what Sebastian said." She shrugged. "Tara was . . . difficult. But Sebastian said it was a sacrifice I had to make. He was right. It was a relief, in a way."

"A relief?"

"To finally see myself clearly. I know who I am now—I'm like Clytemnestra, you know?—or Medea. That's what I'm made of."

"No. No, you're wrong." Mariana turned away. She couldn't bear to look at her anymore. The tears streamed down her cheeks. "You're not a goddess, Zoe. You're a monster."

"If I am," she heard Zoe say, "Sebastian made me one. And so did you."

And then, Mariana felt a sudden force to her back.

She was knocked to the ground, with Zoe on her back. Mariana struggled, but Zoe used all of her weight, pinning Mariana down in the mud. The earth was cold and wet against Mariana's face. And she heard Zoe whispering in her ear.

"Tomorrow, when they find your body, I'll say to the inspector I tried to stop you, that I begged you not to investigate the folly alone—but you insisted. Clarissa will tell him my story about Professor Fosca—they'll search his rooms—find the evidence I put there . . ."

Zoe climbed off Mariana and flipped her onto her back. She loomed over her, raising the knife. Her eyes were wild, monstrous.

"And you'll be remembered as just another of Edward Fosca's victims. Victim number four. No one will ever guess the truth . . . that *we* killed you—*Sebastian and I.*"

She raised the knife higher . . . about to strike—

And Mariana suddenly found her strength. She reached up and grabbed Zoe's arm. They tussled for a moment before Mariana swung Zoe's hand as hard as she could—making Zoe lose control of the knife—

The knife flew out of her hand, and whizzed through the air—disappearing into the nearby grass with a thud.

Zoe leaped up with a cry, and ran to look for it.

While Zoe searched, Mariana pulled herself up—and noticed someone appearing behind the trees.

It was Fred.

He was hurrying over, looking concerned. He didn't see Zoe kneeling in the grass, and Mariana tried to warn him. "Fred—stop. Stop—"

But Fred didn't stop and quickly reached her. "Are you okay? I followed you—I was worried, and—"

Over his shoulder, Mariana saw Zoe rising up—clutching the knife. Mariana screamed.

"Fred—"

But too late . . . Zoe plunged the knife deep into Fred's back. His eyes widened—and he stared at Mariana in shock.

He collapsed and sank to the ground—and lay there, still,

unmoving. A pool of blood seeped out from under him. Zoe pulled out the knife and prodded Fred with it, checking if he was dead. She didn't look convinced.

Without thinking, Mariana closed her hand around a hard, cold rock that was embedded in the mud. She pulled it out.

She staggered over to Zoe, bending over Fred's body.

Just as Zoe was about to thrust the knife into his chest . . . Mariana slammed down the rock on the back of Zoe's head.

The blow knocked Zoe sideways—as she fell, slipping in the mud, she landed facedown—on the knife.

Zoe lay still for a second. Mariana thought she was dead.

But then, with an animal-like groan, Zoe threw herself onto her back. She lay there, a wounded creature, with wide, scared eyes. She saw the impaled knife sticking out of her chest—

And Zoe started to scream.

She didn't stop screaming: she was hysterical, screaming in agony and fear and horror—the screams of a terrified child.

For the first time in her life, Mariana didn't go to Zoe's aid. Instead, she pulled out her phone. She called for the police.

All the time, Zoe kept screaming, screaming—until, eventually . . . her screams merged with the wail of an approaching siren.

3

Zoe was taken away in an ambulance, accompanied by two armed police officers.

The escort was hardly necessary, as she had regressed to being a child: a frightened, defenseless little girl. Nonetheless, Zoe was charged with attempted murder; further charges were to follow. Only attempted murder—because Fred had survived the attack, just about. He was critically wounded, and driven to hospital in a separate ambulance.

Mariana was in a state of shock. She was sitting on a bench by the river's edge. She was clutching a cup of strong, sweet tea that Inspector Sangha had poured for her from his flask—for the shock, and as a peace offering.

It had stopped raining. The sky was clear now; the clouds had rained themselves out, leaving only a few wisps of gray in the pale light. The sun was slowly setting behind the trees, and streaking the sky with pink and gold.

As Mariana sat there, she brought the warm cup to her lips and sipped the tea. A female officer attempted to comfort her, putting an arm around her—but Mariana barely noticed this. A blanket was tucked over her knees. She was scarcely aware of it. Her mind was blank as her eyes drifted along the river—and she saw the swan. It was racing along the water, gathering speed.

As she watched it, the swan spread its wings, and took flight. It flew up into the sky, and her eyes followed it into the heavens.

Inspector Sangha joined her and sat down on the bench. "You'll be glad to know," he said, "Fosca has been fired. Turns out he was sleeping with all of them. Morris confessed to blackmailing him—so you were right. With any luck, they'll both get what's coming to them."

Looking at Mariana, he saw she wasn't taking any of it in. He nodded at the tea. He spoke gently.

"How are you? Feeling any better?"

Mariana glanced at him. She gave a slight shake of the head. She didn't feel better; if anything, she felt worse . . .

And yet something was different. What was it?

She felt alert, somehow—perhaps *awake* was a better word: everything seemed clearer, as if a fog had lifted; colors were sharper, the edges of things more defined. The world no longer felt muted and gray and far away—behind a veil.

It felt alive again, and vivid, and full of color, wet with autumn rain; and vibrating with the eternal hum of endless birth and death.

Epilogue

For a long time after that, Mariana remained in shock.

Back at home, she slept on the sofa downstairs at night. She'd never be able to sleep in that bed again; the bed she'd shared with him—that man. She didn't know who he was anymore. She saw him as a kind of stranger, an impostor she had been living with all these years—an actor who had shared her bed and plotted to kill her.

Who was he, this pretend person? What lay beneath his beautiful mask? Was it all a performance—all of it?

Now that the show was over, Mariana had to examine her own role in it. Which wasn't easy.

As she shut her eyes and tried to visualize his face, she struggled to see his features right. He was fading, like the memory of a dream—and she kept seeing her father's face instead—her father's eyes, instead of Sebastian's; as if they were somehow essentially the same person.

What was it Ruth had said—about her father being central to her story? Mariana hadn't understood it at the time.

But now, perhaps, she was beginning to.

She hadn't been back to see Ruth. Not yet. She wasn't ready to cry, or talk, or feel. It was still too raw.

Nor had Mariana returned to running her therapy groups. How could she presume to help another person, or offer any advice, ever again?

She was lost.

And as for Zoe—well, she never recovered from that hysterical screaming fit. She survived the stabbing, but it precipitated a severe psychological collapse. Following her arrest, Zoe attempted suicide several times, then suffered a massive psychotic breakdown.

Zoe ended up being declared unfit to stand trial. She was eventually committed to a secure unit, the Grove, in North London—the same unit where Mariana had recommended Theo apply for a job.

And it turned out that Theo had followed her advice. He was now working at the Grove—and Zoe was his patient.

Theo attempted to contact Mariana several times, on Zoe's behalf. But Mariana refused to speak to him, and didn't return his calls.

She knew what Theo wanted. He wanted to get Mariana to speak to Zoe. She didn't blame him. If Mariana had been in his shoes, she would have done the same thing. Any kind of positive communication between the two women would be pivotal in Zoe's recovery.

But Mariana had her own recovery to worry about.

She couldn't stomach the thought of speaking to Zoe again. It made her feel sick. She simply couldn't bear it.

It wasn't a question of forgiveness. That wasn't something Mariana could decide on, anyway. Ruth always said that forgiveness could not be coerced—it was experienced spontaneously, as an act of grace, appearing only when a person was ready.

And Mariana was not ready. She wasn't sure she ever would be.

She felt such anger, such hurt. If she ever saw Zoe again, she didn't know what she might say or do; she certainly wouldn't be responsible for her actions. Better keep away, and leave Zoe to her fate.

Mariana visited Fred a few times, though, while he was in the hospital. She felt a responsibility to Fred, and a gratitude. He had saved her life, after all; she'd never forget that. He was weak at first, unable to talk—but had a smile on his face the whole time Mariana was there. They sat together in friendly silence, and Mariana thought how odd it was, how comfortable and familiar she felt with him—this man she barely knew. It was too soon to say if anything might ever happen between them. But she no longer dismissed it quite so out of hand.

She was feeling very differently about everything, these days.

It were as if every single thing Mariana had ever known, or believed in, or trusted, had fallen away—leaving just an empty, vacant space. She existed in this limbo of emptiness, which lasted for weeks, then months . . .

Until, one day, she received a letter from Theo.

In his letter, Theo asked Mariana once again to reconsider her refusal to visit Zoe. He wrote insightfully about Zoe, with great empathy, before turning his attention to Mariana.

> *I can't help but feel it might benefit you as much as her—and provide you with some kind of closure. I know it won't be pleasant, but I think it might help. I can't begin to imagine what you've been through. Zoe is beginning to open up more—and I'm deeply disturbed by the secret world she shared with your late husband. I'm hearing things that are truly frightening. And I must say, Mariana, I think you're extremely lucky to be alive.*

Theo finished by saying this:

> *I know it's not easy. But all I ask is that you consider, on some level, that she is a victim too.*

That phrase made Mariana very angry. She tore up the letter, and threw it in the bin.

But that night, as she lay in bed and shut her eyes—a face

appeared in her mind. Not the face of Sebastian, or her father's face—but the face of a little girl.

A small, frightened girl of six.

Zoe's face.

What happened to her? What had been done to that child? What did she endure—right under Mariana's nose—in the shadows, in the wings, just behind the scenes?

Mariana had failed Zoe. She had failed to protect her—she had failed even to *see*—and she must take responsibility for that.

How had she been so blind? She needed to know. She had to understand. She had to confront it. She had to face it—

Or she would go mad.

Which is why, one snowy February morning, Mariana ended up making her way to North London, to Edgware hospital—and to the Grove. Theo was waiting for her in the reception. He greeted her warmly.

"I never thought I'd see you here," he said. "Funny, the way things turn out."

"Yes, I suppose it is."

Theo led her through security and along the dilapidated corridors of the unit. As they walked, he warned Mariana that Zoe would be distinctly different from when she last saw her.

"Zoe's extremely unwell, Mariana. You'll find her quite changed. I think you should prepare yourself."

"I see."

"I'm so glad you came. It will really help. She speaks of you often, you know. She frequently requests to see you."

Mariana didn't reply. Theo gave her a sidelong look.

"Look, I know this can't be easy," he said. "I don't expect you to feel in any way *benign* toward her."

I don't, Mariana thought.

Theo seemed to read her mind. He nodded. "I understand. I know she tried to hurt you."

"She tried to kill me, Theo."

"I don't think it's quite that simple, Mariana." Theo hesitated.

"*He* tried to kill you. She was merely his proxy. His puppet. She was entirely controlled by him. But that was only part of her, you know—in another part of her mind, she still loves you—and needs you."

Mariana was feeling increasingly apprehensive. Coming here had been a mistake. She wasn't ready to see Zoe; wasn't ready for how it would make her feel—and what she might say, or do.

As they reached his office, Theo nodded at another door at the end of the corridor.

"Zoe's in the recreation room, through there. She doesn't tend to socialize with the others, but we always make her join them during free periods." He glanced at his watch and frowned. "I'm so sorry—would you mind waiting a couple of minutes? There's another patient I must see in my office for a moment. Then I'll facilitate a meeting between you and Zoe."

Before Mariana could reply, Theo gestured at the long wooden bench against the wall outside his office. "Won't you sit down?"

Mariana nodded. "Thanks."

Theo opened his office door. And through the open doorway, Mariana glimpsed a beautiful, red-haired woman sitting, waiting, staring out the barred window, at the gray sky outside. The woman turned and looked warily at Theo as he entered the room and shut the door behind him.

Mariana glanced at the bench. But she didn't sit down. Instead, she kept going. She walked up to the door at the end of the corridor.

She stopped outside it. She hesitated.

Then she reached out, turned the handle—

And went inside.

Acknowledgments

I wrote most of this book during the COVID-19 pandemic. I was so grateful to have something to focus on during those long months, living on my own in lockdown in London. And I was grateful to be able to escape from my flat to this world in my head—partly real, partly imagined, an exercise in nostalgia—an attempt to revisit my youth and a place that I love.

It was also nostalgia for a certain kind of novel, for the books that entranced me as a teenager: the detective story, the mystery, whodunnit, or what you will. So my first acknowledgment is the immense debt of gratitude I owe to these classic crime writers, all women, who have given me such inspiration and joy over the years. This novel is my fond homage to them: to Agatha Christie, Dorothy L. Sayers, Ngaio Marsh, Margaret Millar, Margery Allingham, Josephine Tey, P. D. James, and Ruth Rendell.

It's no secret that writing a second novel is a very different beast compared to a debut. *The Silent Patient* was written in a state of complete isolation, with no audience in mind and nothing to lose. That book changed my life and expanded it exponentially. With *The Maidens,* on the other hand, I felt a good deal more pressure; however, I was not alone this time—there was a small village of incredibly talented and brilliant people around me, giving me support and advice. There are too many people to thank, so I hope I don't leave anyone out.

I must begin by thanking my agent, and dear friend, Sam Copeland, for being such a rock, and a source of wisdom and humor and kindness. Likewise, I'm so grateful for the brilliant and dedicated team at Rogers, Coleridge & White—Peter Straus, Stephen Edwards, Tristan Kendrick, Sam Coates, Katharina Volckmer, and Honor Spreckley, to name but a few.

Creatively, working on the edit of this book was the most enjoyable professional experience I've ever had. I learned so much. And my heartfelt thanks goes to my fantastic U.S. editor, Ryan Doherty, at Celadon; and in London, the equally talented Emad Akhtar and Katie Espiner at Orion. I had so much fun working with you all, and I'm thankful for your brilliant help. I hope we can work together forever.

Thank-you to Hal Jensen, for the incredibly detailed and helpful notes, as well as for your friendship, putting up with me endlessly obsessing about this bloody book. Thank-you to Nedie Antoniades, for all the support and for talking me off the ledge numerous times; I rely on you so much, and I'm truly grateful. Likewise, Ivan Fernandez Soto—thank you for St. Lucy and all the other ideas, and for letting me bounce these crazy plot twists off you for the past three years. And a big thanks to Uma Thurman, for all the great notes and suggestions and the home-cooked meals in New York. I'll always be grateful. And Diane Medak, thanks for your friendship and support and for letting me stay forever. I can't wait to come back.

To Professor Adrian Poole, the best teacher I ever had—thanks for such useful comments, and for your help with the Ancient Greek; and for inspiring my love of the tragedies in the first place. Also thank-you to Trinity College, Cambridge, for welcoming me back so warmly and providing the inspiration for St. Christopher's College.

Thank-you to all my wonderful friends at Celadon—I can't imagine my life without you. Jamie Raab and Deb Futter, I'm eternally grateful to you—and thank you for all your help. Rachel

Chou and Christine Mykityshyn—you're both so brilliant, and so much of the success of the last book was down to you. Thank you. Also to Cecily van Buren-Freedman—your comments really improved the book and I'm very grateful. Also at Celadon, thank-you to Anne Twomey, Jennifer Jackson, Jaime Noven, Anna Belle Hindenlang, Clay Smith, Randi Kramer, Heather Orlando-Jerabek, Rebecca Ritchey, and Lauren Dooley. And thanks to Will Staehle for such a fantastic cover, and Jeremy Pink for getting everything done in such record time. Also a big thank-you to the Macmillan sales team—you guys are absolutely the best!

At Orion and Hachette, I would like to thank David Shelley for all the support. I've felt so encouraged and championed by you; I am so grateful. Also thank-you to Sarah Benton, Maura Wilding, Lynsey Sutherland, Jen Wilson, Esther Waters, Victoria Laws— thanks for your fantastic work! And thank you, Emma Mitchell and FMCM, for the publicity.

A special thank-you also to María Fasce in Madrid, for your insightful and useful notes—and also your encouragement.

Thanks, Christine Michaelides—for the help with the descriptions. Ninety percent of it didn't make it into the book, but I learned something at least! Thanks to Emily Holt for your helpful notes and for being so encouraging. Also, Vicky Holt and my father, George Michaelides, for your support.

And a big thank-you to the fabulous Katie Haines. Once again, working with you is such a delight. I can't wait until we can go to the theater again.

Thank-you to Tiffany Gassouk, for making me so welcome in Paris while I was writing there, and for giving me such great encouragement. Also thank-you to Tony Parsons, for the pep talks and the support. I'm really grateful. Thank-you also to Anita Baumann, Emily Koch, and Hannah Beckerman for the encouragement and helpful advice. And Katie Marsh, kind friend, for your constant encouragement. Also thanks to the National Portrait Gallery, for showing me the picture of young Tennyson. And to Kam Sangha, for your surname. Last but not least, thank-you to David Fraser.

THE MAIDENS

BOOK CLUB GUIDE

Discussion Questions

Greek Mythology in
The Maidens by Alex
Michaelides

DISCUSSION QUESTIONS

1. Now that you know who the murderer was, did you guess correctly? Which red herring was the most convincing? Looking back, what clues did you miss about the killer's identity?

2. What do you make of the ending scene? What do you think happens to Mariana and Zoe after the events of the book?

3. Do you agree or disagree with Mariana's reaction at the end? Do you think she was right to be upset, or do you believe she should've been more compassionate?

   Submitted by Spooky Book Club (Boston, Massachusetts)

4. How do Mariana's memories of her school years at Cambridge influence her actions when she returns there?

5. The book opens with Mariana's assertion of Fosca's guilt. How did this impact your experience and interpretation of the murder case?

6. How did Mariana's expertise as a group therapist help her throughout the book? How did it lead her astray?

7. The book switches between straightforward narration and chapters written as letters. Did you like this choice? What did you make of the letter portions when the book began, and how did your understanding of them change as the book progressed?

8. Who did you think was the male POV in these letters throughout the book? Did your hypothesis change at any point?

   Submitted by The Bookworms (Miami, Florida)

9. There is a lot of Greek mythology in the book. How is the symbolism of the Persephone myth significant in the story?

10. This story explores a number of father-daughter relationships. In what ways are they similar? Different? How does Mariana's own relationship with her father impact how she interprets relationships between other fathers and daughters?

11. Do you think the murderer's actions were a product of abuse?

   Submitted by The Book Queens (Naperville, Illinois)

12. While Mariana is a keen observer, she also misses a number of important things throughout the story. What does she miss, and why do you think she does?

13. If you read *The Silent Patient*, you know that a key character from that story appears in *The Maidens* as well. What other stylistic or symbolic similarities exist between the books? Why do you think the author returned to these themes? As a reader, did you like these connections?

Greek Mythology in *The Maidens*
By Alex Michaelides

Growing up in Cyprus, Greek mythology held a special kind of reality for me. The Greek myths are integral to the culture in that part of the world; Homer and the Greek tragedians are taught in school, in the way Shakespeare is part of the curriculum in the UK. More than this, the fact that the myths are geographically tied to Cyprus made them feel very real to me. As a little boy, I was aware that I was living on Aphrodite's island—and that relics of her were everywhere, from the rock she swam to following her birth off the coast of Paphos to the waterfall where she would bathe. I'm extremely grateful for this early immersion in Greek mythology, as it gave me a mythological imagination to draw on as a writer.

In *The Silent Patient*, I wrote about the myth of Alcestis. I first came across the tragedy by Euripides when I was about thirteen. Alcestis dies to save her husband, Admetus—and then is brought back to life by Heracles at the end of the play. But when Alcestis is reunited with her husband, she doesn't speak. She remains silent. Why? Is it because she is overjoyed to see him? Or is she furious that he allowed her to die for him? Something about this refusal to conclude, to explain, haunted me for years. As did something about Alcestis herself—she was sacrificed, deemed disposable by the man she loved most in the world; and this sense of feeling unworthy struck a chord with me. And so, paradoxically, an ancient myth was somehow speaking an emotional truth that felt incredibly personal and true to me—and not just me, as it turns out, but many others.

And this is what makes the myths timeless: the fact that they still stand up to psychological or psychodynamic scrutiny. That's why they still work as drama today.

Something I wanted to explore in *The Maidens* was how toxic patriarchy can dominate and destroy young people's lives. For me, one of the novel's themes is about what happens when we mistake abuse for love at a very young age, and how this mistake colors the rest of our lives.

Murder, in Ancient Greece, was illegal—unless the victim was a baby. The practice of "exposure" of unwanted infants—the vast majority of whom were female—was common and legally sanctioned.

Baby girls were abandoned on a hillside, literally sacrificed to the elements.

The first historical record of a human sacrifice in Ancient Greece was by Herodotus in 480 BCE. And in the various historical accounts I looked through while researching *The Maidens*, I found a disturbing number of references to the sacrifice of young women in Ancient Greece. Some of the things I read chilled me to the bone: girls in Salamis having their throats ritually cut each year; young women being thrown into the sea and drowned in Paphos for religious rites; Plutarch describing the Orchomenian festival—"a flight and pursuit of maidens by the priest of Dionysus, holding a sword. And he is permitted to kill anyone he catches."

The purpose of religious sacrifice is an attempt to cleanse—to purify an impurity with a symbolic act: the sacrifice of blood to appease raging gods. A young girl was made a container for everything bad and unwanted, everything split-off and disowned: a polluted object, to be sacrificed. It's unsurprising, then, given this historical background, that human sacrifice should work its way into these people's stories—an imaginative reenactment of their psychological traumas, perhaps. As in real life, so in myth: maidens are sacrificed to the Minotaur in Crete; and Hesione and Andromeda are sacrificed to Poseidon's sea monster by their fathers.

In *Iphigenia in Aulis*, by Euripides, Iphigenia is put to death by her father, Agamemnon, in order to appease the gods and thus be able to set sail for the Trojan War. Although this sacrifice is imposed on Agamemnon by the gods, he barely objects to it. He seems oddly resigned to it from the start. Why?

Well, in trying to understand his incomprehensible actions, it might be helpful to remember whose son Agamemnon is. Agamemnon's father was Atreus—and, as a terrified little boy, Agamemnon watched a raging and psychotic Atreus murder each one of Agamemnon's young cousins and cook them in a pot. So not only had Agamemnon been desensitized to horrific violence as a young boy, he was familiar with infanticide.

No wonder, then, that as a grown man Agamemnon wasn't able to clearly see what he was doing to his daughter; on some level did it feel strangely familiar to him, sacrificing his little girl, unaware he was reenacting his own childhood trauma?

And Iphigenia? It always bothered me that this young woman so willingly gives up her life. She says it is "wrong" of her to love life too deeply—and she is the only character in the play who calls Agamemnon "a great man." She doesn't need to be bound or restrained; she willingly sacrifices herself for her father. Why? Is it because she thought that's what love is?

And would Iphigenia rather die, believing that her father loved her, than live and face the terrible, devastating truth—that she had never been loved, not in the true sense of the word—because her father did not know how to love her, because he himself had never been loved; and so on and on, back through the generations. Seen from a psychodynamic perspective, the myths seem to me to be nothing but the story of a large and dysfunctional Greek family, damaged beyond repair, condemned to an endless repetition and transgenerational transmission of trauma.

Iphigenia will go to any lengths to please her infanticidal father—including dying for him. But perhaps this is unsurprising. After all, she grew up in a society where unwanted baby girls were left for birds and wild animals to devour. So Iphigenia learned an important cultural lesson early on—that girls were disposable and sometimes better off dead.

It didn't need to be this way. She didn't need to love and honor this man; Agamemnon wasn't worthy of her loyalty or her respect. She had to separate from him and stop seeing the world through his eyes. But that's one thing to say, and quite another to put into practice.

Without years of therapy, it's unlikely Iphigenia would ever see herself or her father clearly. Had she lived, would she have grown up still trying to please him, still seeing herself as unworthy, as a sacrificial object? Would she sleepwalk her way through life, choosing critical, bullying, unloving partners—men like her father—and would she lie to herself about these relationships, telling herself that this was love? Iphigenia needed to believe in that love when she was a little girl. She needed to believe it in order to survive. But unless she woke up to the truth about herself and her childhood, she would end up sacrificing herself—as she had once been sacrificed. She would live a life free of authenticity and joy, seeking out and enduring toxic relationships, desperately trying—and failing—to please capricious gods, and believing this was love. To me, that's the real tragedy.

It's remarkable, really—these myths are simply timeless: violent and magical and powerful stories, about passion and heartbreak and love and loss. And no matter how fantastical the stories or situations, miraculously the emotions they generate are as real and true for us as they were for the Greeks—thousands of years ago.

Turn the page for a sneak peek of

THE FURY

Available January 2024

Prologue

Never open a book with the weather.

Who was it who said that? I can't remember—some famous writer, I expect.

Whoever it was, they were right. Weather is boring. Nobody wants to read about weather; particularly in England, where we have so much of it. People want to read about *people*—and they generally skip descriptive paragraphs, in my experience.

Avoiding the weather is good advice—which I now disregard at my peril. An exception to prove the rule, I hope. Don't worry, my story isn't set in England, so I'm not talking about rain, here. I draw the line at rain—no book should start with rain, ever. No exceptions.

I'm talking about wind. The wind that whirls around the Greek islands. Wild, unpredictable Greek wind. Wind that drives you mad.

The wind was fierce that night—the night of the murder. It was ferocious, furious—crashing through trees, tearing along pathways, whistling, wailing, snatching all other sound and racing off with it.

Leo was outside when he heard the gunshots. He was on his hands and knees, at the back of the house, being sick in the vegetable garden. He wasn't drunk, just stoned. (Mea culpa, I'm afraid. He'd never smoked weed before; I probably shouldn't have given him any.) After an initial semi-ecstatic experience—apparently involving a supernatural vision—he felt nauseous and started throwing up.

Just then, the wind sped toward him—hurling the sound straight at him: *bang, bang, bang*. Three gunshots, in quick succession.

Leo pulled himself up. As steadily as he could, he battled his way against the gale, in the direction of the gunfire—away from the house, along the path, through the olive grove, toward the ruin.

And there, in the clearing, sprawled on the ground . . . was a body.

The body lay in a widening pool of blood, surrounded by the semicircle of ruined marble columns, casting it partially in shadow. Leo cautiously approached it, peering at the face. Then he staggered backward, his expression contorted in horror—opening his mouth to scream.

I arrived at that moment, along with the others—in time to hear the beginnings of Leo's howl, before the wind grabbed the sound from his lips and ran off with it, disappearing into the dark.

We all stood still for a second, silent. It was a horrifying moment, terrifying—like the climactic scene in a Greek tragedy.

But the tragedy didn't end there.

It was just beginning.

ACT I

This is the saddest story I have ever heard.

—Ford Madox Ford, *The Good Soldier*

I

This is a tale of murder.

Or maybe that's not quite true. At its heart, it's a love story, isn't it? The saddest kind of love story—about the end of love; the death of love.

So I guess I was right the first time.

You may think you know this story. You probably read about it at the time—the tabloids loved it, if you recall: MURDER ISLAND was a popular headline. Unsurprising, really, as it had all the perfect ingredients for a press sensation: a reclusive ex–movie star; a private Greek island cut off by the wind . . . and, of course, a murder.

A lot of rubbish was written about that night. All kinds of wild, inaccurate theories about what may, or may not, have taken place. I avoided all of it. I had no interest in reading misinformed speculation about what might have happened on the island.

I knew what happened. I was there.

Who am I? Well, I am the narrator of this tale—and also a character in it.

There were seven of us in all, trapped on the island.

One of us was a murderer.

But before you start laying bets on which of us did it, I feel duty bound to inform you that this is not a whodunit. Thanks to Agatha Christie, we all know how this kind of story is meant to play out: a baffling crime, followed by dogged investigation, an ingenious solution—then, if you're lucky, a twist in the tail. But this is a true story, not a work of fiction. It's about real people, in a real place. If anything, it's a *whydunit*—a character study, an examination of who we are; and why we do the things we do.

What follows is my sincere and heartfelt attempt to reconstruct the events of that terrible night—the murder itself, and everything that led up to it. I pledge to present you with the plain, unvarnished truth—or as near to it as I can get. Everything we did, said, and thought. *But how?* I hear you ask. *How is it possible?* How can I possibly know it *all*? Not just every action taken, everything said and done—but everything *undone, unsaid*, all the private thoughts in one another's minds?

For the most part, I am relying on the conversations we had, before the murder, and afterward—those of us who survived, that is. As for the dead, I trust you'll grant me artistic license regarding their interior life. Given I am a playwright by trade, I am perhaps better qualified than most for this particular task.

My account is also based on my notes—taken both before and after the murder. A word of explanation regarding this. I have been in the habit of keeping notebooks for some years now. I wouldn't call them diaries, they're not as structured as that. Just a record of my thoughts, ideas, dreams, snatches of conversations I overhear, my observations of the world. The notebooks themselves are nothing fancy, just plain black Moleskines. I have the relevant notebook from that year open now, by my side—and will no doubt consult as it as we proceed.

I stress all this so that, if at any point during this narrative I mislead you, you will understand that it is by accident, not design—because I am clumsily skewing the events too much from my own point of view. An occupational hazard, perhaps, when one narrates a story in which one happens to play a minor role.

Nonetheless, I'll do my best not to hijack the narrative too often. Even so, I hope you'll indulge me the odd digression, here and there. And before you accuse me of telling my story in a labyrinthine manner, let me remind you this is a true story—and in real life, that's how we communicate, isn't it? We're all over the place: we jump back and forth in time; slow down and expand on some moments; fast-forward through others; editing as we go, minimizing flaws and maximizing assets. We are all the unreliable narrators of our own lives.

It's funny, I feel that you and I should be sitting together on a couple of barstools, right now, as I tell you this tale—like two old friends, drinking at the bar.

This is a story for anyone who has ever loved, I say, sliding a drink in your direction—a large one, you'll need it—as you settle down, and I begin.

I ask you not to interrupt too much, at least not at first. There will be plenty of opportunity for debate afterward. For now, I request you politely hear me out—as you might indulge a friend's rather lengthy anecdote.

It's time to meet our cast of suspects—in order of importance. And therefore, for the moment, I must reluctantly remain offstage. I'll hover in the wings, waiting for my cue.

Let us begin—as we should—with the star.

Let's begin with Lana.

About the Author

ALEX MICHAELIDES was born and raised in Cyprus. He has an MA in English literature from Trinity College, Cambridge University, and an MA in screenwriting from the American Film Institute in Los Angeles. His first novel, *The Silent Patient*, spent more than a year on the *New York Times* bestseller list and sold in a record-breaking fifty countries. He lives in London.

CELADON
BOOKS

Founded in 2017, Celadon Books, a division of
Macmillan Publishers, publishes a highly curated list
of twenty to twenty-five new titles a year. The list of
both fiction and nonfiction is eclectic and focuses
on publishing commercial and literary books and
discovering and nurturing talent.